THE

ONE

THING

Marci Lyn Curtis

HYPERION
LOS ANGELES · NEW YORK

First edition, September 2015
1 3 5 7 9 10 8 6 4 2
G475-5664-5-15166
Printed in the United States of America

This book is set in New Caledonia
Designed by Whitney Manger

Library of Congress Cataloging-in-Publication Data
Curtis, Marci Lyn.
The one thing / Marci Lyn Curtis.
pages cm
Summary: After losing her sight—and the future she dreamed
of—seventeen-year-old Maggie meets the one person with the
ability to help her see all the possibilities life still holds.
ISBN 978-1-4847-0902-3 (hardback)
[1. Blind—Fiction.   2. People with disabilities—Fiction.   3. Friendship—
Fiction.   4. Family problems—Fiction.   5. Cancer—Fiction.
6. Conduct of life—Fiction.   7. Musicians—Fiction.]   I. Title.
PZ7.1.C87One 2015
[Fic]—dc23   2015000350

Reinforced binding
Visit www.hyperionteens.com

For my parents, because they
gave me the chance to dream

I'm not a fan of the bouquet. I have nothing against flowers specifically, but once they've been plucked from the ground and clumped together in a grouping, I find them unnerving. Maybe even a smidge creepy. Nothing says *Please admire my beauty while I die a long, slow death* quite like the floral arrangement. Looking back, I realize it was probably some sort of omen that Benjamin Milton was standing beside a bouquet when I first met him. After all, I'd been blind for a full six months, and not once during that time had I encountered a floral arrangement.

Most sighted people are under the assumption that those of us who are completely blind see nothing but blackness. But actually, they are wrong. Those of us who have no vision don't see black. We don't see anything at all. Basically, I see about as much as a fingernail sees: absolutely nothing. No black. No gray. Nothing. So I didn't have a clue what the bouquet looked like when I sat down in Mr. Sturgis's lobby. All I knew was, one, the thing was sitting on the front counter, where I'd plowed into it as I'd checked in, and two, it smelled suspiciously like minced-up old ladies, so I was guessing there were gardenias in it.

As usual, the lobby had me elbow to elbow with criminals and juvenile delinquents. I waited a good thirty minutes or so before the receptionist—Cari or Staci or something that ended in a perky little *i*—finally called me up. I'd never actually seen Mr. Sturgis, my probation officer. In my head he was freakishly tall and he sported a stringy ponytail, a pair of beat-up man-clogs, and a faded peace sign tattoo. But according to my grandfather, he was squat and bald and he had a nasty habit of wearing pants that were about an inch too short. That's the thing about being blind: you see people as they really are.

As I walked into his office, Mr. Sturgis said, "Greetings, Miss Margaret."

"Actually, I prefer Maggie. Remember?" I said as I fumbled my way into my usual seat, folding up my cane and stuffing it in my purse. My full name, Margaret, is the sort of name you'd expect from someone who is three hundred years old. Or in line for the British throne.

"So. Margaret," he went on as I bounced my foot in time to a Loose Cannons song that had been stuck in my head all day. I could hear him shuffling papers around. "Miss Olive tells me that you are finished with your mandatory community service. In her words, she says"—he cleared his throat—"'Margaret is a witty young woman who is highly skilled at looking busy while doing absolutely nothing.'"

A long silence ensued. Presumably he was waiting for me to

comment, but I said nothing. Instead, I brushed a little imaginary lint off my shorts, which was ridiculous, because even if I *had* lint on my shorts, I wouldn't be able to see it.

After a few moments, he went on to say, "How's school?"

"Spectacular," I said. The last day of my junior year was yesterday. So, yes, school was going spectacularly today. I'd slept until noon, feasted on a sleeve of Girl Scout cookies, taken a three-hour shower, and slothed my way to the probation office.

"Care to elaborate about your grades?" Mr. Sturgis said, his pen scratching on his papers.

"Not really."

"What's your current GPA?" he asked, chuckling. He and I had come to an unspoken agreement a couple months ago: I would be magnificently sarcastic, and he'd think it was amusing. Besides, I'd found it was best to keep my verbiage to a minimum when dealing with Mr. Sturgis. If I opened a conversational door, he'd bomb right through it and lecture me to unconsciousness about contributing to society and correcting my karma and whatever.

I shrugged. "Two-point-oh-ish."

It would have been two-point-four-ish if it weren't for my English teacher, who'd hated me ever since I'd caused a little incident in his class several months back. In my defense, I'd been miserable with my abrupt transfer to Merchant's School for the Blind. Partly because I hadn't wanted to leave South Hampton High, and partly because Merchant's was a complete crock. Merchant's was coddling me, patting me on the back, telling me everything was going to be okay. But everything wasn't okay. Out in the real world? I was tripping over curbs I didn't know existed, and I was finding it impossible to tell the difference between a ten-dollar bill and a twenty-dollar bill. I was coming to the realization that I would never kick another soccer goal.

So basically, Merchant's blew. And perhaps the worst thing about the place was my English teacher, Mr. Huff. His breath smelled like the inside of a belly button and he spoke one—word—at—a—time—like—we—were—all—incredibly—slow. A dozen years earlier, he'd had a bout of testicular cancer. So every day in class, he droned on and on about how he was a cancer survivor, and how he could relate to living with adversity, and how he'd overcome obstacles. And I would huff out these monstrous sighs and roll my eyes, hoping he'd get my point.

And then one day, in the middle of one of my huffing-and-eye-rolling displays, he surprised me by saying, "Maggie? Is there something you would like to share?"

Now, I couldn't be blamed for what happened next. I was simply answering his question honestly. Besides, I could've said a lot worse. I was thinking a lot worse. "Actually, I can't seem to grasp the correlation between your nutsack and our eyesight," I informed him, swooping my arm around the classroom to include all the other poor, sightless bastards who had been stuck listening to him day after stinking day.

Naturally, my answer earned me a seat in the principal's office, where I proceeded to tell the principal what I thought of Mr. Huff's nutsack. Next thing I knew, I was spending my afternoons in detention, and Mr. Huff was speaking to me in a pinched voice and handing me an unwarranted amount of crappy grades.

Mr. Sturgis jerked me back to the present. "How's your mother?" he asked.

My head snapped up. "Why? Did she call you?"

"I haven't heard from her. Are you in trouble at home?"

"Nope."

He gave me a probation-officer sigh—slightly suspicious, slightly entertained, slightly annoyed—and then he said, "I'll see you next month. And Margaret? You're a good kid. Keep your nose clean."

2

Grandpa Keith was late. He was supposed to pick me up at Sturgis's office at four o'clock sharp, but my phone had just chimed four thirty. Gramps's tardiness was no huge surprise. He was exceptionally talented in the field of late arrivals. Probably because he moseyed toward his destinations at about half the speed of smell. I was fingering my cell phone, wondering whether I should prod him along, when the door of Mr. Sturgis's crypt-silent lobby opened with a ding.

"Finally," I said, popping up and striding toward the door, not bothering to use the cane I'd tucked into my purse. I discovered almost immediately that some genius had dropped an unspecified, fantastically slick substance on the tile floor and had neglected to clean it up. Naturally, I stepped right in it.

I'd like to say that I fell with the dignity and grace of a self-respecting blind girl—the sort of girl who understands and accepts that, yes, there are hidden dangers out there, and yes, she will probably get a little banged up every now and then. But I didn't. And the four-letter word that came out of my mouth as I hit the floor was extremely loud and so thick that it could've been heated up and drizzled over pancakes.

So my eyes were squeezed shut, and I was lying on my side with the reek of that bouquet all around me, clutching my skull as though it would surely fall apart all over the lobby if I let it go, when I heard a kid's voice say, "That was the most majestic fall I've ever seen."

Gosh, thanks was what I wanted to say to him. But I'd whacked my head on something hard-cornered and it wasn't functioning properly. I couldn't get any words to transit to my mouth. They slid around in my brain, unable to find the exit.

"Are you okay?" he asked. He didn't sound concerned.

"I'm just dandy," I managed after a moment and with some difficulty, sounding more slurred than sarcastic.

The left side of my head was ringing. I stuck a finger into my ear canal and wiggled it around. It didn't help. With a groan, I rolled onto my back.

"Need a hand getting up?" he said.

There was something about the way he spoke—all energetic and lively, as though there were a mariachi band parading out of his mouth—that prompted me to open my eyes. And that was when I realized I was hallucinating from the smack I'd just taken on the head.

Because I could actually see him.

It had been six months since bacterial meningitis stole my sight, six months since I'd seen anything at all. Sure, what I was seeing was a cheesy hallucination, but it was *there*. I should hit my head more often.

A young boy peered down at me. I figured he was maybe eight or nine years old, but I'd never hallucinated before, so my hallucination-age-guessing skills could have been a little off. He was small, golden-toned, and ribby, and he wore board shorts about three sizes too big, a cockeyed baseball cap, and a wide, toothy smile.

I sat up, swaying a little as I came to rest in a seated position. My brain was swimmy and I had a massive headache. "You," I began, shaking an index finger at him, but the kid furrowed his brows at me and I completely lost my train of thought.

I peered at the space around the boy. I wasn't just seeing him. I was seeing several feet around him as well, as though he were a pale gray lightbulb, emitting the sort of muted light that yawns into existence at dawn—almost more the idea of light than actual light. But it had been so long since I'd seen anything that it seemed more like a spotlight.

On the floor beside his sneakers, I could see a crumpled-up Skittles wrapper. Red. The wrapper was bright red. God, I'd missed red. Beside it was a bright blue plastic chair, on which *BITE ME* was carved in big block letters. And above the chair? A soft, buttery beam of slanted late-afternoon sunlight. Beyond that, everything just got dimmer and dimmer, slowly petering out into the void.

Even for a hallucination it was weird.

I looked up at the kid, suddenly realizing that he was supporting himself with a pair of crutches. Not the kind that cram into your armpits, but the short aluminum ones that attach to your forearms. Strangely, they seemed to be a fundamental part of him—if he were standing here without them, he'd look as though he were missing something vital, like a nose or an ear or whatever. He was smiling at me with half his mouth, his expression stuck somewhere between amusement and disbelief. "Are you drunk?" he asked.

I'd never met a hallucination until just now, but I was fairly certain that this particular one was a little presumptuous. Maybe they all were. "I am not drunk," I said indignantly. "I am concussed, which explains your presence here." I swooped an arm around with a flourish, as if introducing him to the situation.

He puffed out his cheeks and sighed. "So then you're a pothead. Crap." Under his breath, he added, "The good-looking ones always have a tragic flaw."

I narrowed my eyes at him. "Excuse me?"

"Well. The thing is? I used to be totally in love with Jessica Baylor. She sat next to me in math. She was *hot*. Like, she had shiny hair and shiny eyes and a shiny smile. But then? She told me she hates cake, and I'm fundamentally opposed to cake-haters. Then there was Hannah. From band? She had *boobs*. They were magnificent. Just thinking about them was enough to make a guy go bonkers. . . ." He blinked once. Hard. Like he was using his eyelids to wipe the image off his brain. "But the thing about Hannah was that I caught her throwing a rock at a squirrel. A squirrel, for Pete's sake. It just wasn't right. Then today, when I saw you—*hello*—I thought you were perfect. That fall? Wow. Just . . . wow. But then I find out you're a pothead." He huffed out another huge gust of air. "It's tragic."

Whoa. I must've really knocked the crap out of my head. "I'm not a pothead," I informed him, although I wasn't sure why I was defending my honor to a young, semiperverted apparition.

"Then why are you staring at me like that?" he asked. "Like, all blank-faced and goofy-eyed?"

Staring? Well, I guess I was. I wondered briefly why pointless social conventions applied to hallucinations. "You'd have to be staring at me to know that I was staring at you," I said. Clearly, he couldn't argue with such logic.

His smile grew wide, commandeering his entire face, and then he said, "You were staring at me first, so you started it. I am just an innocent bystander who is taking note of all your staring."

I tapped an index finger on my chin. There's nothing like a good argument to knock the fog out of your brain. And I could tell by his expression that he noticed my improving mental clarity as well, that he realized his pothead theory had been way off base. "Actually," I said, "when I first saw you? Right after I fell? You were already looking at me, which makes you the one who stared first. My staring, therefore, is just a byproduct of all your staring."

There was a long silence, which then became a longer silence. Finally he whispered, "I believe I've just found my next girlfriend."

I laughed so hard that I let out an unladylike snort. Evidently I had a way with hallucinations. But people? Well, I sort of sucked with people.

A sharp clicking of high heels came into the room. From somewhere behind me, the receptionist said, "What the . . . ? Maggie? Why are you sitting on the floor? Are you okay?"

"Oh, I'm grand," I drawled, not taking my eyes off the kid.

"Never better. Just had a teensy slip, followed by a not-so-teensy fall. Something on the floor is a smidge slippery."

She was dead quiet for a moment, and then she said in a whine, "Oh—no, no, no, no. Not now."

What her problem was I wasn't sure, but I couldn't be bothered. Right now, for some reason, life just seemed to *like* me.

"Benjamin Milton," the receptionist scolded, "stop flirting with the poor girl. Can't you see that she's way too old for you?"

The kid took in a big breath and puffed out his cheeks. Holding up one index finger, he said, "I am not flirting, per se. I cannot help that I am a sexy piece of man-flesh and—"

But she cut him off before he could finish his sentence, her words flying out of her mouth so quickly that I could barely understand them: "Sorry Ben but listen I have to go because I'm late late late and I have three minutes to pick up my son or the day care will charge me and I can't pay them extra or else I'll be short on my rent so be a dear and wipe that stuff off the floor before someone breaks their neck." I flinched as a dingy rag flew out of nowhere from behind me and landed on top of the boy's shoulder. "Thanks a ton I really appreciate it!" She raised her voice and said, "MR. STURGIS I'M LEAVING AND YOUR NEPHEW IS HERE AND DON'T FORGET TO LOCK UP!" Bottle-blond, thin, and middle-aged, the woman half walked, half ran right through my faint bubble of sight. And then she was gone.

For several seconds, I forgot how to breathe. My eyes traveled back to the kid standing in front of me. I felt as though I'd collided with something massive and unyielding and then exploded into a million tiny pieces. I shut my eyes, trying to gather what was left of my sanity. When I opened them, he was still there.

3

I sat there for a few seconds, gaping at the kid. He shifted toward me on his crutches and grinned widely, flashing me his largish set of front teeth. "Why can I see you?" I asked. He didn't answer my question because I didn't actually say it. I tried the words out in my mind, but they seemed too ridiculous to say out loud. I ran a hand over the new lump on my head, wondering whether my fall had knocked something back where it belonged—whether some cog in my brain had been slammed back into the notch labeled SIGHT.

Was that even possible?

I swallowed and let my eyes fall downward. I didn't know what I was expecting to see, but it surely wasn't . . . *myself.* My blindness had caused me to doubt my own existence, made me believe that I'd evaporated into nothingness—a ghost of a person. My hands were bone-white, thin, frail-looking, a single callus on my right index finger from learning braille. I was wearing a white T-shirt advertising my current obsession and the best emerging band of all time, the Loose Cannons, and also the shorts my parents had purchased for me a couple months back. I'd always thought the shorts were comfortable and unique, but now that I saw them I realized why. They were too big, too bunched up in weird places, and too reminiscent of something my mother would wear. My toenails still had a couple specks of Blue Bayou polish on them. It had been my favorite back when I could see. On the side of my right ankle, just north of my flip-flop, was the scar I'd gotten when I'd fallen out of a tree back in the eighth grade. I stared at it for a few heartbeats, long and hard, feeling oddly as though I were standing an inch from a big screen, marveling at every little pixel.

Yup—*yup*—I could definitely see.

Yet.

Why?

Twisting around, I looked behind me. I had maybe a foot of hazy sight, but beyond that, everything faded into oblivion. No waiting room. No chairs. No . . . nothing. I swung my head back, peering at a thin river of frothy light-green substance that snaked its way along the not-quite-white tile floor. Pistachio ice cream, I was guessing. Evidently this was what I'd slipped on. I had never been a fan of pistachio ice cream—nuts have no business hanging around in something smooth and creamy—but in light of current events, I might have to eat a whole carton of it tonight.

Because really.

The kid, Ben, cleared his throat, cranked his head around to face Mr. Sturgis's office, and basically screamed, "UNCLE KEVIN! Mom wanted me to run in and ask whether you could come to dinner tonight, but you're, like, obviously busy working and stuff, so I'll take my new girlfriend instead." All Mr. Sturgis could get out of his mouth was "Um" before Ben interrupted him by saying, "No, it's totally cool, because I want her to meet my family."

"Er. Okay?" Mr. Sturgis hollered back, clearly confused.

"I'm not your girlfriend," I informed him in a low voice, but he just smiled at me like a complete lunatic. And then, chin raised high and spine straight and confident, he lowered himself to the floor with one arm, using the *BITE ME* chair as a prop. His skinny legs folded up limply underneath him.

"So," he said, one eye on me and one eye on the pistachio ice cream he was wiping off the floor, "shoplifting?"

I didn't answer him because his question made zero sense. Also, his head was turned a little, giving me a full view of the writing on his cockeyed hat: ALL THIS AND BRAINS, TOO! I was so idiotically thrilled to see the written word that I read it over and over. Finally, I realized that he was waiting for a comment or an answer or something—to what, exactly, I couldn't quite remember—so I said, "Um. Excuse me?"

"Why are you in my uncle's office?" he said, turning toward me and taking away my brief view of the writing on his hat. "You don't look like an ax murderer or a drug dealer, so I figure you're a shoplifter." He leaned toward me and lowered his voice to a stage whisper. "What did you steal?"

"Nothing," I said sharply. In a normal situation, I would have replied with something quick-witted and smart-assed, but the throb in my head and the sudden one-eighty of my eyesight was interfering with my thought processes.

"I think you are hiding something from me, beautiful," he said.

Well. I didn't know how to reply to that. Mostly because I found it impossible to argue effectively with someone who had just called me beautiful. Even if the compliment had come from a kid.

He stopped wiping the floor and waited for an answer to the shoplifting question. I straightened my posture and said, "I am not a shoplifter. I don't even like to shop. I was...involved in a school prank."

His smile widened, and he laughed in one quick burst that had the sound and the feel of an exclamation point at the end of a sentence. "I love a girlfriend with hidden depths. Please... continue," he said.

"I'm not your girlfriend. I'm way too old for you," I informed him.

"Yes, but you *will* be my girlfriend, so technically it's the same thing," he said, flicking his eyebrows at me.

"Technically, it isn't. Technically, you're, what, nine years old?"

"Ten," he sniffed, as though the one year made a huge difference.

"Technically, you're ten and I'm seventeen, and there are probably laws against ten-year-olds and seventeen-year-olds dating."

He waved me off and said, "So. The school prank?"

There was something in his eyes—a realness or a sincerity, maybe—that I was beginning to notice, if only because it was so lacking in myself. It was this quality, and this quality alone, that prompted me to tell him about the prank.

It went down something like this: Several months ago, while both the faculty and students attended a school assembly, I relocated the obnoxiously huge statue of our obnoxiously huge-headed school founder, Elias Merchant, a few feet across the hallway to the boys' restroom. In front of the urinals, to be exact. Then I coated my feet in the Home Depot's Moon Dust white paint and walked a short trail of painted footprints from where the statue had once stood to where I'd moved it. So basically, it appeared as though the statue had sort of walked off to the restroom and decided to stay there for a while. Okay, so I knew that none of the students would actually see my artistry, but I was certain they would hear all about it. And it was better that way. The embellishments you dream up in your mind are always better than reality. At any rate, it was all in good fun. Until I got caught, that is.

By the time I finished explaining all of this to Ben, his face looked as though it might break in half from smiling. He burst out laughing, a long, loud stream of exclamation-point laughs.

"That's awesome!" he said, using the same chair to pull himself to his feet. After he jammed his arms into his crutches and regained his balance, he froze in place, squinting down at me. "Wait," he said. "You go to Merchant's? Isn't that a school for the blind?"

For the past few minutes, I'd almost forgotten that I was blind. I'd felt so . . . *normal.* More normal than I'd felt in months. Yet I knew: there was so much out there that I couldn't see, so many things beyond Ben and beyond me and beyond the murky ring around us.

I was still blind. Mostly.

After a notable silence, a few words worked their way out of my mouth. They weren't eloquent, but they were words nonetheless. And right now, I couldn't afford to be picky. "Um. Yeah. Merchant's is a school for the blind."

His eyebrows crashed together. "So why do you go to school there?"

I stood up and dusted off my backside, stalling. I had no idea what to say to the kid. Finally, because I didn't have any available brain cells to make up a civilized lie, I told him the truth. "Because I'm blind."

He grinned at me disbelievingly. "Nuh-uh."

"Trust me. I'm blind." To prove my point, I pulled my cane out of my purse and unfolded it. "And if that isn't enough proof, go ask your uncle." I made a little gesture with my hands. "Go ahead."

Without moving the rest of his body, he turned his head toward Mr. Sturgis's office and hollered, "UNCLE KEVIN! THE CURLY-HAIRED GIRL OUT HERE? THE ONE WHO GOT IN TROUBLE FOR A SCHOOL PRANK? IS SHE BLIND?"

There was a muffled, uncomfortable little cough from Mr. Sturgis, and then an affirmative noise.

Ben slowly turned back toward me. He shifted his weight on his crutches, and then his expression changed to something that I could only call enchanted.

"I've been blind since I got meningitis, about six months ago," I explained. "Before I slipped in here today? I couldn't see anything at all. But when I fell, I must've knocked something loose in my brain. Because I can see you, but only you and a little bit around you. Beyond that, there's . . . well, nothing." I squinted along the rim of the dusty circle that surrounded him, where the gray light receded, still mystified by how it just seeped into the void.

"Holy shit," Ben whispered. "It's a miracle."

I opened my mouth to argue with him, but then promptly shut it. The truth of it was that I didn't know why I could see him. I didn't know anything at all, really. I didn't know whether I should tell someone—Mr. Sturgis, my parents, a teacher, a doctor.

A shrink.

I chewed on my thumbnail. Would anyone actually believe me? Probably not. Due to compelling lying practices generally frowned upon by adults, my parents—or anyone else, for that matter—didn't put much credit into the things I told them these days.

Hell, I wasn't sure whether I believed myself. Something about this wasn't quite ringing true. And I had to wonder whether I'd been so desperate for my eyesight that I'd gone straightjacket, whether my neurons had started randomly firing off, creating... this.

I squinted at Ben, at his bucktoothed smile and his floppy blond hair and his crutches, and I swallowed. If I were to be perfectly honest with myself—something I generally strived to avoid—then the answer would be a resounding yes. I'd probably gone out of my nut.

Still, though.

I had no desire to end up in a psych ward while some Egbert dissected my brain. So until I worked out exactly what was happening, I wasn't telling another soul that I could see Benjamin Milton.

"First off, you're too young to cuss," I told Ben. "And secondly, it's not a miracle. When I fell, I hit my head. Hard. It sort of rattled my brain and...um...now I can see you. Possibly."

He wasn't listening to me. He was pacing around, saying, "Holy crap holy crap holy crap holy crap." Finally he jolted to a stop, let his head fall back, stared to the heavens, and bellowed, "HOLY CRAP IT'S A MIRACLE!"

I strode forward and clamped my hand over his mouth. Bending down to his ear, I said in a low voice, "You need to keep this quiet until I figure out what's going on. Can you promise me you won't tell anyone?"

He nodded slowly, eyes wide. My hand fell from his mouth. He murmured, "Okay, Thera."

Thera? "Actually, my name is Maggie. Maggie Sanders."

"But I'm gonna call you Thera," he whispered through nearly unmoving lips. His eyes were still huge bowling balls as he stared up at me.

I pinched the bridge of my nose between my thumb and index finger. I wasn't wearing enough deodorant for this conversation. "Actually, I prefer my real name."

"The thing is," he said, still whispering, "you look just like Thera. On Twenty-one Stones? She shoots lightning out of her fingers and fights dragons with magical weapons."

I scrubbed my forehead with the heel of my palm. "What are you talking about?"

"Twenty-one Stones? The best video game in existence?"

Ah. So I'd been named after a heroine in a video game. What a compliment.

I stood there, arms crossed, as he looked at me as though I were the best roller coaster in the history of roller coasters. Finally he said, "Would you please please please come to my house for dinner? I won't tell my family about the miracle thing. Promise." He jerked his head toward the door. "We can even give you a ride. My mom's right outside." He walked his crutches together and then bent his wrists so his fingers were steepled in an *I'm begging you* position. "Please, Thera?"

Generally, I wouldn't hang out with a ten-year-old unless there was babysitting money involved. Lots of it. But I was desperate to find out whether Ben Milton was just something my brain had conjured up on its own, whether, after months and months of blindness—and like a time-release Tylenol gelcap—some hard protective coating had dissolved and the *crazy* had finally kicked in.

Or whether my sight was returning.

"Yes, I'll go," I blurted. "Just stop calling me Thera."

I called Gramps before we left the building. I got his voice mail, naturally. He was not a *phone* kind of guy. His outgoing message unfailingly made me smirk: at first, there's this long pause, and I can hear him banging around, breathing into the phone, and finally he says, "Heh," and then the line beeps.

Heh was Gramps's word. It was a multiuse word that could mean whatever he wanted it to mean. It could be a question, a statement, a filler word, or an answer. Those of us who really understood Gramps could decipher what his conversational *heh* meant.

"Gramps," I said into the phone. "You were supposed to pick me up, like, an hour ago? Anyhow, I'm going to have dinner at—" I stopped suddenly, unsure of how to categorize Ben. Ben soundlessly mouthed *my new boyfriend's house.* "—a friend's house," I said, rolling my eyes at him. "I'll call if I need a ride home. So. Um. Okay? Bye."

I stared at my phone after I hung up, mystified. It was something my parents had sprung for shortly after I'd lost my sight. A sympathy gift. It wasn't a phone as much as it was a computerized voice that shouted at me every time I touched a key. So I'd hated it at first, and getting me to use it had been a bit like trying to baptize a cat. But I'd come around to it. Sort of.

I gave it one last speculative glance before stuffing it in my pocket and glancing at Ben. He was just a couple feet away, still smiling idiotically at me. Feeling strangely as if I were taking something that had never been mine, I said, "C'mon, kid. Let's go. And remember: mum's the word."

He pried one hand free from its crutch, twisted an invisible key to lock his mouth, and then tossed it over his shoulder before we stepped out the door.

4

When I first lost my sight, I spent an inordinate amount of time holed up in my room, sleeping and listening to music. This did not go over well with my parents. So after a good week of my refusing to leave my room and my refusing to go to school and my refusing to do basically everything, my parents yanked me out by way of Hilda, an orientation and mobility specialist whose main purpose was to teach me to navigate the world, whether I wanted to or not.

Hilda was ridiculously intense and ridiculously bad-breathed, and she had this creepy Romanian accent that turned her Ws into Vs, which was entertaining in an immature sort of way. Hilda and I disagreed on several key points when it came to my training, namely the long white cane. While I detested the thing, she adored it. She called it a "theoretical extension of my fingers," which was somewhat of a coincidence because whenever I used my cane, I wanted to extend my middle finger.

Canes, I believed, were made for old people. Frail people. People who didn't mind announcing their blindness as they walked down the sidewalk. I didn't want to announce anything as I walked. I just wanted to *walk*. So I accepted the cane with great disdain. Even now, as I made my way out of Mr. Sturgis's office, it felt heavy in my hand, cumbersome even, and I fought the urge to fold it up and cram it back in my purse.

I didn't see Ben's mom—a bright-eyed, fair-haired, roundish woman wearing feather earrings and hospital-type scrubs—until we were practically on top of her. It was disconcerting to be walking along in Ben's little bubble of muted gray light, seeing only asphalt and car doors and litter, and then—*boom*—suddenly there was a woman standing right in front of me, leaning against a banged-up burgundy minivan and chatting on a cell phone. Yet there she was, plain as day. And she, like Ben, was so beautifully, desperately *real*. Everything about her, from the warm tones in her voice to her welcoming smile, was screaming *I like baking cookies and going to PTA meetings!* at me. Could my mind fabricate something like that?

Yes. No.

Maybe.

Ben introduced us. "Mom, this is Thera. Thera, Mom." And then he added rather indelicately, "Thera is blind."

Resolved to see this through as planned, I did my best to focus on her left ear instead of her eyes as she dropped her phone into the front pocket of her scrubs. Her face exploded in a smile, as if I'd done something exceptional just by existing. "Oh! Nice to meet you, Thera!" she said. She threw herself toward me, taking me completely off-guard by giving me a massive hug. She was soft and squishy, and I sank in to her—like she was an honest-to-God hugger and I was an honest-to-God huggee and this was something that was actually happening.

I didn't know what to do with my hands, so finally I settled on giving her an awkward pat on the back. "Maggie, actually. My name is Maggie," I said into her shoulder.

She took a step back and considered this, her face scrunched up and her feather earrings swaying in the breeze. "Actually, you look more like a Thera."

Ben appeared thoroughly pleased with himself. To his mom, he said, "So. Uncle Kevin is busy working tonight, but Thera can take his place at the table if that's okay?"

She clapped her hands as if someone had just informed her that she'd won a brand-new, ding-free minivan. One that didn't look as though it would keel over if a bird landed on the antenna. "Yes! Absolutely," she said.

Ben swung his way to the back passenger-side door and waited for his mother to unlock it. But I stayed rooted where I was, suddenly terrified as I stared down at myself, where the outer rim of fragile gray light dissolved my body, quite literally, in half. Albeit muddy and faded, the left side of my body prevailed as per the norm, but the right . . . well, it fell into oblivion.

None of this made sense.

I wiped my palms on my shorts. Maybe I didn't want to figure it out right now. Maybe I just wanted to go with it and see where it took me. Minutes ago, when I'd sat in Sturgis's office talking to

Ben, I'd forgotten all about my blindness. My blood had seemed carbonated, all light and fizzy, and I'd felt more like myself than I had in ages.

Maybe, just for a little while, I wanted to be *Maggie* again.

I could do that. Having a wedge of my eyesight back, hallucination or no, was so distracting, so exhilarating, that I could easily stop thinking about all the whys and the hows for a while and just be myself. After six months of nothing, I deserved that.

Taking one bold step toward Ben, I bent over and whispered in his ear, "Remember: keep the eyesight thing on the down-low."

He saluted me. "Alas, I shall speak of your secret to no one," he said, all serious.

I rolled my eyes.

....

The van wheezed as it fired up. Once it got going, it rattled like there was a loose marble rolling around in the engine. The upholstery was layered with a thick dusting of animal hair. Also, animal cages and kennels and such were crammed all over the place. Ben's mom explained that she worked for a local veterinary hospital and occasionally had to pick up wounded animals from the streets.

The Miltons lived out in Chester Beach, about fifteen blocks, a long causeway, and a million miles from where I lived. There were two types of people who hung out in Chester Beach: there were hippies, and then there were hippies. My grandma Karen used to fall into the hippie category. Back when she was alive, Gran used to pluck me out of bed at an ungodly hour to greet the sun as it crept up over the water. Not exactly a morning person, I would grouse the entire fifteen-minute car ride, only to be hushed to silence by the sun bursting over the ocean and flinging yellows and reds and oranges into the sky. So I'd always liked Chester Beach. It reminded me of Gran. Even now—sitting in a hooptie of a minivan with a scrawny, bucktoothed kid who appeared to light up roughly a four-foot radius and his strangely affectionate mother—I thought of Gran. Not for very long, but I did think of her.

What I could see of the Miltons' yard was weedy, scraggly, over-grown. The house seemed to sag on its foundation, its wooden clapboard siding slathered in a single layer of white paint that was chipped and weathered. On the front door, the brass knocker had been ripped off and reattached with duct tape. Regardless of all that, it was a comfortable sort of place that didn't echo when I stepped through the front door, quite unlike my own house, which, I'd noticed since I lost my sight, yawned out in front of me when I walked inside.

The place smelled faintly of incense. A massive collage of snap-shots dominated the entire entryway. It was crammed full with photos upon photos of Ben and an older, good-looking, dark-haired boy.

"Is that your brother?" I whispered, pointing.

"Yup," Ben said, smiling brightly. "But I'm the bestest and the brightest." He gestured to the photos and lowered his voice. "My mom is a freak about pictures. They're everywhere."

He was not exaggerating. The place was festooned in photos, most of which were slightly off—a little blurry or a little off-center or whatever. You'd think that, with all the practice, Ben's mom would be a half-decent photographer.

Ben led me across the foyer, past an old-school upright piano, and down a hallway to his room. At his doorway, he pried an arm from its crutch and balanced with one side of his body. Sweeping his free hand out in front of him with a flourish, he said, "Welcome to my inner sanctum."

From what I could see, it was the sort of room that would belong to a kid who spent far too much time studying. The tiny space was crammed full with solar system models, posters of Einstein, NASA memorabilia, and books up the wazoo.

"Ben? *Ben*. Tell me these aren't your encyclopedias," I said, squatting down and squinting at the spines lined along his bookcase. "Tell me you are storing them in your room until your mom sells them to a wrinkled-up eighty-year-old woman at a garage sale."

Ben waved me off with his still-free hand. "Duh. They're in my room, aren't they? Of course they're mine."

I cracked up. "Aren't you aware that there's this new encyclopedia nowadays? It's really compact and easy to use. It's called the Internet," I said, standing up and turning toward his closet. You can tell a lot about a person from his closet. Due to my limited scope of sight, I could see only the right-hand corner of the space, which was crammed full with a colossal stack of hats that sported a variety of semicatchy phrases. At the base of Mount Saint Hat was a soccer ball. It was the kind that kids use—the smaller, nonstandard size—but it was a soccer ball nonetheless. I swallowed and turned my back to it.

"Internet's for sissies," Ben said. "I started reading encyclopedias when I was eight."

I snorted loudly. "Seriously? You read them for fun? Wow. That's . . . that's . . . vaguely pathetic."

He dismissed my comment with a grunt. "What do you read, Thera?"

I hadn't been ready for that question. I'd given up on books. Braille was too much work and I wasn't very good at it, so I read with my fingers only when absolutely necessary. At school, usually. So basically the only words I'd actually tackled lately were on the computer, where I'd spent hours trying to figure out the next concert venue for the Loose Cannons. And that hardly counted, seeing as how my computer did all the reading for me. Finally, I answered the question as I would've six months ago. "Anything funny with a happy ending," I said. "I hate reading stuff that is depressing or morbid or in any way crappy. That's what life is for."

He raised his eyebrows like, *Well, aren't you little miss sunshine and rainbows?* "So you don't read books about dragons?"

I shook my head.

"Sorcerers?"

I rolled my eyes.

"Mystics? Astronauts?"

I harrumphed.

"Wow, Thera. You need to get a life," he said. He was smiling as he said it.

"This from the kid who reads encyclopedias for fun," I pointed out.

"It's entertaining," he said indignantly. "When I had my last back surgery? I was, like, stuck in a hospital bed forever. Bored.

The only thing worth a crap in the library at Memorial was their encyclopedia set. So I read the As for two weeks straight." He smiled his toothy smile and gestured to the bookshelf, to the first book in the set. It was rather thick. "There are a lot of As. Now? I have my own set. And except for the Qs, which"—he paused for half a beat and his grin fell, just a little, but then it bounced right back and he continued—"I don't have, I've made it clear to the Rs. And things are starting to get interesting, what with the rail-babbler and Arkady Raikin."

"Do I want to know what those things are?" I asked, not bothering to hide my amusement.

"The rail-babbler is a goofy-looking Malaysian bird—"

"So it's the Ben of the bird kingdom?"

He went on as if he hadn't heard me. "And Arkady Raikin? You haven't heard of him? The Soviet comedian?"

"I haven't had the pleasure," I said dryly. Just what I needed: a ten-year-old friend whose SAT scores could blow mine out of the water.

He shook his head and clucked his tongue. "Thera, Thera, Thera. You've been missing out."

I just nodded. I couldn't agree more.

5

Ben wanted me to meet his dog. Since dogs weren't exactly my thing, I told him that introductions were completely unnecessary. But he didn't listen. Leaving me in front of his encyclopedias, he swung off to retrieve his dog from the backyard. He took my sight with him, the room ebbing away to nothing as he stepped into the hallway.

I knew there was a whole room full of the sort of crap that brainy ten-year-olds find fascinating, but I felt as though I'd been left alone with nothing but the soccer ball I'd seen inside Ben's closet. Tripping over God knows what, slamming my shin into something hard-cornered, and cussing creatively, I finally came to a stop with one hand on the doorjamb of Ben's closet. I stared into the void, seeing the soccer ball all too well in my mind's eye.

My phone rattled to life in my back pocket. Startled, I flinched and sucked in my breath, heart throbbing in my chest. Yanking the phone out, I fumbled my way across the room and stuffed it in my purse. It was Clarissa Fenstermacher calling, no doubt. A fellow student at Merchant's. A couple weeks ago, Mr. Huff had paired us up to work together on a summer research paper about illiteracy in America, and Clarissa had been hounding me about it ever since. I'd been doing my best to avoid her.

I didn't hear the distinctive *tink tink tink* of the dog's nails approaching until the mongrel slammed into me. Ben's dog, Wally, was a monstrous, shedding, yellow thing who slobbered all over Ben until dinner. While I was admittedly no expert in dogology, I was reasonably certain that he was a yellow Lab or some variation thereof. Whatever he was, he barked at random items—ink pens, scissors, the hem on Ben's shorts—and then he followed us to the dining room, where he planted his oversize ass on the floor at Ben's feet and panted as though he'd just run the Iditarod, stealing all the good air and replacing it with dog-breath air. It wasn't as though I hated dogs, exactly. I'd just prefer they were smaller, calmer, and cleaner. With a long, skinny tail and a meow rather than a bark. That would be the perfect dog.

Ben's mom had changed into a gauzy blue dress that billowed around her when she walked and made her look like a gypsy. She'd prepared quinoa enchiladas. She pronounced the word *quinoa* like "KEEN-wah." I'd never heard of the stuff before, and it must've shown on my face, because she went on to explain that quinoa was a "healthy grain."

Now, I was generally opposed to health foods. In my experience, they tasted like either dirt or air—like something nasty or like nothing at all. Also, I figured the preservatives in my diet would keep me alive longer, just by virtue of the fact that they were, well, preservatives.

With one eye on Ben's mom, I covertly spun my plate a quarter turn, so my enchilada was positioned at exactly twelve o'clock. It was purely out of habit and completely unnecessary, but I did it anyway. Meals had been a challenge for me since I'd lost my sight, and if my main dish wasn't sitting at exactly twelve o'clock, where I could locate it easily, everything just felt screwy.

Anyway, I'd just taken my first bite of my twelve o'clock, healthy enchilada—which, for the record, had nothing on a bag of Cheetos, but was surprisingly okay—when I heard massive footsteps approaching the dining room. Loud and clunky, they came from some area in the left of my non-eyesight. Suddenly, Ben's older brother—the good-looking, olive-skinned boy I'd seen in, oh, fifty million or so pictures around the house—emerged from the nothingness and sat down directly across from me.

If I had just one word to describe him, it would be *big*. Not fat, mind you. Just large. Muscly. He was tall, probably six feet or so, and he towered over my hundred-pound, five-four frame. He wore a black V-neck T-shirt, jeans, and these monstrous boots that somehow succeeded in making him appear even larger. His dark hair was scratched into universal messiness—in a way that may or may not have been intentional, and in a way that made me want to stare at the little angles created on his head. Ignoring me completely, he scooped a guy-size portion of enchiladas onto his plate and dug in.

Okay, so I was fully aware that this entire evening might be something my brain had conjured up on its own, that there was a possibility—more probable than not—that I was still lying on

Mr. Sturgis's floor, dreaming or hallucinating or whatever it is that crazy people do when they've completely lost it.

Still.

There was something about this guy, invented or not, that made me keenly aware of all my physical imperfections. I was too short, too boring-faced, too disheveled. I hadn't combed my hair all afternoon, and I was relatively certain that by now it resembled the hair inside a man's armpit. Also, I was wearing those baggy mom-shorts, a well-worn Loose Cannons T-shirt, and the oldest flip-flops known to mankind. I was complete disarray.

"Mason, this is Thera," Ben said to his brother by way of introduction, gesturing grandly toward me.

Without even a glance in my direction, Mason jerked his head up in a nod. "Hey," he said in greeting, the long vowel sound rolling smoothly and richly off his tongue.

Strange. He was such a huge, broad-shouldered guy that I'd expected his voice to be gravelly. Regardless, something about his tone was vaguely familiar, but I couldn't place it. I was replaying it in my mind, picking apart the timbre, when I realized that I hadn't replied. Staring above his head like a proper blind girl, I said, "Hi. Actually, my name is Maggie."

When his eyes finally flickered toward me, taking in my ratty hair and my ratty Loose Cannons T-shirt and my ratty everything, I caught a flash of something that I couldn't quite put a finger on. Anger, maybe? I wasn't sure. But I knew this: it was the first real expression he'd had since he'd sat down at the table. Half a second later it was gone, replaced by a certain coolness.

If I were a lesser woman I would have squirmed in my chair. Blushed. But I didn't. Chin held high, I tossed his aloof attitude right back at him and casually carved off a bite of my enchilada. I didn't know what his problem was, but I couldn't be bothered.

"Where do you go to school, Maggie?" Mrs. Milton asked me as I pretended to have difficulty scooping up a glob of my enchilada filling. There was something questionable in there, something brown mixed in with the quinoa. Either meat or mushrooms.

"Merchant's School for the Blind," Ben answered loudly, going overboard in advertising my lack of eyesight. Then he nudged me in the foot. He was a smooth one, this kid.

"Merchant's," I repeated, only because it should have come out of my mouth in the first place.

"Mason goes to Brighton," Mrs. Milton said cheerfully.

In a normal, polite conversation, this would be the point where Mason would jump in and add something. But he didn't. I could see him in my peripheral vision, ignoring my presence with utter indifference.

Now, I'd never been especially skilled at reeling in my temper. Particularly in situations that involved arrogant males. So I turned my head and glared at him. Dead in the eye. Mason crossed his arms and leaned back in his chair, keeping one skeptical eye on me for the remainder of the meal.

I drummed my fingers on the table, keeping time with the drip-drip-drip of the kitchen faucet. Fine. Whatever. He probably wasn't real anyway.

Mason said only a few words after that: *sour cream* and *um-hum* and *nope*. Every time he spoke, I made note of the velvety way his vowels rolled off his tongue. And every time he spoke, I kicked myself for making note of the velvety way his vowels rolled off his tongue. Because clearly, the guy was an egotistical jackass.

I was sitting there, tapping out an aggressive faucet song and eating my quinoa-and-maybe-meat-or-maybe-mushroom enchilada, when Ben said to his mom, "So in swim practice last night? I kicked ass." He glanced at his brother for confirmation. "Right, Mason?"

Mason made an affirmative noise, and Mrs. Milton shot Ben a disapproving look and said, "Benjamin Thomas Milton. Language."

Ben took in a monstrous breath and puffed out his cheeks, making his face almost completely circular. And then he leaned toward his mother, both palms flat on the table. "Sorry," he said. "It's just that I beat my time from last year. That crappy backstroke one? And now I come in only a few seconds after everyone else."

"You swim?" I said disbelievingly.

He sat up a little taller. "I'm on the swim team at North Bay Aquatic Club. The Dolphins?"

"Benjamin has spina bifida," his mom explained to me. "He was born with it. The bottom half of his legs are pretty much paralyzed, but his upper body is strong. He's been on the swim team since he was three."

"Wow, I'm impressed," I said, my voice quieter than I'd intended.

Ben's mom smiled. "Clearly, he gets his athletic ability from his father. I can hardly walk the dog without tripping. But Ben's dad? He was quite an athlete." The way she said *was* left me with the distinct impression that Mr. Milton was no longer living.

There were a few seconds of heavy silence in which Ben squirmed in his seat and Mason cleared his throat, and then Mrs. Milton said, "Oh, I almost forgot—" She bolted to her feet and hustled into some unspecified area of my non-eyesight, leaving her sentence open. But Ben and Mason seemed to know what was coming. There were two groans, the loudest of which was from Mason, who put his fork down and rubbed his forehead with his palm. Before I knew what was happening, Ben's mom popped back into my vision, holding a camera. A flashbulb went off in our faces.

"Mom," Mason complained. Just the one word: *mom*.

Mrs. Milton shot him a look. "Tonight is special," she said. "We have company. And enchiladas. Life moves too quickly. If I don't capture it, well . . ." Her voice faded away and her expression turned wistful. Finally, she took a deep breath, gave a bit of a forced smile, and said, "I want to remember tonight."

6

After dinner, Ben and I went to his room, shut the door, and played video games. As it happened, I did look a bit like Thera, the badass dragon slayer in Twenty-one Stones. But she was unquestionably the better looking of the two of us, even though she was animated. Yes, she had my curly auburn hair, and yes, she had my fair coloring, but she had one of those cute button noses, whereas I had a chubby, unfeminine-looking nose. And she had boobs, while I was still waiting for mine to grow into something respectable.

Ben's dog rested his muzzle on Ben's leg, his nostrils working, and stared unblinkingly at Ben while we played Twenty-one Stones, which, in my opinion, was a little strange. After several minutes of the staring thing, I jabbed my thumb in the direction of the mutt and said, "What's with the dog?"

Ben spoke to me in the inconsistent, erratic way that kids speak while playing video games. "HURRY UP AND SHOOT YOUR FIRE OUT BECAUSE HERE COMES WYVERN—SHOOT HIM—NO WITH FIREBALLS—Who? Wally? He's my dog. Duh. I'm, like, his favorite person—WAIT, DON'T GO IN THERE. YOU'RE GOING TO GET US KILLED!"

"Don't you think the way he's staring at you is a little weird?"

Ben rolled his eyes. "Wally was a stray that some assnozzle left at the veterinary clinic where my mom works. So she brought him home. He's been totally—TURN AROUND—HE'S GOING TO INCINERATE YOU—my dog ever since."

"Well, he ought to be off doing dog stuff—like barking and running around in the backyard and chasing cats and whatever," I muttered under my breath, one eye on Wally.

"He does that, too—HIT THE DRAGON BETWEEN THE EYES—THAT'S WHAT KILLS HIM!" Changing the subject, he said, "So. I must know everything about you, starting with the most important matter: what's your Thing?"

"My Thing?"

"Yeah. Everyone has a Thing."

"What sort of Thing?"

"You know, like, what is the Thing that makes you the happiest?—WATCH OUT BEHIND YOU!—What's the Thing that makes you *you*? Your Thing. My Thing is swimming. Like, obviously."

"Okay, then. That's easy. My Thing is soccer," I said with an air of finality. I used to be amazing at soccer: the sprinting down the field, the dribbling of the ball with the inside of my foot, the scoring.

He considered this for a moment, and then he said, "When was the last time you played soccer?"

"Like, six months ago, maybe? Right before I lost my sight?" I said, sort of defensively.

"Then it isn't your Thing. Not anymore."

I shrugged, trying not to let his words sink in enough to bother me. But they trickled in anyway, through the wide, jagged cracks the blindness had cut into me. They left my stomach pinched and my mouth dry. "Okay, so then I don't have a Thing," I said, hoping he'd drop the subject.

But he didn't. He set down his controller and stared at me, aghast. On the screen, his character got incinerated by a purple dragon. "Thera. Everyone has to have a Thing."

"But I don't," I argued. My life had been so stuffed full of soccer that I'd had little time for anything else. I grant you, I'd tried other things. Summer yoga camp. Snowboarding club. A decade's worth of piano lessons. But for countless reasons, they hadn't cleaved to me like soccer had.

"What about the Loose Cannons?" he said, gesturing to my T-shirt. "Are they your Thing?"

"The Loose Cannons are a band," I explained. "They can't be my Thing."

"Why not? Do they make you happy?" he asked.

"Well, yes," I said. "I guess. They're my favorite band. They just seem to get me. But that doesn't make them my Thing."

"Have you ever been to one of their concerts?"

I rolled my eyes. "No." Rather than having conventional concerts, the Loose Cannons played impromptu in completely random places—like the mall or the bank or whatever—and then uploaded the footage online. Five months ago, when they'd burst onto the music scene by posting their first concert on YouTube, they'd snagged a million hits. Their second concert? Three million. But as big as they were right now, the only way you could see one of their concerts was to uncover the band's obscure online clues to where and when they'd play next, which was something I'd been trying—and failing—to do for months on end. "Seeing the Loose Cannons in concert is next to impossible."

Ben shook his head and picked up his controller. His on-screen character immediately jumped up and started running through a cave. My character followed. "Thera," Ben said, "seeing the Loose Cannons is totally possible."

"Sure. Uh-huh. Right."

"Woman. Your words wound me greatly. You've already seen them—or one of them, anyway. My brother is the lead singer. Hel-lo? Mason Milton?"

Mason Milton.

That was when reality fell over me like a suffocating wool blanket. I had to be hallucinating. I'd spent the better part of the past several months either pining for my eyesight or pining for the Loose Cannons.

Of course I'd conjure up both of those things when I cracked.

Of course I would.

On top of that, the Mason Milton I'd met tonight looked brutally close to the one I'd pictured over the past several months. I huffed and let my head fall back. Fine. *Fine.* It was time for me to wake up or whatever it is that happens when crazy people realize that they are crazy.

I didn't, though. I just sat there and continued to be crazy.

A half hour later, Mrs. Milton knocked on Ben's door and pleasantly informed him that she was dropping him off at swim practice in "exactly forty-two minutes" and he needed to find his suit "and use the restroom, because the pool is not a toilet."

Ben looked mildly embarrassed. "Mom. I have plenty of time. We can even drop Thera off at her house on the way. She just lives in . . ." He turned to me. "Where do you live?"

"Bedford Estates," I said, and his eyebrows shot up.

"Bedford Estates," he informed his mom. "So we have plenty of time."

It wasn't until after we piled into the backseat of the Miltons' minivan, and after we pulled out of the driveway, and after I gave Ben's mom directions to my house, that Ben leaned over and whispered in my ear, "You seriously live in Bedford Estates?"

"Yup."

Our house was just like the others in Bedford Estates, outrageously huge and sort of gaudy. We'd moved there when I was four, and even at that tender age I thought the place was outrageously huge and sort of gaudy. So I spent most of my time upstairs in my bedroom. It was a dreamer's room that stared out at the great maple in our front yard. It had slanted ceilings plastered with a couple dozen glow-in-the-dark stars and a little cutout in front of the window, the perfect place to read. A thousand memories lived there now, all in suspended animation: pictures of friends slapped on a corkboard, a half-deflated soccer ball wedged in the corner, books jumbled on the nightstand. I'd set foot in it only once after meningitis took my sight, and it had felt as though it belonged to someone else. Someone with possibility. So I stayed downstairs in the boxy, functional room my parents had set up for me before I came home from the hospital.

After we came to a stop in my driveway, Ben leaned out the window, craning his neck to peer up at my house. He whistled, long and low. "Sweet," he said, dragging the word out as though he were talking about a skateboard trick or a new video game.

And then, silence. Ben and his mom were waiting for me to climb out of the car.

I swallowed. This was it: the end. The dream of the past couple hours had freight-trained past me in a blur of normalcy. All those minutes and seconds were gone now, and I felt like I'd squandered them. I wasn't ready to let them go. I swallowed again, louder this time, and looked around, taking in the back of Mrs. Milton's head and Ben's skinny legs and the cracked vinyl seats.

"Um. Thera? I'm gonna be late for swim practice," Ben prompted.

I flinched. "Right," I said, yanking down on the door handle and stepping out of the van on wobbly legs. With one last aching look at the colors and the textures and the *life*, I said good-bye.

7

Grandpa Keith's first words that evening were directed at an auto auction on TV: "Nineteen sixty-eight Dodge Ram. Absolute piece of crap." (Technically, the first thing he said was, "Your dad just called. He wants to know where you've been all afternoon and why you aren't answering your cell phone." But that little spiel was just the sort of thing that I didn't want to deal with right now, so the "absolute piece of crap" comment was the first thing that I actually paid any attention to.)

I was sprawled out on the sofa in an unladylike tangle of legs and hair and confusion. My cat, Louie, the laziest feline in the feline cosmos, was a massive lump of sleeping fur beside me. Gramps had commandeered Dad's overstuffed, overused armchair, something he did every evening just before Dad got home from work. If I didn't know any better, I'd swear that he was getting even for all the childhood grief Dad had put him through. But Dad was the most ho-hum guy on the planet, so the only thing Gramps could possibly be avenging was getting bored to tears all these years.

Gramps was a TV nazi and he guarded the remote control with his life. So I was stuck listening to the auto auction. I wasn't paying attention to it. I was...well, I wasn't sure what I was doing. Trying to convince myself that what had happened today was real, maybe?

I wasn't having any luck.

The more I thought about it, the more outrageous it all seemed. I mean, really. Banging my head and suddenly reclaiming part of my eyesight? Mason Milton's just *happening* to be Ben's brother? Of course I'd fabricated the entire thing.

Except.

Where had I been all afternoon if I hadn't been at the Miltons'? How had I even gotten home from Mr. Sturgis's office?

"Gramps," I said suddenly. "Did you happen to see the van that dropped me off?"

"Van? No. Why?" he said suspiciously.

"No reason," I said. I wiped my palms on the sofa and then cast around for a change of subject. "So. What did you do today?"

"Went to Manny Grayson's funeral." Gramps was obsessed with funerals—what sort of coffins people chose and what was written on their tombstones and whatever.

"Who's Manny Grayson?" I asked.

"One of Hank's friends—went along as a plus-one."

I scrunched up my nose. "A plus-one...at a funeral?"

Gramps ignored me. "Played polka music during the service." He scoffed. "Polka music. Heh. Who plays that crap?"

I winced inwardly. I played it—or I *had* played it, rather. Not because I'd wanted to, but because my ex–piano teacher, Mr. Hawthorne, had an affinity for crap music. Problem was, I'd been physically unable to strangle such dusty sounds out of a piano. So I hadn't. I'd improvised the pieces in spectacular fashion, reaching into his concertos and mazurkas and mixing them up, scattering the notes like leaves in the wind. My creativity didn't fly with Mr. Hawthorne, however, and so after nearly a decade of arguing with him over starchy piano theory, I lost interest and quit. I don't know which one of us had been more relieved.

At exactly seven thirty, my mother stepped into the house. I knew this not because I actually knew the time, but because I knew my mother. She was nothing if not regimented. Giving me a cursory greeting—just a hand running across the top of my head—she unloaded on the arm of the couch, all sighs.

I swung my feet around to the floor. My cat hit the carpet with a wide-pawed flump. "Hey, Mom. How was your day?"

"Exhausting," she said. Her customary reply these days. Particularly while ducking conversation about her job—head coach of the women's soccer team at the University of Connecticut. Clearing her throat, she changed the subject. "Hilda called me today to set up an appointment with you. Said she's left you several voice mails and you haven't gotten back to her?" When I failed to reply, she went on. "Anyway, she said she'll be here at eleven o'clock tomorrow."

"In the *morning*? I have plans." Which, in fact, I did not. But I could have some plans if I really wanted to.

While I might be lacking in marketable skills, I happened to do a bang-up job when it came to lying. Unfortunately, my mother was aware of my talent. I could practically hear her eyebrows hike up. "What plans?"

"Stuff."

"Well, change your stuff," she said tiredly. And then her phone rang: her assistant coach. With a grunt, she stood up and paced away, talking backpasses and kick-and-runs and shoot-outs.

Back in the day, my mother had played soccer for the women's national team. She'd been a middie, the fastest on the field, and we had a box of old DVDs to prove it. When I was real young, I used to sneak into the basement late at night, put the TV on mute, and curl up under an afghan to watch them. Back then she was my hero. My biggest and grandest memory of her came from when I was five. It was fall, and the sky was a crisp, cloudless blue, almost too blue to be real. My mother's team was playing against Norway in the quarterfinals of the Women's World Cup, and the United States was hosting. The critics considered Norway the favorite that year, but my mother proved them wrong. She scored the only goal in the game. When the last buzzer sounded, she ran to the sidelines at full force—just a blur of sweat and smile and ponytail—threw me on her shoulders, and paraded me across the field. I'll never forget how I felt on her shoulders: strong, pretty, smart.

In the stadium's parking lot that same evening, some punk slammed into her, snatched her purse, and bolted off at a dead sprint. Yes, Dad was right beside her. And yes, he stood there like a complete dumbass while the guy took off. Mom, however, tore after the guy, screaming at the top of her lungs. It didn't take long for her to catch up to him. She seized him by the arm, yanked her purse free, and said through her teeth, all up in his face, "Your mother must be so *proud*." Then she clobbered him on the side of the head with the purse and stomped off.

She was huge to me that night, larger than life. Magical, even. Her confidence and energy on the field leaked out into everything she touched. It was as though she could do anything, be anything, conquer anything she wanted to, and I wanted nothing more than to become just like her. But then a couple days later, just before the semifinals, she tore her Achilles tendon. I remember all too clearly the thin set of her lips when she was told she would never again play competitive soccer. She'd always been so strong and so centered that I didn't expect the injury to change who she was. Which was exactly why the following weeks were so strange. She just got . . . distant. Hardened. There was something haunting and sharp-edged about her facial features. She refused to see her friends, sulked in her room, stayed in her pajamas the entire day. She was suddenly this person I didn't know, and it terrified me. Dad assured me that she was going to be fine, that she was just going through some sort of grief process. A big part of her—her dreams, her talents, and her strengths—had died.

But all that changed when I turned six and started to play soccer. I wasn't a natural, like she had been. I spent long, arduous hours outside, banging the ball against the garage door and practicing footwork. "You're doing it wrong," she told me one day from the back porch while I worked on my finish into a makeshift goal. When I glanced up at her, hair every which way and clothes rumpled, I noticed something different in her eyes—a hope or a yearning or a need.

I scratched a mosquito bite on my collarbone. "Can you help me?" I asked.

And that was all it took.

My mother's demeanor started to improve as soon as she walked down the porch steps that day, and so did my soccer skills. With Mom's tireless coaching, I became unstoppable with the soccer ball between my feet, scoring eight, nine, ten goals per game. I loved watching the expression on her face when I scored. It was the same face I used to adore: bright-eyed, explosive, and full of energy. Even back then I knew—I was her second chance. I could picture myself, nothing but sweat and smile and ponytail, running across the field toward her after the last buzzer of the World Cup finals. To celebrate with her. To give her what she'd been cheated out of. To give her back the life she had lost.

But six months and five days ago, all that changed. And she lost her dream again.

I didn't remember much from that first week in the hospital, but I remembered what was important. I remembered the steady rhythms of the machines beeping behind me. I remembered the thick odor of disease that hung in the air. I remembered the way my head had felt—like it had been cleaved in half with a rusty hatchet. But most of all, I remembered overhearing a conversation that hadn't been intended for my ears.

"Do you think she knows yet?" a nurse said as she adjusted my sheets.

Something that sounded like heavy machinery rolled across the floor. I could smell coffee breath in my face as another nurse said, "That she's blind?"

"No. About her mom leaving town."

Heavy sigh. "She doesn't know much of anything right now."

"What sort of mother just takes off while her kid is in the hospital? What sort of mother *does* that?"

I didn't believe it at first, that my mom had gone. But for several days running, as I lay in a medication stupor, I listened for Mom, waited to smell her linen perfume or to feel her take my hand and whisper that everything would be okay. But she didn't.

Dad was there, though, more often than not—a solid, protective presence at my side, pleading to God under his breath. This was so typical of him. The praying. He was so characteristically down-to-earth and no-nonsense that most people never would guess he prayed all the time. But I remembered it so clearly from my time in the hospital—Dad's pleading for me, for Mom.

For the happily ever after.

And he got it. Almost.

When I finally started to pull through, Mom appeared out of nowhere, complaining to the doctors that I needed more pain medicine and grumbling about the room temperature and making me wonder whether I'd imagined it all. And by the time I got released from the hospital, I wondered if maybe I did.

8

I was sitting in front of my computer when the doorbell rang the next morning. I ignored it completely. I'd grown to despise answering the door. It was too much of a crapshoot. Could be the Pope. Could be a serial killer. I had no way of knowing, no peephole to peer through. And anyway, since I'd rolled out of bed I'd been particularly engrossed in the Loose Cannons' website, where I'd learned that the band had performed last night on top of an abandoned building in Bridgeport.

And I'd missed it.

The biggest difference between my computer and a sighted person's computer was that mine was armed with software that converted what was on the screen into speech—like, every link, every piece of text, every everything. In other words, it had taken me an exhaustingly long time to tab my way through the website using keyboard shortcuts to find . . . basically nothing.

Rumor was, clues to the band's concert times and locations were embedded somewhere in the site, though I'd never been able to unearth one. Today I'd found a short post from the band, thanking the fans who'd attended the concert—nothing cryptic there. A couple quotes from last week's newspaper, which had featured the band—ditto. And the link to the concert's YouTube video.

The doorbell rang again.

I hit the link, and "Lucidity," the first song in last night's concert, snaked into my room. With a sigh, I tabbed down to the video's comment section. Hardcore fans in the know haunted this spot to brag indecently about having attended the concerts. Today was no exception. There was a post from some superfan who called herself Pink Pistol, boasting that she'd gotten Mason's autograph after the performance. Another from Tommy X, who claimed that the concert had been "mind-blowing." After that were probably a half-dozen posts from brainless bastards such as myself, begging both Pink Pistol and Tommy X to divulge how they'd found the clue.

The doorbell rang again.

I navigated down to Tommy X's reply: "In order to keep the mystique alive, I can't disclose the Big Secret. But I'll tell you this: you have to look beyond the surface."

I leaned back in my chair, exhaling in irritation. I'd spent months combing through the band's website. Months. I knew it forward and backward. If there were a clue—on the surface or not—you'd think I would've bumped into it long ago.

The doorbell rang again.

And again.

And again.

I cursed under my breath, jerked to my feet, and stomped to the front door. My manners were always a couple steps behind my mouth, so I swung the door open in all my glory—hair, like a squirrel had been running through it; pajamas, like a homeless guy had been wearing them for a month straight; expression, like it was teetering on the edge of a four-letter-word—and said, "I don't speak English." Then I slammed the door shut.

It was quiet for a beat or two, and then I heard a familiar burst of strong Romanian consonants: "Neither do I."

I yanked open the door. "Hilda," I breathed. "I forgot about our session."

"Oof," she said, pushing past me.

During the first session, right after I'd lost my sight, she'd burst into our house like a hurricane, ordering my parents to relocate furniture, barking at them to reorganize the kitchen and closets, and urging them to vandalize the cabinets with braille, all of which had been pretty entertaining. After that, though, she'd started in on me, and our relationship had gone downhill.

"Put on your shoes and grab your cane," Hilda said gruffly. "Today we will go outside."

"Outside? Why?"

"To learn."

I waved a dismissing hand at her. "I'm pretty happy with the inside, actually."

"*Pish.* You cannot stay inside for the rest of your life."

Oh, but I could. Inside our house, I was a rockstar. I knew where to walk, which drawer held what, whose footsteps were banging through the entryway. I didn't even need my cane. But outside? Well. That was completely different. And I had no desire to take the show on the road.

"Actually, I've become what you might call indoorsy."

Hilda grunted. "Outside."

This woman could ruin a morning like Hitler could ruin a mustache.

With a loud sigh, I lumbered to my room and got dressed. Several minutes later I collapsed on the couch, shoes in hand, and said, "Um. What are we going to do outside?"

"Learn to navigate sidewalks."

I winced. "So we're going to wander up and down the sidewalk so people can get a good look at me before they run me over?"

She grunted. "We could walk to a friend's house, no? If you have a friend nearby?"

A friend.

The words left a bitter taste in my mouth. My "friends," most of whom had been on my soccer team, and most of whom had treated me like a charity case when I'd lost my sight, were a part of my past, not my present. Even my two closest friends, Sophie and Lauren, had drifted away from me, remaining somewhere out of reach, off in the background, as though waiting for some huge miracle to occur.

But it hadn't.

And in the meantime, I'd had to relearn how to be a person: how to get dressed, eat, take a shower, identify objects. I'd had to figure out how to take those first steps into unknown emptiness. And honestly? My first successes had been too embarrassing to share with Sophie and Lauren: "Hey guys, learned how to use a fork today without shish-kebabing my face." So instead, I'd shared my achievements with Hilda, but only because she had been the one forcing me to discover them in the first place.

"Ready?" Hilda grunted.

"Not exactly."

"You cannot hide in your house for the rest of your life."

"Actually, I kind of can."

I could hear her pacing in front of me, something she did when I was annoying her. Finally she blurted, "Tell me, where do you see yourself in ten years?"

A little voice in my head—the same voice that encouraged me to say mildly inappropriate yet potentially amusing things—was cheering me on to ask whether this was a trick question. But I decided against it. While I couldn't prove it scientifically, I was pretty sure that Hilda was the most uptight person on the planet.

Mistaking my pause for confusion, she said, "Your life. How do you envision your life?"

I scraped a toe across the carpet. I didn't want to think about my future until sometime in the future. Or perhaps sometime after my death. Stalling, I said, "You mean, like, family and career and whatever?"

She shot a heavy gust of nasty breath in my face. "Yes. Family. Career. Whatever. Your *future*."

I waved a palm at her, making light of the topic. "I don't have to worry about that for a long time."

She cleared her throat vigorously enough to cause bleeding. "Oof. You must begin planning now." And then she went on and on about Missouri State University, and how it was voted the best college for the blind, and how I could grow up to have a career and a husband and children, and how I could use public transportation to get to work and to do my errands, and so on and so on and so on, and then I realized that I couldn't even hear her anymore because all I could think was *There's no way in hell I can live like that.*

9

I'd left my phone in my room while I was out tripping over rogue fire hydrants, and when I scooped it off my bed I found that I had ten missed calls and two voice mails, all from the same number. Phone in hand, I walked straight down the hall and out the sliding glass door. Settling on the wooden steps of our deck, I retrieved my messages.

The first one: "Thera. It's Ben."

Ben.

My hand started shaking so badly, I could hardly hold the phone as Ben went on to say, "You know, Ben Milton? Your boyfriend? The charming, good-looking one? Anyway, one word for you: Doritos." He paused, all dramatically, and then went on. "The thing is, Thera? I just had one of those aha moments. The ones Oprah is always talking about? I just realized that the Dorito is the perfect chip." There was this crunching sound on

Ben's end of the line, like he was killing a bag of Doritos in my ear. "Just the right amount of salt," he said. "Intense flavor. They go perfectly with water, milk, juice, or soda. And, if I don't brush my teeth after I eat them, I can taste them for approximately ten hours. What's better than a chip in your mouth for ten hours? Nothing. That's right: nothing. That's frigging perfection. I believe that the masterpiece known as the mighty Dorito may just be your Thing. You must eat a bag of them immediately. Actually? No. Don't just eat the chips—eat them while honoring their excellence. Please call me back at your earliest convenience. Good-bye."

I sat there for the longest time after the message ended, trying to keep myself from getting overly hopeful. But Ben's personality had practically crawled out of the phone and shaken me by both shoulders.

He was real.

But that doesn't mean I saw him.

I chewed on my thumbnail as I listened to the second voice mail: "Thera. You should probably get some sort of privacy block for your phone number because any jackwad can just look it up online. Not that I'm a jackwad. I am probably the least jackwaddish person I know." He paused as though he was waiting for me to chime in and defend his honor. "Anyways, I was wondering whether you knew when guys start growing armpit hair? I think I have an armpit disease, because I don't have any hair. Not. A. Single. One. And by the way, FOR A GIRLFRIEND, YOU TOTALLY SUCK AT RETURNING PHONE CALLS. That is all."

Calm down, I warned myself as I saved his number in my phone. *This doesn't mean anything. Not yet.*

I called him back. He picked up after only one ring. "Thera, my love!" he basically screamed.

"Ben!" I hollered back, smiling like a lunatic.

"Did you try some Doritos?" he asked.

"Haven't had the chance," I said. I felt oddly as though I'd just found another fraction of myself, a piece that had been torn up and discarded months ago.

He sighed into the phone. "Thera. This is serious. You don't have a Thing. You can't be walking around without a Thing. It's unnatural. You'll develop a limp or a cough or something." When I cracked up, Ben hollered over me, "I'm not kidding, Thera. This is big. People are supposed to have Things. Heck, even Mason has a Thing."

Mason. Well. That shut me up.

I jerked to my feet and paced across the deck, my flip-flops making a joyful little *clap clap clap* rhythm that was completely at odds with the sudden twist in my gut. If Ben was real, then Mason was—

"Anyway," Ben went on, crunching on Doritos again, "I was thinking to myself this morning, 'Self, Thera would love to see your swim meet today.'"

"I would?" Of course I would. Truth was, I'd curated a couple dozen ulcers since I'd said good-bye to Ben, believing that yesterday had been some sort of elaborate fantasy—something I'd wished for and wished for until my brain finally broke down and believed it. I needed to sort out what was going on. I needed to discover whether there was a chance that maybe, just maybe, my sight was returning. I needed answers.

"Yup. You would," Ben said. "It's at two o'clock, at North Bay Aquatic Club. See you there." And he hung up.

....

I was somewhat familiar with North Bay Aquatic Club. I'd taken a handful of swim lessons there when I was fourteen, back when my mother was convinced that I needed to vary my cardio workout to prepare for soccer season. My instructor was a middle-aged guy who was huge and lumpy, built like a trash bag full of walnuts, and he had a sour yet surprised expression permanently etched into his features—like he'd just taken a sip of what he'd presumed was Sprite, but to his shock discovered that it was instead grape-fruit juice.

On the first day of lessons, he made the mistake of teaching me how to float on my back. From that point on, I was completely done. Why flail around, gasping for breath, struggling to improve my already stellar soccer skills, when I could lie on my back and float peacefully? So float I did, through that first swim lesson and every swim lesson that followed. It was a fantastic waste of my mother's two hundred dollars.

Now, as Gramps pulled his truck to a stop in front of North Bay Aquatic Club, I tried to keep my eyes from sweeping the area for a little dot of eyesight, but failed entirely. I didn't see anything, though, and as Gramps got out of his truck and guided me inside the building to the pool, I grew more and more tense.

I was psycho.

They were going to chuck me into a nondescript white-on-white building with all the other whackjobs, and I'd end up rocking back and forth in some activity room while drinking Capri Suns and mindlessly crocheting doilies and—

"You want me to walk you to the bleachers?" Gramps asked.

Just then, Ben blinked into being. Whether the crowd had hidden him or I simply hadn't been at the right angle to catch sight of him, I didn't know. All I knew was that suddenly there he was: walking along the edge of the club's cobalt-blue pool, concrete under his bare feet and a bushy-haired boy at his side, laughing at an unknown joke.

I sucked in my breath.

"You okay, kid?" Gramps asked.

"I'm fine," I murmured. Which was true. I was fine. I was perfectly sane.

I could feel my sweaty hand on Gramps's elbow, and I could hear the steady rhythm of the spectators' feet stamping in the stands, and I could smell the chlorine and cocoa butter–scented sunscreen. And I could see Ben. All of these things were occurring at the same time. And I was completely sane.

"Mags," Gramps said loudly. And from the impatience in his tone I got the feeling this wasn't the first time he'd called my name. "Want me to walk you to the bleachers?"

I waved him away and said good-bye, staying right there, wherever *right there* was, as realization swept over me. If I was really seeing Ben—really seeing him—then who's to say that I couldn't see in other circumstances? Hope expanded in my chest like a hot air balloon.

I could reclaim the soccer field.

And my friends.

My school.

My life.

Suddenly, something waist-high that reeked of Elmer's Glue and Pop-Tarts jabbed me in the thigh and said, "Are you gonna get out of my way sometime this century?" Sounded like a little girl. A mouthy little girl. By means of answering her, I yanked my cane out of my back pocket and unfolded it with a flick. "Oh. Okay. I get it. So you're blind," she said through a distinctive lisp, stubbornness still lacing her tone.

"That I am."

"How come you don't have a guide dog?" she challenged.

"Who says I need one?" I said, one eye on the pool, where Ben was cheering on the current race.

"*I* do," she argued. "Blind people have dogs. How come you don't have one?"

Massaging my forehead with my knuckles, I said, "Because I don't like dogs."

"How come you don't like dogs?"

I was tempted to ignore her. Everything in me itched to get closer to Ben, closer to my eyesight. "Because they're slobbery and hairy and barky," I said, trying to catch Ben's eye.

She grumbled under her breath. "Where are your dark glasses?"

Evidently common sense wasn't very common. Couldn't she see that I had more important things happening here? "Not all visually impaired people wear dark glasses," I told her. The truth was, wearing dark glasses is a personal choice. Some of us wear sunglasses because we have discolored or distorted irises, while others are light-sensitive regardless of the visual impairment. None of which needed to be shared with this kid.

She said, "I thought blind people were supposed to be nice. You aren't very nice."

Well. That was the most accurate thing she'd said so far.

Ben looked up and saw me. He beamed at me in a way that looked like it might fracture a smile muscle, and then he headed toward us, my eyesight ghosting behind him like a comet tail until he swung to a stop in front of me.

And just like that, I felt whole again. I couldn't stop beaming.

Ben was wearing a pair of slate-blue swim trunks, a toothy grin, and—crammed sideways on his damp sandy hair—a baseball cap that said THE VOICES IN MY HEAD ARE TELLING ME THAT YOU'RE AN ALIEN!

"Thera!" he screamed. The kid looked like a skinny stork in a swimsuit—all knees and elbows and whatnot.

"Ben!" I yelled back, and then I let my gaze drift downward. I found myself looking at the stubborn face of a young girl— probably around six or seven years old, I was guessing—who had an army of freckles but only one front tooth. She was wearing a scowl, jean shorts that were creased where they met her pelvis, a white T-shirt with hearts stamped all over it, and a glittery purple tiara. She suspiciously pursed her lips at me for half a tick, and I glanced away, realizing that I was staring at her like a sighted person.

Leaping toward Ben, she hugged him at the waist—crutches and all. "Ben!" she bellowed.

"Hey, Samantha," he said.

She blinked up at him. "Will you play with me? Pleaseplease-pleaseplease? I'm so bored."

"I will absolutely play with you. Later on," said Ben. He nodded in my direction. "Right now, I'm sort of busy with Thera."

She turned to glare at me. I smiled innocently at her shoulder. And she took off, back to wherever she'd come from. Probably Satan's lap.

10

Ben introduced me to his best friend and teammate, Teddy—a short, bushy-haired kid wearing swim trunks identical to Ben's. I couldn't help but notice that the right side of Teddy's face was covered in puckered, rubbery-looking scars, which were creepy and compelling, all at the same time. I'd like to say that I wasn't the sort of person who would stare at them, but, well, I couldn't stop staring. They were just so…there. Finally, he turned his head slightly and his moptop hair swept over them a bit, freeing me from my moral non-dilemma.

"When I met Teddy, he was ass-up in a hospital bed," Ben informed me after introducing the two of us, "getting skin harvested from his butt cheek to graft to the burn spot on his face."

How was I supposed to respond to that? I snuck yet another glance at Teddy, who seemed perfectly at ease with the subject matter. "Oh. Well. That's . . . um . . . interesting," I finally said. And then naturally, I afforded myself a quick look at his face again to inspect the skin, which, incidentally, did not look like the skin of a kid's butt.

Ben went on to say, "He was my roommate—room two twenty-two at Memorial. I was there for some testing and bored out of my goddamn skull."

"Ben. Don't cuss," I said, but both boys kept yammering on as if I hadn't spoken. They bantered back and forth about Teddy's white ass—Teddy claiming that it was more handsome than Ben's face, and Ben submitting that it was whiter than the white incisors on a white polar bear, and so on and so forth.

And then finally Teddy said, "Dude. Admit it. The only reason you decided to be my best friend was so you could get away with calling me 'butthead' without getting in trouble." I laughed so hard that I started making squeaky dolphin noises.

Then there was a rather loud announcement about an upcoming race, and Ben said, "Gotta run, Thera." He pointed with his head to the pool. "It's time to carpe my diem."

"What do you know about carpe diem?" I said through a chuckle.

"Everything. I read all about it in the Cs."

I laughed again. It sounded like Ben's exclamation-point laugh, which was sort of weird but sort of nice.

"I'll be in the water in five minutes," he said. He saluted me, Teddy said good-bye, and then the two boys took off, disappearing into a throng of bathing suit–clad kids.

. . . .

The first words Ben's mom said to me that afternoon were, "Careful, I have dog poop on my scrubs." Which was disturbing because she said them during another one of her surprise-attack hugs. She did not, in point of fact, reek of dog crap. She smelled vaguely of incense and peppermint and kindness. As soon as she pulled away from me, she led me to a set of metal bleachers, next to—to my complete and utter humiliation—Mason. Seeing as how I'd shown up at his house last night wearing a Loose Cannons T-shirt and poorly faking my blindness, I figured he thought I was a lunatic fan who had weaseled my way into his life by pretending to be blind so his little brother would take pity on me. Which was mortifying even though it wasn't true.

All right, so maybe the lunatic fan part was true. I mean, if I happened to stumble upon a hint today that helped direct me to the next Loose Cannons concert . . . well, let's just say I wouldn't be upset.

At any rate, Mason failed to acknowledge me when I said hello. Actually, check that; he acknowledged me by immediately sliding away from me, presumably cramming himself next to some woman, because I heard a surprised little "Oh!" as he moved.

I chatted idly with Mrs. Milton, keeping tabs on Mason with my senses (while appearing not to be keeping tabs on Mason with my senses). I could practically feel the aggravation crawling out of his pores, could hear his choppy, annoyed breaths.

Honestly.

Sure, he'd become something of an instant celebrity recently, but just how arrogant was he to believe I'd come to the swim meet just to be around him? I silently fumed, tapping my foot in time with the *swoosh-swoosh-swoosh-swoosh* of the swimmers cutting through the water. Mason's aversion to me was maddening, frustrating, and . . . well, sort of absorbing. Did he really believe I was a crazed fan, or did he just find me atrocious-looking? Probably a little of both. I didn't bother with makeup anymore. There were too many little bottles and too many little tubes and too many little opportunities to turn myself into a clown.

Whatever the reason, Mason refused to speak to me. He did, however, exchange pleasantries with another spectator and offered a hand to what sounded like a little girl who was struggling up the bleachers. "Whoa, there," he said, and I felt the bleachers rise slightly as he stood. There was something genuine in Mason's voice. Something authentic. It made me feel strange for some reason—either hurt or confused or exposed. I didn't know what it was, exactly, except that there was a lot of it.

I grumbled under my breath for letting him get under my skin. Mason was not just a complete egotistical jerk—he was a complete egotistical jerk who obviously believed that I idolized him. And he was dead wrong. Sure, I loved his music. And yes, I'd likely give up my right kidney to learn the location of his band's next concert. And of course, I thought he had an amazing voice. But that didn't mean I *worshiped* him, that didn't mean I'd go to such ridiculous lengths just to be near him.

Mrs. Milton nudged me with her elbow. "Ben's race should be coming up any second."

"Yeah?" I said, glancing covertly at Ben. He stood next to the pool, his entire body rocking with laughter as Teddy made faces at him. "Has he always loved to swim?" I asked, reaching down to scratch my calf. In my haste, I inadvertently brushed my arm against Mason's. It was the smallest of touches and lasted only a fraction of a second, but something inside me lurched as a sharp bolt of electricity reverberated between us. I jerked away and folded my arms across my chest.

"Actually," Mrs. Milton said, her voice slightly guarded, "a few months ago Ben went through a bit of a swimming funk because of a falling out with another kid on the team."

I felt my mouth drop open. "Ben had a *falling out*? For real?"

Mrs. Milton muttered, "It was a girl."

"Ah."

"Ben had a huge crush on her," Mrs. Milton explained, "and you know how Ben is when he likes someone. He goes all out, even if they aren't the least bit interested. He saved his allowance for months to buy her a video game."

"Twenty-one Stones?" I asked. Suddenly I didn't want to hear the rest of this story.

"That's the one," Mrs. Milton confirmed. "Anyway, when he gave it to her, she didn't react the way he'd hoped." While her words were matter-of-fact, I could hear fierce maternal protectiveness hiding in her tone.

"What did she do?"

"Threw it in the trash and called him a . . ." She stopped, regrouped, and then tried again. "She called him a 'stupid retard.' He was heartbroken."

I felt a sharp pang in the hollow of my chest, a clog in my throat. I whispered, "Is she still on the team? That girl?"

"No," Mrs. Milton said in a sigh. "Coach has a strict policy about the kids treating one another respectfully." She patted me compassionately on the leg. "Oh, don't get upset, hon. The kids at school prepared him for this kind of thing. He's kind, trusting, an easy target. And anyway, he has Teddy, and now you—someone who can appreciate what it feels like when life throws you curveballs."

I nodded woodenly, and, eyes closed, tried to pull myself together. Beside me Mason was still as stone, but I'd swear I could feel his breath feathering against my cheek. I'd swear that he was facing me, that his eyes were on me. Was he staring at me?

I dipped my head, letting my hair curtain my face for a few seconds. Then I raised my chin. I still felt his eyes on me—scorching like the desert sun. I twisted my hands in my lap. Why was he staring?

Trying to take my mind off Mason, I peered across the nothingness to where Ben was getting ready for his race. He now sat on a wooden bench alongside the pool, so stuffed full of smiles that they just spilled out of him. He pulled on a pair of red swim goggles that warped his face a little, like those mirrors that distort your chin and make your head look fat in all the wrong places. Pumping one fist high in the air, he cheered for someone in the pool. There was something about the upward curve of his mouth that filled me with an overwhelming, protective affection. Some people have so many layers to them that you can hardly see who they are. But when I looked at Ben, I saw everything that made him *him*.

Why would anyone intentionally hurt someone like him?

When they announced the next race, Ben approached the water. There was a long pause while he climbed the podium. He moved slowly and deliberately, as though savoring the moment. When he finally made it to the top of the podium, he stood there for a long fragment of time. Supporting himself with the metal rails of the podium and peeling off his crutches, he scanned the crowd until he found us. And then he smiled.

Instinctively, I smiled back and began to lift my hand to him, but I stopped, midwave, and ran my fingers through my hair.

Too late. Apparently Mason had already seen it. He made an irritated sound in the back of his throat.

I felt as though I should play it off, so with my gaze facing the pool and with all the innocence I could muster, I said, "Are you okay, Mason?"

He bit off a "Yes" through what sounded like clenched teeth.

Well. At least he'd spoken to me.

Ben, oblivious to my bonehead move, stretched his toes toward the water, leaning over the edge. I held my breath. Beside me, Mrs. Milton's camera fired off pictures, one after another in rapid succession.

There was a loud pop, a monstrous splash, and the stands erupted in cheering. Ben didn't appear partially paralyzed in the water. He looked strong and confident, like any other kid, yet so insanely different. As the race went on, I caught snatches of swimmers passing him. Though Ben moved slowly, deliberately, he had an obvious advantage on another swimmer, a chubby kid at his ankles. When Ben turned around at the far end of the pool to make his final lap, he glanced behind him. And then, little by little, he slowed his pace, letting the kid gain ground on him.

I couldn't believe it. He was deliberately letting the kid beat him.

This really shouldn't have surprised me. Not really. Ben was just . . . good-hearted. CEO of the National Society of Encyclopedia Britannica Readers, president of the Department of Constant Bucktoothed Smiles, grand pooh-bah of Letting the Fat Kid Win.

Who was I? I didn't know.

O nce I allowed myself to harbor the hope that I might completely regain my vision, the idea possessed me. That evening, my mind hopscotched between the ways my life would stitch back together if my sight fully returned, how I'd reclaim the soccer field, the hallways at my old school, the afternoons with Sophie and Lauren. How my troubles with my mother would dissolve.

Doubts snuck in there, too. I worried that my newfound sight was temporary, transient. That maybe nature would realize its mistake and return me to complete blindness. That if I didn't hurry up and figure out all the whys and the hows and the wheres, my little island of eyesight, along with the explanation for it, would disappear just as quickly as it had come.

Best I could guess, the crack I'd taken on my head had been the catalyst. Yet I wasn't exactly dying to field-test this theory. Bashing myself on the skull with a hammer for another inch of vision? No, thank you. My luck, I would knock myself right back into complete blindness. Besides, I couldn't shake the feeling that I was overlooking something crucial. I felt oddly as though I were a moth stuck in a lamp shade, bumping around the light but missing the bigger picture.

By the time I wandered into the living room, where Gramps and Dad were listening to an ancient Beatles album and swapping conspiracy stories about John Lennon's death, I was complete wreckage. I felt compelled to see Ben again, which then made me feel guilty because he was just a good-hearted ten-year-old kid who didn't deserve to get used just so I could see, which then made me feel frustrated because currently I *could not see* one freaking thing, which then made me long to see Ben again, which then made me feel guilty for wanting to see Ben again, which then made me realize why I usually ignored my goddamn feelings. I groaned quietly and buried my face in a couch pillow.

"What's wrong, honey?" Dad asked.

I was so close to telling him the truth—honest, I was—but the words seemed too twisted to make sense coming out of my mouth, so in the end I replied that everything was fine, that I had a headache, and I walked back to my room and shut the door.

I paced a little. Sat on the edge of my bed a little. Listened to the radio a little. And then I lurched up, unloaded in front of my computer, and signed on to Dr. Darren's website.

This wasn't the first time I'd turned to Dr. Darren. I'd always skewed a bit toward the hypochondriac side of the wellness scale. Back in the fourth grade I'd had imaginary thumb cancer for a while. And then flesh-eating disease of the ankle. In middle school I'd acquired a touch of fabricated tuberculosis, which, given my track record for medical misadventures, my parents had not taken seriously. I'd therefore done what most paranoid quasi-tuberculosis sufferers would do: I'd signed on to the Ask Dr. Darren website and requested advice.

From what I remembered of his website photo, Dr. Darren was a gray-haired, leather-skinned man who had long, scraggly eyebrows that must've grown tired of lying down flat because they stuck straight out of his forehead. He had a strong, direct manner of answering questions—a convincing sort of approach that always managed to help me sort out my preoccupations. And that was what I needed right now.

It took me forever to navigate through his website. When I finally located the Q and A section, my fingers hovered over the keys for a moment before I typed in my question: "Hello, Dr. Darren. I was wondering whether it's possible for a blind person to get their sight back from a head trauma?"

I gnawed on my thumbnail while I waited.

And waited.

And waited.

Jerking out of my chair, I paced back and forth in front of my desk, shaking out my hands and trying my best to keep from becoming too optimistic. Finally: a little ding of an incoming message. I collapsed in my seat and tabbed down the screen to find his reply: "Good evening, Maggie. I'm afraid the answer is no."

I rubbed the back of my neck for a moment and then typed my response: "Not even part of their sight?"

Dr. Darren: "Part of their sight?"

Me: "Just around one person. Like, if I hit my head and then afterward I could see someone."

Dr. Darren: "If you hit your head and you're suddenly seeing things, you've suffered a traumatic brain injury and you are hallucinating. Or"—the screen reader paused for some time, so long that I bolted to my feet again and crossed my arms—"you have a psychiatric disorder."

I collapsed on my bed and threw my forearm over my eyes. This was exactly what I'd feared would happen if I turned somewhere for answers. I was on my own.

12

The feminine hygiene aisle in Target wasn't the best place to be marooned. Gramps was in the store somewhere. He'd shoved me into this aisle, muttering that "the sort of things" I was looking for were right in front of me. And then he informed me that he'd be right back, that he needed fishing supplies and also something that had sounded like toenail clippers, but I couldn't be certain. His words generally came out a little muffled, so half the time I didn't know what he was saying.

In contrast, my other grandfather, Grandpa Brian—whom I called Repeat Grandpa because everything he said came out of his mouth twice ("How was school? How was school?")—made his words difficult to miss. Repeat Grandpa lived in California and was not very grandpa-ish because he was tall and skinny, and he rarely cussed. In order to be a grandpa, you should be old and grumpy and bald and opinionated and fat, like Gramps. Or at the very least, you should have a big potbelly, the tendency to grouse about people who drive too fast, and an affinity for the phrase "goddamn it all to hell." But that was just me.

Gramps had been my best friend since I lost my sight. He offered me a couple of things that girls my age could not. One, he didn't feel sorry for me, and two, he wasn't about to treat me differently because I couldn't see. I could not say the same for my old friends.

Anyway, a half hour earlier, Gramps had hollered into my room, "Going to Target. Need anything?" At the time, I'd been camped on the Internet for a good three hours, first trying to figure out the Big Secret by, as Tommy X had suggested, looking "beyond the surface" (i.e. going all the way back to the band's first official website post and then picking through it for clues), and then, after coming up empty, moving on to listening to my screen reader recite entries from an online encyclopedia. I'd started with the Ds rather than the As to pay homage to the Dead Eddies. Back in the day, the Dead Eddies were the band that had first gotten me into music. I mean, their song, coincidentally enough called "The Beginning of It All," was singularly responsible for transforming my life. And so: the Ds, out of respect. At any rate, I was cursing Tommy X and perusing the Ds when Gramps came into my room and asked me the Target question. Naturally, I was in dire need of some girly things. And naturally, Gramps wasn't about to set foot in the girly aisle for me. So I'd had to go along.

Gramps drove a Ford truck that was so old it had probably driven Moses to church. But he refused to replace it. He claimed the old stuff was sturdier than the new. Which was probably a good thing, because Gramps's driving skills were a little on the sketchy side. Just last year, he'd gotten into a fender bender with his barbershop. As he'd pulled into the shop's parking lot, he'd hit the gas instead of the brake. It had ended up being a very expensive haircut.

"Mom at work?" I asked Gramps as we pulled out of the driveway.

"Yup," Gramps said. "Left at dawn and said she'd be working late tonight."

My chest knotted up reflexively, like it always did when Mom spent long days away from home. It was childish and paranoid, but ever since she'd disappeared while I was in the hospital, I wondered whether this would be the time she wouldn't come home, whether my blindness had scared her away for good. I cleared my throat and said, "What about Dad?"

"Left for work at five thirty." This didn't surprise me. Dad got up with the chickens to commute to Manhattan. He was an intellectual property lawyer. Whatever that was. He'd dutifully explained it to me one day, and I'd dutifully forgotten.

It took only a couple of minutes in Gramps's passenger seat for me to start to yawn. When I first lost my sight, I spent a lot of time yawning, and in turn I spent a lot of time wondering why I was yawning, which just made me yawn all the more. It took a doctor to explain this phenomenon: I was yawning because of my sudden lack of visual stimulation. My brain thought that nothing was going on, so it figured it must be nighttime. In other words, my life was so freaking boring that my brain thought it was time to sleep.

I figured that I was yawning now because all Gramps talked about was the weather and the weather and the weather some more. And after that he gave me an update on his trick knee, which, for those who do not speak Prehistoric Doofus, is not a magical knee but a knee that locks up once in a while. Finally he said, "So. Why are you hanging out with the crippled kid? A bit young for you, if you ask me."

Gramps didn't have a batter-up circle for his thoughts. He just opened his mouth and struck out. Swing and a miss. No political correctness whatsoever.

"Gramps," I chastised, suddenly the moral one in our relationship. "He's not crippled—he has spina bifida. And as far as his age goes, he's actually pretty mature."

Gramps harrumphed. "I hear he sucks at swimming."

"Who told you that?" I asked, feeling weirdly protective of Ben.

"Hank." Hank was Gramps's friend. Without fail, the two of them met for coffee and donuts every morning.

Pinching the bridge of my nose, I said, "How would Hank know about Ben's swimming?" Though I already knew the answer to this question. Hank was the town gossip.

"Hank's mailman's son told him," Gramps said, and I rolled my eyes. "The whole family has had a rough go. The older boy? Mason? A hothead. Suspended from school a couple years back. After his dad died. In some local rock band called the Squeaky Guns."

"The Loose Cannons," I muttered, not appreciating the reminder of Mason.

I was quiet for the remainder of the ride. And now, as I stood stranded in Target, Mason Milton was still on my mind. Which was to say that I was standing there like a complete mindless idiot. Huffing out a monstrous gust of air, I reached up, miscalculating the location of the shelves and knocking what sounded like a thousand boxes off the Great Wall of Tampons. I squatted to pick them up, grumbling under my breath. Gramps's dumping me off here felt more than a little premature. Hilda had yet to teach me how to navigate in stores. Hell, I'd barely walked down the sidewalk yesterday without breaking my face.

Footsteps rounded the corner behind me. And then a girl's voice: "Oh wow. That's . . . wow. Want some help picking those up?" There was an awkward pause in which I deliberated whether to decline the offer, a pause just long enough for her to discover she knew me. *"Maggie?"* she said, clearly surprised.

Now, if I were the observant type, I would have already recognized Sophie's voice. Lord knows I'd heard it a million times out on the high school soccer field, and a million times before that. It brought back memories of normalcy. Memories of slumber parties and laughfests and summer camps.

Sophie and I had known each other for what felt like an eternity, but I was reasonably certain we were seven when we first met. It was during our first soccer practice for a coed league, where all great friendships are born. That day, one of our teammates, Trevor Wilson—a boy with tumbleweed-looking hair and one lazy eye that had spread to his entire body—kept tripping Sophie. He and his friends thought it was funny. A game. But I did not. I have this thing about bullies. They infuriate me. So after he tripped her a half-dozen times, I marched up behind him and tapped him on the shoulder. When he turned around, I kneed him in the groin. That was the end of the tripping thing and the beginning of Sophie and me.

Sophie was exceedingly tall and exceedingly red-haired, and she had these slender fingers that she drummed against her chin when she was trying to figure something out. I knew this because

I'd seen her do it, oh, a thousand times on the soccer field when our plays went awry. I suspected that she was tapping her chin right now. Which was exactly why I felt the urgent need to escape.

"Hey, Sophie," I said.

"Um, hi," she said.

Painfully long pause.

The only sound was Dad's favorite Foreigner song, wandering out of the overhead speakers. I clung to it, desperately bouncing my heel to the beat.

She blurted, "God, I haven't seen you since . . . I mean, I haven't seen you in forever. You look great." That was the thing about Sophie. She was nice. This was why I'd liked her. Back in the day, I'd informed her of this. And she'd told me that she liked me because I was not nice. Whether that had been a compliment or an insult, I'll never know.

"Thanks. So do you," I joked. She was quiet for a beat too long before she laughed. And her laugh was screechy. All wrong.

We stood there for a moment in thorny silence while the conversational walls closed in. I shifted my weight. I'd never been good with small talk. It had always been sort of painful for me. Made me feel as though I were trying to shove a boulder through a funnel. And generally, all that came out of my funnel was the sort of dust that made me choke. Besides, talking to Sophie just didn't feel natural. Not that it felt natural to talk to anyone these days. Except for Ben, of course. The long and the short of it was this: my lack of eyesight made people uncomfortable. Self-conscious.

Awkward.

Sophie plowed on, her voice muffled as she picked up the boxes for me. "Um," she said, her voice shaking a little. "We haven't been the same without you."

By "we" she'd meant "the soccer team." We'd all been friends. Usually when you're on a soccer team, there are one or two players who are too girly or too fake or too gossipy or too irritating, but I'd honestly liked everyone on my team. When I first got out of the hospital, my friends told me they wanted to stand beside me while I adjusted to my sudden blindness. We were a team, for Christ's sake. One for all and all for one and all that crap. But without my eyesight, my friendships spun off-kilter. They were unpleasant. Everyone felt it. But I was the only one with enough balls to do something about it. I started brushing off their phone calls, their attempts to visit, and their invitations to get-togethers, claiming I was too busy to spend time with them.

Okay, so I had been the one who had turned away from my friendships. But it had been so easy. And now, as I stood facing Sophie in the store, I felt a thick, bitter glob in the back of my throat. Now, I wondered why Sophie had given up on me so quickly. Now, I couldn't help but think: Why had she stopped trying? I'd had to try to walk, navigate new school hallways, fight my way through the void. I just hadn't wanted to try with friendship.

"Lauren's going to freak when I tell her I ran into you," Sophie said.

It took a concentrated effort for me to not roll my eyes. Lauren had been the easiest one to walk away from—almost like she'd been relieved.

Silence.

More silence.

The Foreigner song gave way to some Kenny G disaster. Suddenly my breath felt like it was strangling me.

Sophie cleared her throat. "So my mom is waiting for me in the car? And I have to go. But it was nice seeing you."

"You too," I muttered. "Um. Before you go?"

"Yes?"

God, this was humiliating.

I held up the box. "Is this super plus?"

There was a pause in which I figured she was reading the box. Then: "Um. Yeah. It is, actually."

We said good-bye and I made my way to the end of the aisle. While I waited for Gramps, I squinted and swiveled my head around and generally tried to will back my eyesight, tried to see something—anything. I was in such deep concentration that I actually flinched when some dirtbag of a guy shuffled up to me and said in my ear, "You blind?"

I shamelessly ignored him. I was an authority on ignoring people. It was one of my hobbies. Plus, it was one of the few perks to being blind. Generally, strangers will speak to you only once before giving up, figuring you're also deaf. Or too slow to form a coherent response.

"You blind?" he asked again, louder this time, his breath in my face. He reeked of stale cigarettes, crappy English, and about a quarter century of failure.

I turned my head away from him and twirled my cane against the floor, signifying that I had better things to do than talk to him. What those things were, I wasn't exactly sure.

He went on to say, "You know, you're pretty hot for a blind girl."

This guy was the perfect example of why they print directions on shampoo bottles. "Gee. Thanks," I said.

"Welcome."

Gramps showed up at that precise second and rescued me, saying in a low, gravelly voice, "I might be old, but I'm strong." The next thing I knew, the guy was gone.

13

That night, I wandered outside to the timeworn Adirondack chair on the back deck. I came out here sometimes in the evening, when the house felt too lopsided to hold me upright and when the weather was agreeable, either listening to music or just eavesdropping on the crickets. Tonight I could hear the neighbor's sprinkler hissing as I unloaded into the chair and folded one leg underneath me. The air was gluey and promised rain, but I'd spent too long in our brutally air-conditioned house this afternoon, too long trying to keep myself from calling Ben and inviting myself into his life again. And while it had been several hours since I'd run into Sophie at the store, I still felt as though I were tripping over all the loose strings of our failed friendship.

And so: the deck, where I could breathe.

I didn't use headphones anymore—they heisted far too much of my hearing—so when I fired up my iPod, the Loose Cannons'

"Transcendence" emerged through the tiny wireless speaker in my lap.

My entire body exhaled.

The Loose Cannons' music had been the glue that had held me together over the past several months, the only thing that made sense to me anymore. I closed my eyes, whisper-singing the lyrics until the end of the song, the keyboard solo. Then I pressed my fingers down on my thigh in time to the notes. Though I hadn't sat in front of a piano in a good couple years, I could still pluck notes out of the air and put them exactly where they belonged on a keyboard.

The sliding glass door opened and exhaled a burst of air-conditioning and my mother, who had evidently just gotten home from work. "Mind turning that down?" she asked, ghosting across the deck in what sounded like her standard rubber-soled Coach Sanders shoes.

I almost got up and left, just slunk back to my room. Being alone on the deck with my mother dredged up all kinds of painful memories—all of a sudden there I was, lying on that hospital bed again, half-dead and newly blind and miserable, wondering where she had gone. Wondering whether she'd ever return.

I pushed the recollections aside. "Whatcha doing?" I said, turning down the music and putting both feet flat on the wooden slats. There had been a time when I hadn't been able to walk barefoot across the deck without collecting at least a dozen splinters, but the years had worn the boards smooth so they were soft and creamy on my feet.

"Watering," she said tiredly, her voice now coming from the far end of the deck. We had an eight-thousand-year-old fern that lived there every summer—the only thing my mother had ever succeeded in growing. It was gigantic and sprawling, the sort of beast that could swallow a small child whole. Come September, she'd roll it back inside to its winter home at the bay window. She sighed. "Fern looks droopy."

"Maybe it needs to be watered twice a day," I suggested, like the fern expert that I was. The last time I'd picked up a watering can had been years ago, to squash a spider. In a dream I'd had.

"Maybe," she said vaguely.

Silence.

More silence.

It's conversations like these that make a person look forward to standing in line at the DMV.

I cleared my throat. "Feels like it might rain," I said.

"Mmm. Little bit," she said.

This pretty much summed up 99.9 percent of our chats since I'd lost my sight. We spoke, but we never really said anything. Our exchanges had never been like this when I'd been able to see—so full of holes. We used to stuff soccer balls into every gap, so we'd been able to navigate practically everywhere. Now every time I took a step I plunged into a crater.

Sure, Mom had eventually come back from wherever she'd gone while I was in the hospital, and maybe she'd even tried to make up for it in her own way. She'd been all over me when I'd first gotten home, working with Hilda to blind-proof our house and getting me set up with a new computer and whatever. But then she'd tiptoed out the door and gone back to work.

And the quiet settled in.

None of us ever mentioned her disappearance. And we didn't speak of her quick exit back to work. We just adjusted to a new norm. Dad was the one who worked from the house for a couple months while I got established both at home and at Merchant's. It should have been reassuring, having him there, but he spent an abundance of that time following me from room to room and chattering away, something he'd done only once before, when Gran was sick. Gramps brought home bags upon bags of cookies from Big Dough, my favorite bakery downtown. Everyone did their best to fill in the gaps. But even so, I spent the first several months of blindness alone, palms flat on the walls of my boxy new room, searching for a door that didn't exist.

....

The next morning, Dad found me in the kitchen, hunched over a bowl of Cap'n Crunch, my favorite cereal out of sheer laziness. Squat and fat, the box was easy to differentiate from the others on the shelf.

"Good morning, honey," Dad said jovially.

"Morning," I muttered back, not sure what was so good about it. Getting up at hideously early hours was not something I generally did during summer vacation. In fact, I loved sleep so much that it was the first thing I thought about when I woke up. But the past several nights my sleep had been fractured, fitful, and I knew why. It had been a couple days since I'd seen anything.

I'd hoped beyond hope that my eyesight was going to trickle back to me as time progressed, that eventually I'd see something else—anything else. But after a couple days' worth of nothing but my fumbling blindness, I was beginning to feel like I was sinking in murky dark water.

And I hated it. Hated having some sort of hope thrown at me and then discovering it could very well be heavy enough to sink me. So I'd broken down and texted Ben last night, inviting myself to his house. I wasn't proud of it, using Ben. But at this point I was starting to doubt I'd even seen him. At this point, I was starting to panic.

"Coffee?" Dad asked as he tromped past.

"God, yes."

Awkward and soft-spoken, Dad had the grace of a yeti. He was the sort of guy who grew up playing *backup* for the backup right fielder on his Little League team. A real man's man. Interestingly, his parents had given him two middle names, Melvin and Samuel, both of which sounded less like a middle name combo unit and more like a stodgy debate that his parents had gotten into while Dad was in utero.

"You're up early," Dad said, banging around in the cabinets. Although our kitchen had been meticulously mapped out, organized, and defaced with braille, he still fumbled to find even the simplest of items. Like cream and sugar. By great force of will, I refrained from standing up, taking four perfectly measured strides to my left, and producing the sugar from the cabinet—second shelf from the bottom. The fact of it was, I let him do it for me because he felt like he needed to. "Have a session with Hilda this morning?" he asked.

"Nah. Tomorrow at noon," I said, making a mental note to cancel the appointment. Yesterday she'd informed me that our next lesson would cover How to Cross a Street, which, as fascinating as it sounded, would have to wait until hell froze over.

Dad said, "You got some mail yesterday. It's on top of the microwave."

"Like, snail mail?"

He plunked a coffee cup down in front of me. Hazelnut steam wafted in my face. Dad's tone was forced-casual as he said, "Just some DVDs from a few colleges."

"Must've come by mistake. I haven't contacted any schools."

"Your mother did on your behalf, after researching the best programs for students with disabilities." This was classic Mom. She'd had every opportunity to tell me this last night on the deck, yet she hadn't. "Cal Poly looks awesome. Also, Missouri State."

A few months back, I'd thought I had the perfect excuse for not sending out college applications: I was the juvenile delinquent who'd defaced Merchant's. But then my counselor had informed me that the prank was only a misdemeanor—something many colleges would overlook if I explained the situation honestly and apologetically during the application process.

I sighed and said, "I don't want to go to those schools."

"Where do you want to go?"

Nowhere. "I don't know."

Last year, college scouts wouldn't leave me alone. Even phoned once a month to grill me on whether I'd chosen a school. Back then there hadn't even been a question. I was going to UConn. I'd enjoy my last four years playing for Mom, and then I'd go straight to the national team. But now, college seemed like a distant dream. Completely unobtainable. I said, "I'm busy today, so maybe I'll check them out tomorrow or the next day?"

I could almost feel his eyebrows jerk up. "You have plans?"

"Going to visit a friend."

"Really? Who?" he asked hopefully.

I took a sip of coffee to avoid the question. What he really wanted to know was whether I was planning on hanging out with Clarissa Fenstermacher. Ever since my little brush with Old Man Law, my parents had been pushing me to spend time with her. Clarissa, who had been blind since birth, had a "lovely attitude," and she was the sort of person who would help me "make peace with my blindness." So I fundamentally didn't want to hang out with her.

"Nobody you know," I said dismissively. Truth be told, I'd never been much for the students at Merchant's, particularly Clarissa, whose cheerful, glass-half-full, unrelenting chatter made me wish I could unsubscribe to my own ears. "What are you doing up so early on the weekend? Working on a big case?"

I heard his breath hitch a little. I heard his coffee cup rattle too loudly against the counter. Then I heard the lie come out of his mouth: "Just have a bunch of errands to run, actually."

A sharp pang seized my chest.

The only thing Dad and I had ever had in common was our love of music. He was obsessed with classic rock, which, combined with his fascination with old-school vinyl and his enthusiasm for a great bargain, made the garage sale his biggest weakness. He'd hover at my bedside first thing on Saturday mornings—just a hulking shadow framed by hallway light—and say, with a passion that, though not exactly charming first thing in the morning, was awfully infectious, "Thirty garage sales today! Thirty! And fifteen of them claim to have vinyl!" And minutes later, I'd find myself stumbling out of bed and getting dressed. Scouring garage sales for old albums was the one thing we'd done together, the one piece of him that had been entirely mine.

And now it was gone.

I wasn't sure how it all stopped, whether he'd stopped asking me to go along or I'd turned him down too many times, only that it did.

Dad cleared his throat. "Anyway. I'd better get going. See you tonight?"

I nodded, and—even though I'd been awake for a couple hours, gotten dressed, and eaten breakfast—went back to bed.

14

I was uncharacteristically quiet for the remainder of the morning. Sure, there was the creative cussing when I stubbed my toe on a doorjamb, and there was the singing of three Loose Cannons songs while I took a shower, and there was the asking of Gramps to drop me off at Ben's house, but other than that, complete quiet. Until I arrived at Ben's, that is. Because the second I returned to my little cloud of vision, I fell right back into myself again.

So Ben and I were crutch-to-cane at the Miltons' kitchen counter, preparing English muffin pizzas, and Ben was extracting words from my mouth by way of a Would You Rather? game, which, for all intents and purposes, was just a ridiculous barrage of questions that forced me to choose between two unpleasant hypothetical actions ("Would you rather catapult down a slide made of razor blades or have seven nails hammered into your tongue?").

All the while, I was doing my best to avoid looking at Mason, who was slouched in a chair at the kitchen table, strumming random chords on his guitar. Which was to say that I was totally looking at him. In my defense, an hour ago, when I'd walked into the house, I'd discovered that my tiny ring of eyesight had expanded since the last time I'd seen Ben. And I'd be damned if I wasn't going to enjoy looking at everything around me.

Including Mason.

As much as I hated to admit it, Mason wasn't good-looking in a conventional way, but in an interesting way. Whether it was intentional or not, his dark hair had a messy look to it, like he'd been sweating and he'd raked a hand through it, and it had just stayed like that, stuck up in fascinating angles all over his head. His face was all olive tones, with sharp edges that a girl could never pull off. I tried to categorize him, but I came up short. He had the broad chest of a weight lifter, the dark eyes of an emo kid, the hair of an actor. Nothing fit, but—annoyingly—everything fit.

Realizing my brain had skewed off in an uncharted, reckless direction, I turned deliberately away from Mason and stared hard at the space around Ben. Which, I reminded myself, was the reason I'd come here in the first place. To find answers.

Gone was the murkiness that had surrounded Ben when I'd first met him. Now he burnished the room in buttery sunshine, and the vibrant light, though brightest around him, bled right through the kitchen walls and into the next room before it petered away into the nothingness. I couldn't help but hope that my eyesight would continue to grow, that eventually I'd see everything.

And I couldn't help but worry that it would leave as mysteriously as it had come.

I sighed quietly, staring down at my feet. Years ago, whenever my soccer team was losing, my coach used to gather us all together and say in an intense, knowing tone, "The universe is conspiring in your favor, so just go out and play hard." She'd embezzled the first half of this pep talk from a novelist named Paulo Coelho, and the second part was just some cheesy attempt to get us out of our own heads. Regardless, most of the time it had worked: once we gave up our chokehold on the circumstances, once we just played, we usually came back to win.

And now, as I stood in the Miltons' kitchen, I realized that the more I groped for answers regarding my eyesight, the more those answers eluded me, slipping through my fingers, as inconsequential as tinsel. If I let it all go, if I just relaxed, enjoyed my eyesight, and waited for the answers to come to me on their own, everything would work out.

The universe is conspiring in my favor.

And I had a little chunk of eyesight to prove it.

I exhaled, the tension in my neck and shoulders dissolving instantly.

"Thera," said Ben, jerking me back to the game. "I asked if you'd rather wake up naked in a crowded coliseum or suck the snot out of a dog's nose? Also, I asked if you like extra sauce? Also, also, I asked if you'd mind grabbing the cheese from the right-hand drawer in the fridge?"

"I don't know, yes, and sure," I said as I turned toward the fridge.

I was relatively certain that Mason had come to the kitchen for a front-row seat to the Maggie Faking Her Blindness Show, so I moved toward the fridge slowly and gracelessly. Still, as I fake-fumbled around in the fridge, pretending to have difficulty finding the shredded cheese, Mason momentarily stopped playing the guitar, huffed out an irritated blast of air, and grumbled something indecipherable under his breath. Cheese finally in hand, I slammed the fridge shut and shot the stink-eye in his general direction. Which probably didn't help my case, but it made me feel better.

I wished Mason were more like the flaky Mrs. Milton, who forgot I was blind half the time. Mrs. Milton, who thought it was perfectly normal that a seventeen-year-old girl was hanging out with her youngest son. Mrs. Milton, who didn't scrutinize my every move. Mrs. Milton, who made me completely comfortable. Since she kept me at ease, I rarely made mistakes around her. I'd become a master of averting my eyes while speaking to her, of using my cane as a ridiculous prop, of stumbling around every now and then for good measure. But Mason? Well, he was a completely different story. And now, as I made my way back to Ben, I was making a concentrated effort to avert my eyes from Mason's bare feet, which were stretched out in front of him. They were wide and monstrous, and his big toes arched up every time he hit a complicated chord. There was just something about the motion that was annoyingly complex.

"Hello? Earth to Thera? For the zillionth time: Would you rather wake up naked in a crowded coliseum or suck the snot out of a dog's nose?" asked Ben, jerking me back to the game. "And before you ask, the answer is no."

"What was I going to ask?"

"Whether you can pass on the question. You can't pass. Naked or snot?" he said, balancing on one crutch and snatching the cheese from my hand.

Maybe Mason had grown tired of hearing the same question. Maybe he had strong opinions when it came to dog snot. But for whatever reason, he chose this moment to give his own answer to Ben's question: "Naked."

Two things happened to me instantaneously: one, I was unhinged from all rational thought, and two, my cheeks burned with what felt like a very sophisticated five shades of deep red. Luckily Ben had spun around to face Mason so he didn't notice. "You'd choose naked over dog snot? Seriously?" he asked Mason.

Mason shot Ben a comical look that was full of the sort of subtext you can only get from a decade of bonding in the backseat of the car during family vacations, and he said, "Of course. You, on the other hand, should go with dog snot, what with that monstrous birthmark you have on your ass." This was immediately followed by a scuffle that started with Ben leaping toward Mason, and ended with laughing, shouting, and wrestling on the kitchen floor.

"Knock it off, you two," Mrs. Milton chastised lightly. Wearing a pair of Birkenstocks and a dress that appeared to have been forged from a burlap sack, she stepped into the kitchen, a half-dozen fabric grocery bags swinging from her arms.

The two boys scrambled to their feet, looking guilty. "Just goofing off, Mom," Mason muttered. And then he greeted her with a kiss on the forehead.

And as Mason slid the grocery bags from her arms, I could see something genuine in his eyes, something sincere. Something that made me question every opinion I'd ever had of him. Something that seared me with a brief, burning thought: *Mason is a good person.*

I swallowed.

All of the Miltons were, actually, especially Ben. Whom I was currently taking advantage of. It was painful to admit this, even in my own head—like gravel grinding against the inside of my skull.

"Um. Thera?" Ben said. "I think your phone was ringing?"

I hadn't even heard it.

I dragged myself away from my eyesight and down the hallway to check my phone for voice mail. Rounding the corner to Ben's room, I stood there for a moment—longer than proper, really—just breathing and trying to collect myself. And then I swung the door shut and slid my hands up the wooden surface, in search of the hook where I'd hung my purse. It was gone, replaced by a damp towel.

Strange.

"Thera," Ben said with what sounded like a full mouth, his crutches squeaking down the hallway toward me, "you have to try these with ranch. It's the shit."

Thanks to Ben, my eyesight hit the edge of the room and ghosted toward me, bleeding through the walls as he made his way down the hallway.

I wasn't in Ben's room.

I was in Mason's room.

I froze as my vision drifted over the space, toward the wall that separated it from Ben's room. Though my sight dwindled along the curved outer borders, I could probably still see a good half of the area.

And it was unsettling.

Surprisingly sparse and neat, it reminded me of an adult's room. There were no piles of dirty laundry. No posters of half-naked girls. No *Sports Illustrated* magazines. The space was punctuated by three pieces of sturdy-looking mahogany furniture: a squarely made bed, a dresser, and a desk. A photograph of Mason and his father—framed in mahogany, naturally—was the only thing adorning the walls. From the thousands of pictures scattered all over the house, I knew that dark-haired, dark-eyed Mr. Milton had looked like an older version of Mason, and I knew that he'd often worn athletic shorts and UConn T-shirts. But none of the pictures I'd seen were like this. The photo had been taken years ago, given Mason's young age—maybe three or four years old, tops. Mason was perched on his dad's lap as they sat on the wooden planks of a pier, bare feet dangling toward the water. Mason grinned at the camera, but his father was ducked down as he kissed the crown of his son's head, his emotions shaken up like dice and spilled all over the scene—acceptance, devotion, reverence.

My eyes blurred with tears and I turned away, took an unsteady breath, and tried to regroup by looking around. All in all, Mason's room resembled a hotel room: overly tidy and overly clean. Still, for some reason I could picture him here, curved over a laptop with his brows drawn together in thought and his fingers moving purposefully over the keyboard. I could see him striding into the room after a shower, towel wrapped around his waist, shoulders dotted with little water droplets, and still-wet hair sticking out in one intriguing direction after the other....

I grumbled under my breath. Even when he wasn't around, Mason made me feel like an idiotic version of myself.

"Thera?" Ben hollered from his room. "Where'd you go?"

I didn't answer. As I stared down at the things piled neatly on Mason's desk, a thought hit me so hard that I almost stumbled sideways. *What if Mason has a list of concert venues in here?* Months of obsessing over the Loose Cannons, and it came down to this: me in Mason's room, gawking at the papers on his desk, knowing that without a doubt I was closer than ever to discovering one of music's best-kept secrets.

At first glance, I saw nothing related to the Loose Cannons. A checkbook paper-clipped to a stack of bills, all of which were addressed to Mrs. Milton, and all of which were opened cleanly with either a knife or a letter opener. A dark-brown leather day planner that outlined Ben's swim practices and Mrs. Milton's work schedule. A stack of glossy pamphlets—Skydiving at Night, Parachute Operations 101, Connecticut Skydiving, and Parachute Sense. A single sheet of notepaper, where Mason had left a half-finished poem, "November."

Wait. Not a poem. A song:

Winter and spring are all but gone/but the bitter wind never stops playing that song/so I fall back to November every time it blows. Yeah my dad never meant to go/and as strong as he was he never could know/that I'd fall back to November every time it blows. I know I know I know/it's always November/I know I know I know/it's always November. Sure his memory fades in me/but I know deep down I'll never be free/'cause I fall back to November every time it blows/I fall back to November every time it blows/yeah I fall back to November every time it blows.

An ache so bottomless that it seeped off the paper settled into my chest, crushing my heart and lungs. I don't know what did it—the pain in the lyrics, the way Mr. Milton's photograph had tugged at my gut, or just the shock that I was actually standing in Mason's room, hoping to stumble across some sort of hint that unlocked the secrets of the Loose Cannons—but suddenly I felt light-headed. I closed my eyes and groaned quietly. I was too overcome to hear the front door opening, or to pay attention to the parade of footsteps coming down the hallway, or to take note of the approaching voices. Until I heard the doorknob turn. Then all at once my mind snapped back to me.

And I panicked.

My eyes flew open at exactly the same time as the door. Mason and three other boys tumbled into the room, laughing and shoving one another. They stopped short when they saw me. Shock flitted across Mason's features. It was replaced quickly with contempt. He took one intimidating step toward me.

"What the *hell* are you doing in here?"

15

My heart clubbed in my chest, and I stood there for several miserable seconds, frozen and mute, praying for the floor to open up and suck me in. All the while, three unfamiliar boys, all roughly my age, sauntered forward and regarded me with various degrees of interest. To my left smirked a heavily pierced, slim-shouldered boy, his eyebrows hiked up clear to his hairline. Just behind him was a red-faced stocky kid who shifted hesitantly back and forth on his feet. The tallest of the three boys—a lanky, tattooed guy who twirled a set of drumsticks between his fingers—ogled me as though I were a souped-up 1968 Mustang. Oblivious to his friends' antics, Mason just stood there glaring at me, anger rolling off of him like thick, suffocating smoke.

"I got lost," I said finally. Which was actually 100 percent true.

"You got lost," he said.

I swallowed. "That's what I said."

Mason did not answer. He just stood there, skewering me in place with his eyes. Tattoo Guy, openly disregarding Mason's hostility, scratched his chest with his drumsticks, jerked his chin in my direction, and said to Mason, "Bro. Been hiding your new girl from us?"

Mason shut his eyes, and I had the strangest sense that he was trying to hurdle over some sort of conflicting emotion. He drew in a slow breath, and his guitar, which hung by a strap on his shoulder, swung forward as his chest expanded. In his exhale and with his eyes still closed, he said, "This is not my girlfriend. This is Maggie, Ben's friend. She's blind." His words were overly measured and overly quiet and overly enunciated, and I could hear implied air quotes when he said "Ben's friend" and "blind." Which totally infuriated me. Why did Mason always have to think the worst of me? Why couldn't he *ever* give me the benefit of the doubt?

I focused my gaze in the general vicinity of Tattoo Guy, and, forcing a smile and doing my best not to speak through my teeth, I said to the boy, "Nice to meet you. And you are...?" I knew Mason's eyes were open now because I could feel the heat coming off of them. And I couldn't care less. I couldn't remember the last time I'd had this sort of outrage clawing its way out of me—years ago, maybe, while fighting with my mother?—and it left me feeling dangerously out of control.

Tattoo Guy, looking oddly entertained by the animosity in the room, smirked and said, "David Slater. Pleasure to meet you, m' lady." He swooped a palm out in front of himself and bowed theatrically, as though he were so grandiose that even the blind could see him.

The pierced-up kid rolled his eyes at David. Clearing his throat, he held both arms out, like he was a gift or something, and announced grandly, "But more importantly? I'm Carlos Santiago, keyboard virtuoso." He cuffed the shy-looking kid on the shoulder. "And this is Gavin Alexander."

Members of the Loose Cannons. I recognized their names, even though I'd never actually seen them.

I nodded a shocked hello.

Mason threw the guitar on his bed. The strings made a discordant sound when they struck his pillow. Then he said two words, and two words only. They were directed at me through tight lips: "Get out."

That was when I knew I was going to tell Mason the truth.

Right now.

I couldn't take it anymore. I couldn't take his accusations, and I couldn't take his holier-than-thou attitude, and I couldn't take his snide tone. I'd spent the past several months learning how to be a person again, for Christ's sake. Learning how to match my clothes, pour my own milk, find my way to my goddamn room. I'd had to figure out how to *live*. And Mason? He had everything and he didn't even give a shit.

I straightened my spine, leaned forward, stabbed an index finger in his direction, and said in a low, menacing tone, "You think you know what's really going on, you arrogant, self-absorbed sonofa-bitch? You have *no. freaking. clue.*"

He grabbed my hand and leaned toward me, daring me to

continue. We were too close to each other—a couple inches. Energy ricocheted fiercely between us, and there was something burning behind the amber flakes in his eyes, something I'd never seen before, an ache and a fury.

"There you are, Thera! You get lost?" Ben bellowed from the doorway, breaking the spell as he swung into the room. "Oh, hey, guys."

Mason's grip sprung free from me and we both took clumsy steps away from each other.

There was an awkward silence, which then stretched into a painfully awkward silence. David cleared his throat, the corners of his lips turned up, and then offered his fist to Ben and said, "Hey, broseph."

Ben, crutches and all, gracelessly fist-bumped David, and then he said to Mason, "Please tell me the band didn't come here to rehearse."

Mason sighed and knuckled his forehead. "Gavin's neighbors complained about the noise last week, so, yes, we're rehearsing here tonight."

Ben lifted his chin. "I hereby complain about the noise," he proclaimed, and Mason scoffed. Ben leaned toward his brother. "No, seriously. Thera and I were going to watch-and-or-listen-to a movie tonight, and you guys are too loud and obnoxious when you practice."

Carlos winced. "Harsh."

Mason pinched his eyes closed for a moment. "Well, you're just going to have to deal with it for tonight. We don't have any other options. Carlos lives too far away, Gavin's mom has a book club meeting, and David's place is too small." Then he stood there, arms crossed, and waited for us to exit the room.

....

I could hear the loud voices of Mason's bandmates as soon as I stepped into the hall, the "Dude, what the hell was *that* about?" and the "What's the story with the two of you?" and so on and so forth. So I hauled ass down the hallway before I could hear Mason's explanation. It would be optimistic to the point of foolishness to believe that Mason wouldn't tell them I was a pathetic groupie snooping around for information on their concerts, and I couldn't stand being around to witness it. Sure, just moments ago I'd been right on the verge of screaming the truth at Mason, but now—as I followed Ben into the kitchen, where he pled his case to Mrs. Milton—I realized that telling Mason the truth would have been a tragic mistake. It would have sounded like a desperate lie coming from me right now, a lie he wouldn't have believed.

Hell, I hardly believed it myself.

I huffed out a sigh, thinking about the lyrics I'd seen in Mason's room. I suppose I couldn't really blame Mason for being distrustful of me. Not really. He was still reeling from the loss of his father, and it had clearly left him bruised, suspicious, jaded. And I knew that more than anything, he was just trying to protect Ben, who had been mistreated and hurt in the past. Still, it didn't give him the right to treat me so poorly. To sound so condescending. To make me feel so small. I collapsed into a kitchen chair beside

Ben's mom and massaged the epicenter of the headache that was growing between my eyebrows.

"Mom," Ben whined to Mrs. Milton, who was hunched over a recent stack of photos and a mug of leafy-smelling tea, "this is my house, too—isn't it? I have just as much right to be here as Mason."

Mrs. Milton didn't answer right away. This was one of the things I liked about her. She wasn't the sort of parent who blurted out canned responses. Leaning back in her chair and looking speculatively at Ben for the space of several breaths, she said, "I understand how you might be feeling unimportant." She considered the situation for a few more moments, taking a sip of tea and crinkling her nose at the steam. "But it isn't as though you have to leave the house, is it?"

"Well, no. It's the *principle*, Mom," Ben said helplessly. "Why do I have to cancel my plans just because Mason wants to practice his crap music here?"

Well. Never thought I'd see the day. Saint Ben was jealous.

Mrs. Milton nodded as though she completely understood Ben's plight. "Yes. Of course. The principle." Running one finger around the rim of her mug, she said, "Don't you want your brother to succeed?"

Ben let his head fall backward, all dramatically, and he stared at the ceiling. "Maybe," he grumbled.

"Hasn't Mason supported you in *your* pursuits?" she said, watching Ben closely. "Chauffeured you back and forth to swim practices? Sacrificed many an afternoon to go to your meets?"

Ben straightened up, looking as though he were biting back

several inappropriate words. Finally, balancing his weight on his crutches and letting his feet swing back and forth, he muttered, "Maybe."

She took another sip of tea and smiled gently. "So I'm sure you understand then."

Ben's lips twisted, but he said nothing.

She smiled. "It's settled: I'll drop Maggie off at home and you two can watch your movie tomorrow."

16

Since I couldn't sleep that night, I padded down to the basement and listened to one of Mom's old soccer DVDs. Most of my insomnia was because of Mason—I suspected that he'd already told everyone within shouting distance that I was a fraud—but some of it was because I'd become hyperaware of my upstairs bedroom. Whether it was my confrontation with Mason or the emotions I'd been wrestling with, I wasn't sure, but when I'd crawled into bed that night, I'd felt my old bedroom looming above me, dark and ominous.

Anyway, since the house had been picked through and organized and blind-proofed ad nauseam, I knew exactly where to find the DVDs—in the cabinet right underneath the TV. In the past, I'd always watched them on mute, overly concerned that I might wake my mother. I hadn't wanted to remind her of the past she'd buried. But now, mute wasn't even an option for me.

Not that it mattered. I'd felt so disconnected from my mother the past several months, so excluded from her list of priorities, so defiant, that I cranked the volume up louder than necessary, willing her to discover me here.

For the first several minutes, I had no clue which DVD I'd chosen. All I heard were the sounds that accompanied professional soccer games—the crowd noise, the buzzers, the vuvuzela horns. But then: Dad's voice.

Dad used to morph into a totally different person at soccer games. Between his armchair reffing and his constant hollering, he was obnoxious enough to tick off roughly a fifty-seat radius. It was a side of him I used to love to see, a side of him I missed desperately since I'd stopped playing soccer, and listening to it now made me feel lousy and ecstatic, all at the same time.

The game was old, international. In Spain, most likely, given the announcer's language. I could hear a tiny voice, my voice—God, I must've been a toddler—say, "Mommy is fast, isn't she, Daddy?"

"She's amazing," Dad said in a reverent tone.

"When I grow up, I'll be amazing, too," I vowed.

My chest twisted. I'd always believed that I could be amazing. That Mom's magic would rub off on me. That I was invincible. And I was, at least for a little while. Sighing, I pulled an afghan over me, yanking it clear to my chin, and, feeling small and broken and frail, I remembered my very last soccer game.

It was November, junior year. We were playing our rivals, McDonnell Prep, some swank private school just outside of town. My teammates and I had been playing with one another since rec ball, so we practically moved together without thinking, as part of the same machine. And that night we were amazing. We won in the sort of grandiose fashion that is boring as hell for the spectators—a 20–2 score at the final buzzer. Afterward, Sophie, Lauren, and I rolled out of the stadium on a massive high, loafing around in the parking lot far longer than necessary as we clung to the last few seconds of the soccer season.

Sophie had just gotten her driver's license, and her parents had gifted her with a monstrous black Chrysler that the three of us called Bertha. Bertha's most redeeming quality was her gigantic hood. And that night, we sprawled across it indelicately, in an unladylike fashion that is perfectly acceptable when you're sweaty and dirty and you've just spanked the crap out of a bunch of hoity-toitys from McDonnell Prep. The late-November air had a bite to it that promised winter, but the sun had just set, so the hood was still warm.

Lauren sat up, dangled her legs off the side of the car, and looked at me. "So what gives, Sanders? When the hell did you learn that bicycle kick? I've never seen anything like it." She slapped the heel of her palm on her forehead, her eyes bugged out. Thin and attractive, Lauren always made these crazy faces, which drove me a little nuts, and she had long blond bangs that hung in her eyes, which drove me a little nuts, and she had great boobs, which drove me a little nuts. Regardless, I liked her. She was passionate and full of life.

I shrugged, gazing up at the night's first stars, completely embarrassed and yet completely elated by her reaction. But this was the way it had always been with Lauren. She was forever fangirling something—Nick Jonas's abs or Maroon 5's newest song, or, more currently, me. Lately I'd burst into a whole new level of soccer. It had shocked me almost as much as everyone else. I didn't know how I'd done it, only that I'd stopped thinking about what I was doing on the field and started reacting instead. Taking a long swig from my Gatorade bottle, I said, "I don't know. I guess it just happened?" I'd crossed in front of the goal and seen the ball coming toward me—in slow motion, like it was hanging in the air waiting for me. I'd jumped and kicked in two beats, an upbeat and a downbeat. It had been a rhythm, was all, the last two notes in a chord of music. To my body, it had made perfect sense. It had been intuitive.

Sophie, who always knew how to cut through the bullshit in a conversation, bumped me with her shoulder and said, "You should have seen your mom. She went *insane.*"

My eyes jerked to hers. "Yeah?"

She smiled and nodded, and something huge and warm and perfect swelled in my chest. Suddenly I couldn't wait to get home, couldn't wait to sit with Mom at the kitchen counter and dissect the game over a shared spoon and a gallon of ice cream. Soccer was the biggest and best part of both of us. It wound us together into a singular person, a stronger person. A Maggie-and-Mom.

I hummed along to a Dead Eddies song trailing out of Sophie's open window while Lauren rummaged around in her backpack, extracting an expensive-looking French lip balm. She slid the balm generously across her lips, smacking them together when she was finished. Lauren's mom worked at the makeup counter at Nordstrom and had no problem whatsoever hijacking cosmetics from the store. And Lauren had no problem whatsoever hijacking them from her mother's bathroom.

Sophie stared pointedly at Lauren's lips and huffed out a tremendous sigh. And then she spun her car keys around her index finger. Spin, *clunk*. Spin, *clunk*. She was our self-appointed mother figure. With Sophie, I'd always let anything slide. She deserved a little leniency. She was the best of the best, my rock, a straight-A report card made flesh. She was allowed a personality flaw or two.

While Sophie was ridiculously serious and Lauren was ridiculously social, I straddled the line between the two, my grades just good enough to be considered mediocre and my mouth just loud enough to be entertaining. Which, as far as I was concerned, was a great place to be. Sure, I didn't have a long wake of ex-boyfriends—if you counted Dillon Young, from the fifth grade, my ex-boyfriend count would be an almost-respectable five—but I was a soccer god, and that was what was important.

"Can you believe," Lauren said, changing the subject, "that we only have one more soccer season until—"

"Don't say it!" I hollered. "You'll spoil the moment. Remember? We just handed McDonnell Prep their *asses*."

"I know, but the thing is—"

I held up a palm to stop her again. Even though it was a year and a half away, Lauren was already getting sentimental about the prospect of graduation. About breaking up our team. Going our separate ways. She'd always been emotional—teetering between the highest of the highs and the lowest of the lows—but she'd been treating our impending graduation with the same sort of dread generally reserved for root canals. Personally, I couldn't wait to graduate. Move on to college ball. National ball.

I felt unstoppable. Like a miracle.

And now, as I huddled under an afghan in my dusty basement, knees pulled up clear to my chin, I remembered how I had put both hands on Lauren's shoulders that night and looked her confidently in the eyes. I remembered that she had smelled like watermelon bubble gum and Serum de Rouge Lip Treatment. And mostly, I remembered telling her, "It's all going to work out, you know."

As it turned out, that had been the biggest lie I'd ever told her.

17

For a woman who struggled to pronounce "twelve o'clock," Hilda sure knew how to materialize on my doorstep at exactly twelve o'clock. On the dot. Since the Mason debacle had eclipsed nearly every aspect of my life, I'd forgotten to cancel my session with her, so I ended up spending a delightful afternoon learning How to Locate the Right Street and How to Cross Intersections. Both of which felt about as easy and as natural as navigating on and off a ski lift with a newborn baby in one arm and a carton of eggs in the other.

So after an hour or so, my brain went on recess, and I began to wonder whether my U12 soccer coach still had a muffin top, and whether Hilda's teeth had ever visited the dentist, and whether Nutter Butters were better than Fig Newtons. And then Hilda, who had evidently taken notice of my daydreaming, said in a surly voice, "Tell me, Maggie, where are we?"

All I knew was that, one, we had been walking long enough for my hand to start sweating all over Hilda's elbow, and that, two, Hilda had been rambling on about "stepping onto the curb" or "stepping over the curb" or "side-stepping curbs." It had definitely been something about both stepping and curbs. So I said, "Err . . . I believe we are beside a curb?"

She blew a big gust of Romanian breath in my face and said, "Tell me about your surroundings."

Now, I'd spent a lot of time with Hilda over the past several months, and I'd learned that the easiest way to get her to shut up was to tell her what she wanted to hear. So I soberly said, "There are traffic sounds in front of us, so we must be facing a busy street."

She muttered a long string of foreign words under her breath. "More."

I bounced my foot to the faint beat of a flag fluttering some-where to my right, mixing the rhythm with the music that was always in my head. When I first lost my sight, I thought my other senses would instantly sharpen. But that never happened. It was Hilda who showed me how to pay attention to the world around me, Hilda who taught me to extract clues from my environment.

"We're between a couple buildings?" I said finally, after tak-ing note of the funneled breeze against my skin. I gestured with both arms, like a traffic director. "There's a flag flapping over there, and—um—it smells like French fries? So we are down-town, between, like, the courthouse and a McDonald's?"

"Oof" was all she said in response, which could mean one of two things: I was either very right or very wrong.

. . . .

Ben's first words to me when I picked up the phone that evening were not "What's up?" or "Hey, how's it going?" or anything remotely close to normal. They were "The manatee." It was strange how he could make me smile with just a couple words.

"Ben. What are you talking about?" I said, spinning a slow circle in my desk chair while silently mouthing the words to "Eternal Implosion," the new Loose Cannons song on the radio.

A massive sigh, then, "Thera. The thing is? There is something seriously wrong with the master plan of the universe, and it's called the manatee."

As I stood I got a whiff of dried sweat from my clothes. Blech. "Um. Why?" I asked Ben, shuffling to my closet. The labels on my clothes were marked with fabric-painted dots that described the color (one dot for black, two for blue, three for red, and so on and so forth), something Hilda had engineered in an effort to prod me into efficiency in the morning. It hadn't worked.

I found a blue T-shirt and yanked it over my head. When I returned the phone to my ear, Ben was saying, "Just think about it, Thera. The manatee: piglike snout, flip-flops, blubber, tail, and a goatee. I don't think he was meant to be invented. I think he was invented accidentally."

"Maybe he was invented at the last minute?" I said, smiling into the phone. "Like, after all the decent animal parts were already used up?"

I heard him snap his fingers. "Thera. I think you are on to something. God was like, 'I'm supposed to meet the guys for poker in five minutes, and I have all this extra animal-making crap left over. I'll just slap it together and call it MANATEE.'" I could practically feel him grinning like a lunatic. "I feel so much better now." Then

I heard a muffled sound on his end of the line, and Ben grumbled, "Why so early?" He sounded as though he were talking through a tunnel, so I figured his hand was over the receiver. "Okay. Fine. *Fine.*" Then his voice came booming back to me. "Mason is insisting that we leave for swim practice in ten minutes," he informed me. Then he raised his voice. "WHICH WILL PUT US THERE TWENTY MINUTES EARLY. WHICH IS STUPID." My stomach twisted involuntarily as I remembered the scene in Mason's room. A full twenty-four hours had passed, and I still had no clue what I'd say to Mason the next time I saw him. "So," Ben went on. "What's happening in Theraville today?"

I cleared my throat, thankful for the distraction. "Well. I ate half a bag of Doritos—which, incidentally, are really great but they are not my Thing—and then I checked out a couple online encyclopedias, and then I had a session with Hilda."

"No shit? Encyclopedias?" he practically yelled, paying no mind to all the other stuff.

"Ben. Don't cuss," I said, which, okay, was sort of hypocritical coming out of my mouth, but whatever. He was only ten and I was practically a legal adult. "Yes, encyclopedias," I told him. "I looked up the Phantom Keys after one of their early songs came on the radio. That one about the ocean? 'Stealing the Wave' or something like that? Because really: that song. It's insane. After that I went to the Qs to read up on Peter Quigley, their keyboardist. Did you know he plays with only his left hand because his right hand was injured in a car accident back in the nineties? *Only his left hand,* for crap's sake. And he's so good."

I figured Ben would give me grief about skipping around the alphabet, stalking musicians and whatever. I was wrong.

"EXCELLENT!" he hollered excitedly. He prattled on about the *P*s for a while, about how the term "penal servitude" has nothing to do with male body parts, and about how the famous Pedros take up page after page after stinking page, and about how the color pink is technically not a real color, since scientists say there is no such thing as pink light.

"I don't know," I said. "I'm sort of partial to the *Q*s. That entry on Peter Quigley? The *best*."

Silence spread over the line.

"Ben?"

"Yeah?" he said quietly.

"What's wrong?"

There was another odd hiccup of silence, and then Ben cleared his throat. His voice about fifteen octaves too high, he said dismissively, "Nothing. It's just that I don't have the *Q* encyclopedia."

"Oh. That's right. What happened to it, anyway?"

Silence again.

"Ben?" I said finally, feeling strangely as though I'd hurt his feelings, though I wasn't sure how. "You still there?"

"Yeah," he said. He cleared his throat. "It's just . . . Some assnozzle at school thought it would be funny to steal the *Q*s from my backpack and rip the pages into a hundred trillion pieces."

A swell of sadness crashed into my chest and dragged it out to sea. "Ben, I'm so sorry," I whispered.

"It's fine," he said, sort of loudly. "Totally fine. I mean, some people are just . . ." He exhaled. Tried again. "Some people are just assnozzles, you know?"

"Yeah. I know," I murmured.

My heart had been flooded with water. It was drowning.

We didn't speak for a beat or two, and then Ben exhaled, coughed, and abruptly changed the subject. "Thera, when you were completely blind—like, before you hit your head and could see me and stuff—what did you miss seeing the most?"

"The sky," I said. "And I still miss it."

"What do you miss about it?"

I took in a big breath and exhaled, puffing out my cheeks, and then I said, "I miss those minutes right around twilight, when it isn't quite daytime, but it isn't nighttime, either. It feels magical somehow, like you could do something phenomenal without even trying. I miss the scarlet in sunrises. And clouds. Stars. God, I miss stars." I sighed, a tired sound that sagged my body. I hadn't meant to give him such an honest answer. "Do you ever think about what you would like to do if you could walk without crutches?"

His answer was instantaneous. "Nope. When I see something I want to do, I just do it."

. . . .

After we hung up, I killed some time on the Loose Cannons' website. There hadn't been a post since the one I'd already ransacked, so I returned to the video's comment section I'd been on the other day, hoping to find some insight from the superfans.

I did not.

All I found was a smattering of crowing, boastful comments about last week's concert and a few remarks from some random jackass who called himself Cannon Dude. He gossiped like a housewife, first claiming that, one, Mason was in dire need of a haircut, and then that, two, Carlos had left the concert without as much as a word to the rest of the band, and, most notably, that, three, it was Gavin who held the key to the Big Secret.

I rolled my eyes. Please. Gavin—the timid kid who played bass guitar and sang backup—was far from the sort of scheming architect it would take to mastermind something like that. Hell, he'd hardly been able to look at me when I'd met him.

When Mom stepped into my room, I was sideways on my bed with my legs dangling off, moping and grousing and generally feeling sorry for myself while listening to last week's concert. Hollering over the music, Mom said, "Mr. Fenstermacher called me today. He said Clarissa has been"—she sighed heavily and walked past me, turning down the music—"trying to get in touch with you about your English paper, and you've been dodging her."

I opened my mouth to reply, but then closed it again. Talking to Mom was a bit like trying to fold a fitted sheet: no matter how hard you try, it always ends up a lumpy, crooked mess. So why even bother? Mom sat down on my bed, her tiny frame hardly moving the mattress. I was reminded suddenly of how alike we were—both of us petite, small-boned, both of us topped with the same riot of chestnut curls.

"Maggie," she said tiredly, "remember our bargain with your principal to keep you from expulsion? We promised him you would stay out of trouble and pick up your grades." Out of nowhere something in me felt close to breaking down. She must've seen it in my expression because her voice became hesitant, awkward. "Look," she said, clearing her throat, "your father and I don't want to ground you."

"What would you even ground me from?" I asked. I didn't know why I'd said it. Maybe because she was sitting so close to me. Or because I was still frustrated about missing another concert. But for whatever reason, the question had just emerged from me, probably surprising me as much as it surprised her. And now that I'd said it, I was shocked by how badly I wanted to hear her answer. My parents hadn't even punished me after I'd gotten busted for my prank. They'd only spoken to me in a quiet, disappointed tone as we'd driven home from the police station, and then they'd sent me to my room. Fact was, there hadn't been anything for them to take away from me. I'd already lost everything that mattered.

"Maggie," Mom warned wearily, evading the question.

And I had my answer.

I wasn't crying. Not exactly. But I was finding it impossible to swallow. I wrapped my arms around my torso as she went on to say, "Look, can you just promise me you'll call Clarissa today and get started on the project? You can't afford any more bad grades."

I closed my eyes and nodded once, waiting for her to leave before I dialed Clarissa's number.

Clarissa answered on the first ring. "Hey, Clarissa," I said.

"Maggie! *Holy crow*—I'm so glad you called!" she chirped, and suddenly my phone felt like an inflating balloon with her big, bright voice bursting out of it. I wedged it against my ear as she went on. "It's so nice to hear from you! How have you been? Are you mad at me?"

"Um no?" I said. Which was barely even a sentence. In fact, in long-division language, it would probably be considered a remainder. But then, sometimes trying to get a word in with Clarissa was like attempting to leap between the ropes in a game of double Dutch—she didn't pause long.

"Phew! I've probably left a hundred billion messages on your voice mail, and I never heard back," she trilled. "Anyway: I've missed you! Have you been busy? *Dude*, I've been so, so busy— book club and cake-decorating class and Girl Scouts." She paused for half a beat to catch her breath and possibly to scoop up another thousand words to jam into my ear. "I've been hanging out at Bean and Gone Coffeehouse," she said. "They have a new barista who's absolutely *gorgeous*. I know what you're thinking"—she dusted her voice with sarcasm in an attempt to sound like me—"'Clarissa, how do you know he's gorgeous if you're blind?' And I'll submit this to you: it's the way he asks me whether I want extra sugar in my iced coffee." She sighed, all dramatically. "It's like a poem, the way he says it. A *poem*, Maggie. Swoon. Element."

There was a short delay in which I realized she was waiting for me to comment. "Really?" I said. Which was all I could come up with. Discounting my lack of eyesight, I didn't have anything in common with the students at Merchant's. Particularly not Clarissa, who was . . . well, Clarissa: naturally happy, like a yellow Lab. A yellow Lab that had just chugged a refrigerator's worth of Red Bull. She had no problem accepting her blindness. Didn't even have a clue what she was missing. I wondered what that sort of ignorance would feel like, wondered what it would be like to not yearn to see the things I loved—the sky and the colors and the *life*.

"Yes," Clarissa sang. "He works there Wednesday afternoons. You should come with me next week! Ooooo . . . you should totally come." She unloaded a rather large breath in my ear. I could hear her drumming her fingers on something. "Except, do you know what? Our project. Wednesday afternoon is the only possible time this week that I can come over to work on it."

"You want to come over Wednesday afternoon?" I said, stalling, my face pointed toward the ceiling. *God, I promise to be a better person and to keep my grades up and to stop cussing and to get out of bed before noon if you could please please please give me another partner for my English paper because this one is too hyper and too bubbly and too talkative and too everything and I'm pretty sure that my brain will melt out of my ears if I have to sit in a room with her for hours on end.*

But apparently the only person listening was my mother. Because right then she cracked open my door and said, "Tell Clarissa that Wednesday will work just fine."

18

I didn't see Mason for several days, although he might as well
have been lurking over my shoulder the entire time by the
way he weighed on my mind. I spent an indecent amount of
hours wishing I'd stood my ground in his room that day, wishing
I'd screamed or stomped off or slammed the door or whatever,
instead of slinking out like I'd done something wrong.

Which I hadn't.

For the most part.

Anyway, by the time we finally ran into each other, I had a half-
dozen defensive sentences already worked out in my head. I was
ready for battle. I expected fireworks, after all. Confrontations.
But what happened when we first crossed paths in the Miltons' living room was . . . nothing. Mason just breezed by as though totally
unaware of my presence. After he'd walked past, I turned to stare
at his back, swallowing my words. Arguing my point now would

just make me appear desperate, guilty. And so I said nothing. And the next day? Nothing, nothing, and nothing some more.

And so it went, day after day: Mason and I ignored each other.

Okay, so he ignored me while I pretended to ignore him. But it was virtually the same thing. In my defense, he was hard to figure out, so he was hard to ignore. It wasn't just the Loose Cannons thing. It was everything about him. He always wore black T-shirts and jeans. Always. Even when it was ridiculously hot. Also, I'd noticed that there was something interesting in his gait that suggested *I have important things to do* while at the same time said *I'm in no hurry*. Furthermore, he had this peculiar yet adorable habit of sucking on his lower lip when he was deep in thought. Which—I was embarrassed to admit, even to myself—completely disconnected me from my brain.

Regardless of all that, there was something about the condescending set to his jaw whenever I was nearby, something about the way he always stood with his back toward me, something about the sound of his size-Sasquatch boots slamming into the floor as he walked past that left me with the distinct impression that I'd come out on the losing side of our argument. And it grated me to no end.

And so several days later, as Ben and I sat next to each other on his floor playing video games, I said, "I'd appreciate it if you would kindly remove the burr from Mason's ass," to which Ben said, "He's only being a jerk because he thinks you are faking your blindness," to which I said, "You'd better tell him otherwise, Benjamin Milton," to which he said, "I did, like, twenty thousand times, but he doesn't believe me."

So that was that. Mason thought I was a pathetic, lovesick,

starry-eyed fan who was using his little brother to get near him, and there was nothing I could do about it.

Naturally, Ben defended his brother. "He'll come around to you at some point, Thera," he said. "It just takes him longer to get to know people. He's been a little quiet since Dad died." This was the first time Ben had mentioned his dad. I'd been respecting his silence. After all, I knew what it felt like to have a closet stuffed full of skeletons. I had an entire graveyard crammed into mine. So I just sat there and let Ben talk. "It was horrible when he died," he went on. "I cried like a volcano for days."

"A volcano?" I asked.

He raised his chin and straightened his posture, suddenly looking like a forty-year-old man crammed into a skinny, ten-year-old frame. "Yeah. Like, sort of explosively, you know? When stuff like that happens, you have to get it out. So you can move on. It took me a while, but I'm okay now. I miss my dad, but I'm all right." He sighed and stared out the window for some time. "But Mason?" he went on, turning toward me. "He never cried. He kept his feelings inside. The only time he was a volcano was when some kid at school teased him about failing three chemistry tests in a row, and he hauled off and punched him. Square in the jaw. Knocked him out." Another sigh. "He got suspended for a week."

I chewed on my lip, feeling slightly less angry with Mason, but no less irritated with him. And while I was fully aware that, yes, on one level I sort of despised him, I was also aware that on another level I was completely infatuated with him. And it was infinitely annoying. What bothered me most was that I knew he could act like a kind, decent human being. I'd witnessed the phenomenon. So why couldn't he cut me a little slack?

Okay, so I wasn't a model citizen. I didn't always make the best decisions. I wasn't the kindest person in the world. But still. If I were a groupie, wouldn't I be falling all over myself when Mason was in the room? Yes. Did I fall all over myself when Mason was in the room? No.

At least not visibly.

What Mason and I needed, I decided finally, was to clear the air a little. Talk. While it was unwise to tell him everything, I could tell him what was important—that I wasn't using Ben to get near him. I owed Mason that much. So a couple hours later, when Ben headed to the bathroom with an extra-thick encyclopedia, I went looking for Mason.

It wasn't difficult to find him. I crept quietly toward a guitar riff that drifted from Mason's bedroom, stopping short when my feet hit the doorway. I'd been hoping I wouldn't be able to see Mason, that maybe Ben's light, which had swelled some over the past few days to bleed through much of the house, would not include Mason's room—the scene of the crime.

But it did.

And while I was cautiously optimistic about the steady growth of my eyesight, the dim outer edge of light that graced Mason's room lent it a mysterious, dusky quality that made me nervous for some reason. Mason was sitting on his bed, his guitar in his lap. Not reclining against his headboard, but sitting cross-legged in the middle of the bed—a position shockingly childlike and straightforward. He had a vague, tender honesty about him, an openness. He was young. Vulnerable. Simple.

He reminded me of Ben.

Clearly unaware that I was watching him, he was humming

softly—using that same alluring tone that twisted my stomach into exquisite knots every time he opened his mouth, the tone that I hated and loved with equal ferocity. Other than an occasional rustle of encyclopedia pages from the bathroom, the rest of the house was a silent audience, listening along with me. Biting my bottom lip, I stayed right there, one hand on the doorjamb, and watched him. I'd never actually seen him play the guitar. Not like this. Sure, a few days ago he'd sat in the kitchen and plucked absently at his guitar while Ben and I had played Would You Rather? But this was something more. Tonight his expression was lost somewhere in the space between notes. Tonight he was just Mason. Finally I wiped my palms on my shorts, stepped into the room, and said, "Um. Mason? I was wondering if we could, you know, talk."

The humming stopped, and Mason's fingers hitched slightly on the guitar strings. And then, without even a glance in my direction, he continued playing.

I'd been expecting this. And in some ways, it made things easier. I straightened my posture and said, "Look . . ." I kept thinking that the rest of my sentence would crawl out of my vocal cords on its own, but that didn't happen. So I cleared my throat and forced it out. "I just wanted you to know that I really care about Ben, and I'd never do anything to hurt him. He's been hurt enough in the past."

My chest squeezed as feelings for Ben crowded in my heart. I hadn't counted on this affecting me so much. But for some reason my emotions had been sitting right on the surface lately, sharp and intense. I felt exposed. Fragile. It took several seconds to organize my thoughts enough to continue, and Mason didn't speak. Why, I wasn't sure. But he wasn't the easiest person to figure out. Like me, he was damaged. He'd just done a better job adjusting than I had. Maybe because he'd been forced to adjust, for his family's sake. He was the scaffolding of his family, the support that helped hold everything together.

What was I to mine?

I blinked up at the ceiling, focusing on the white stucco as my words came tumbling out. "Anyway, if I've offended you in any way I'm really sorry. It's been sort of a tough few months for me—" My throat closed up and tears clouded my vision.

Shit.

I could feel them now, the tiny cracks that were starting to form in me, fractures of a self I wasn't sure I knew anymore, a self I'd divided in half over the past several weeks, a self that was too broken to stand in front of Mason.

I had to get out of here.

"So anyway, your brother has been sort of a lifesaver for me," I went on quickly, my words piling up on top of one another as I backed out of the room. My voice shook and gave out and did that awful thing that voices do when you talk while crying. "He's . . . well, he's just Ben, you know? He's kind and sweet and funny. I keep thinking that, if I hang around him long enough, he'll start to rub off on me." Laughing without humor, I groped for the doorjamb and then clung to it as if it were a life preserver. Mason's huge form swam in my vision. "Anyway, I guess I just wanted you to know that I don't plan on stepping out of Ben's life just because you don't like me." I brushed the back of my hand down my cheek, swiping away the wetness. And then, spinning on one heel, I left him there. And I noticed, as I ran down the hall toward Ben's room, that Mason had finally stopped playing.

I was standing outside on the deck that afternoon, wholly adrift in my thoughts, digging my iPod out of my pocket while reconstructing and deconstructing my meltdown in front of Mason, and also trying to decide whether it was worth accidentally-on-purpose twisting my ankle to get out of my next session with Hilda, when the sliding glass door jerked open and a female voice behind me hollered, "Maggie?"

I shrieked—like, literally shrieked—and lurched around, my iPod skidding off to some unknown area of my non-eyesight, probably never to be found again. "Who's there?"

"Clarissa!"

Clarissa.

Was it Wednesday already? Oh dear God: it was Wednesday. I rubbed the back of my neck. "Oh, hey, Clarissa," I said, working to keep my tone sociable.

Tapping her way toward me until her cane thunked against my feet, she greeted me by taking my right hand between both of hers. I had no idea how she'd found it. It had been propped on my hip, directly across from my left hand, which, by no great coincidence, was propped on my left hip. Squeezing my fingers excitedly, she said, "*Heeey.* Hope you don't mind that Dad dropped me off a little early? He had, like, only a quick break before his afternoon rounds at the hospital to give me a ride. Cripes, my backpack is *so. ridiculously. heavy.* Too many books! Think we can go inside and get started?"

Extracting my hand, I wiped it on my shorts. Which was juvenile, but I did it anyway. "Um. Sure," I said.

When we got to my room, she unloaded herself on my bed and launched into one of her erratic, exclamation-point soliloquies about our illiteracy paper, during which I set about ignoring her by means of thinking about what I'd said to Mason. And also thinking about the way he'd looked. And sounded. With a sigh, I turned my attention back to Clarissa. She was still talking. She'd moved on to a full discourse about Iced Coffee Guy. I thought that maybe she'd stop there, that maybe she'd realize she was oversharing, but she didn't. She slid right into a painfully long description of the buttercream frosting she'd made in cake-decorating class. Finally I said, "You're seriously taking a cake-decorating class?"

"Yes," she sang with a friendliness that made me feel slightly guilty. "Why wouldn't I?"

"Just seems like it would be hard, is all," I said, shoving my hands in my pockets, and then pulling them back out, and then folding them over my chest. I cleared my throat. "I mean, you can't even see what you're doing, so what's the point?"

"Frosting," Clarissa trilled. "Frosting is the point. Ganache and citrus curd. Whipped cream. Fondant. And—*oh*—meringue. Besides, cake decorating is so much fun! And supereasy. You just have to go slowly and pay attention to what you're doing—the position of the decorating bag, the amount of pressure you put on it, yada yada yada. Want to come to my next class? You should totally come. You're so hilarious—the ladies there will love you. Doesn't even matter if the cake turns out hideous, because really: still tastes like cake!"

"Huh," I muttered noncommittally as I made my way toward my desk, determined to fire up my computer and get working on this paper. Halfway across the floor, though, I tripped on Clarissa's massive backpack, which she'd evidently deposited in the middle of my room. Grunting, I pushed it aside and said, "What the hell is in your backpack?"

I heard the rattle of ice in a cup—iced coffee, I was guessing—and a pronounced swallow. And then she said, "In order to get a ride here, I had to go with Dad to work for a couple hours. He had patients to see. Somebody's bladder to stitch up or whatever. So I brought my books, because it pains me to sit there for hours, listening to him talk to his coworkers about prostates and penises and hurtias."

"Hernias," I corrected, and then, like the child that I was, I smirked. Because: penises.

"Whatever. Hernias," she dismissed lightly. "Anyhoo...the books! I'm reading two simultaneously because they both came in the mail at the same time and I couldn't choose. They both sounded *so* good. Do you like to read? I'll loan them to you when I'm done. You'll freak—just keel over and die. I mean, the *romance.*"

"No, thanks," I said, not particularly keen on exploring the ins and outs of romance at this particular juncture. And besides, thus far I'd managed to conquer only Grade 1 braille, which worked like a simple substitution code. Most books these days were written in complicated, twisty Grade 2 braille, which I was still learning.

"Sure?" she chirped. "You'd fall in love with the guys! The one in *Enchanted Kiss* is in this crazy-good indie band that totally reminds me of the Loose Cannons! The drummer is so insanely talented. And the lead singer is Mason Milton all the way, so swoony and—"

I coughed like I'd just swallowed my tongue.

"You all right?" Clarissa said.

I clapped my hands together overzealously. "Yup. Totally fine. I just . . ." I cleared my throat. Twice. "You like the Loose Cannons?"

She snorted. "I have an unhealthy amount of like for the Loose Cannons. In fact, the Loose Cannons take up so much Like Space in my brain that there is hardly room for anything else besides baked goods."

I sat down hard in my chair. "Huh."

"Yeah," she said. "I mean, the Loose Cannons' lyrics? They slay me. 'Eternal Implosion' goes to some crazy-deep places, Maggie. Brilliance. Factor."

"Huh," I said again. Because I was verbose like that. But honestly I didn't know what else to say. I was too shocked. Clarissa just didn't seem the type to like my kind of music. And anyway, she started talking again so it didn't really matter.

"A friend of mine—Jase Crenshaw?" she said. "He knows Mason Milton. I know, right? *Mason Milton.* They go to school together at Brighton."

My chair squeaked sharply as I jerked toward her. "Has Mason told him the Big Secret?" I practically shouted.

I heard her collapse on the bed. Drum her fingers on my wall. "No. He hasn't, no." She blew out a loud exhale. "What do you think he's like? I feel like he's superhot. Or else superintense."

"Both. Definitely both," I said with a sigh.

A sigh.

Dear God. I could hardly stand myself.

"Anyway," Clarissa sang, "I feel like the Big Secret can't be all that hard to figure out. There's probably this *gigantic* clue right in the middle of the website somewhere—so easy that it's hard, you know? We should totally hang out more so we can brainstorm."

"Sure," I said immediately. Because the truth of it was, there were certain sacrifices I was willing to make to attend a Loose Cannons concert. And hanging out with Clarissa Fenstermacher was one of them.

19

While I had a closetful of perfectly acceptable shoes, I'd worn nothing but flip-flops since I lost my sight. Even in the winter. I wasn't sure why exactly, but I presumed it was because their thin soles helped me to get a sense of my environment, to detect tiny changes in the landscape and the slope of the ground and whatnot. Or maybe I was just too lazy to tie my shoes.

Whatever the case, I liked the statements that my flip-flops made. They said, *I think my toes are pretty*, and they said, *I don't plan on dressing up any time soon*, and they said, *I have no intention of trying to outrun law enforcement today*.

At any rate, since my feet were always exposed they tended to be constantly cold, which in turn made them ghostly white. And as Ben and I sat side by side on his living room floor in front of the TV, they looked practically see-through next to Ben's exceedingly tanned, exceedingly dirty feet.

"How come your feet are so grimy?" I asked, leaning against the couch.

He shrugged. "Haven't been wearing shoes much lately because I found out my shoes are sweatshop shoes. I need some new, non-slave-labor ones, but Mom has been busy with work. And so: I have been barefoot."

"Sweatshop shoes?"

"Duh, like the kind made in third-world countries by five-year-old kids. It was on the news the other day. Turns out, my favorite shoes were glued together by slave labor. I may give up shoes altogether. I may become shoeless." I rolled my eyes as he went on, pointing with his head to a pair of white sneakers by the front door. "If you put them to your ear, you'll hear the voices of a thousand disadvantaged kids forced to work for a penny a day."

My reply was interrupted by raucous laughter coming from the direction of Mason's room, where Mason and David had been holed up the entire time I'd been here. Although Mason and I hadn't actually spoken since my unbecoming breakdown in his room, in the past few days I'd noticed less tension in his shoulders when I was around, and he'd seemed to surface in the same room as Ben and me more often. Consequently, I thought maybe my little speech had made an impression. I grant you, it was just one flimsy, splintered piece of plywood slid across the giant ravine between us. Not enough to support the weight of either of us, but just enough to tell me that we weren't as far away as I'd once thought.

Grumbling at myself for getting distracted by Mason again, I kicked Ben's grubby foot, just lightly. "It's a good look for you, the dirt," I teased.

"Glad you're finally coming around, Thera. Maybe we can reconsider that kiss?"

I stabbed him in the ribs with my elbow and said, "Reasons that I will not kiss Ben Milton—GO: One, he's seven years younger than me. Two, although he isn't my brother, he feels like my brother. Three, he has grilled cheese sandwich stuck in his front teeth."

"Shit. Really?" he said, scrubbing his teeth with an index finger.

"Four, he's too young to cuss, but he cusses anyway. And five"—I lowered my voice—"I found a Loose Cannons CD hidden under his bed yesterday."

"Shit," he said again, louder this time, making his Flabrador retriever—who had his legs spread out behind him like a frog and his nose propped on Ben's knee—raise his dog-brows.

I shot the dog a look. Honestly. Wally was a little too reliant on Ben for attention.

"Please don't tell Mason about the CD," Ben whispered like we were in a James Bond movie and I'd just uncovered the truth about a top secret file.

I would have gladly tortured him for a while, but Mrs. Milton stuck her head into the living room and said, "Benjamin Thomas Milton, what did I ask you to do today?"

Ben's head fell back theatrically and he stared at the ceiling. "Scrub my toothpaste out of the sink?"

"And?" she prompted.

He filled his cheeks with air and then let it out all at once, flapping his lips. "Vacuum the Doritos out of my carpet before the room"—he made quote fingers—"turns into an ant pile?"

"Could you take care of that now, please? I have the early shift tomorrow and I need to go to bed soon. I don't want to be listening to the vacuum at midnight, like the last time you cleaned your room."

Ben gave me an apologetic shrug and took off, leaving me in the dusty, indiscriminate outskirts of my eyesight. But it was enough to just barely make out Mason, minutes later, as he came loping down the hallway, passing by the living room without noticing me. He headed straight out the front door, leaving it open for David, who was a few paces behind. David's eyes snagged on me just before he crossed the threshold. He jerked to a stop.

My breath hitched. What had Mason told his bandmates after I'd left his room the other night? That I was a stalker? A lunatic fan? Suddenly, I felt like one of those jackasses who had resolved to ride out a hurricane in a trailer park. A storm was knocking on my front door, and now there was nowhere to go.

David put a hand to his chest. I held my breath, waiting for the ax to fall. "Be still my heart," he said. "Maggie Sanders: the mystery girl. You look as lovely as ever." Then he loped over and crashed down beside me, bumping his shoulder against mine. "Do me a favor and explain that little scene in Mason's room? Mason won't tell us jack shit."

I blinked. Mason hadn't told his friends about his suspicions? I waved David off with one hand, and, staring at the tattoo on his forearm, said, "It was nothing, actually. Just, you know...a misunderstanding."

"Then you and Mason don't have a thing?"

I felt a weird tickle in my throat. I swallowed over it. "Nope."

He kicked his spindly legs out in front of him and laced his hands behind his head, leaning against the couch. "Is there a

reason you're here at eight P.M. on this beautiful summer eve-
ning, listening to reruns of . . ." He glanced at the TV and cringed.
"Holy crap, it's even worse than I thought: *So You Think You Can
Dance?*"

I shrugged.

"You know it's Saturday night, right?" he asked.

"So?"

"So we are heading out to the Strand. The Dead Eddies are
playing a reunion show there tonight and you should come with."

"The Dead Eddies? No shit?"

He smiled with one side of his mouth. "I shit you not."

"Wow." The Dead Eddies were . . . well, they were the *Dead
Eddies.* I'd loved them since forever. Still, the thought of being
around Mason without the benefit of sight made a hard knot settle
in my stomach. In fact, the thought of being around Mason at all
made a hard knot settle in my stomach.

I swallowed. "Are Carlos and Gavin going, too?" I asked.

David picked casually at a loose fray on his jeans. "Gavin's tied
up at some dinner soiree with his parents, and we haven't seen
Carlos since he stormed out of rehearsal a couple days ago."

"You guys have a fight?"

David shrugged, a motion that involved the entire upper half
of his body. "Sometimes he doesn't see eye to eye with the rest of
us. He was hell-bent on changing an arrangement, we disagreed,
and he took off. His usual MO," he said dismissively. "Anyway:
the Strand?"

"Um," I said, stalling. "Isn't the Strand that place in Bridgeport?
The over-twenty-one club?"

"Yup," David said.

"You guys have fake IDs?"

"Yup."

"Well, I don't have one, so I guess I'm out."

"Yeah, but here's the thing: I know a guy who knows a guy who owes me a solid. I can get you in."

Grasping now, I blurted, "I forgot my cane at home."

He shrugged. "You can borrow my elbow for the evening. Or Mason's."

I swallowed so loudly that I swore he could hear it. "But Ben—"

David let out a massive sigh, like I was being extremely thick-headed. "Ben is ten and you are seventeen. He will completely understand." And before I could protest or even say good-bye to Ben, he yanked me upright, out the door, and into the driveway. As he guided me into the backseat of Mason's car, he said to Mason, "Hey, man, I invited Maggie to come along."

"Ah," Mason said. Which was technically only an acknowledgment of both my existence and the fact that I was tagging along. Still, Mason didn't sound mad or upset or broody, and so it felt like a victory.

20

If I were to jump up and down on a pogo stick while wearing four-inch heels, on the up-bounce I'd probably be just tall enough to hold on to David's elbow without reaching. So when I stumbled on the steps of the Strand's back entrance, I sort of dangled from his arm. Mason, who was directly behind me, steadied me by the waist while I regained my footing. "You all right?" he asked, taking his hands away but leaving what felt like two burning palms on my sides. I responded with something that sounded an awful lot like "Gumph," to which he replied, "Good," as though I'd uttered an actual word. Which only proved that he was accustomed to starstruck girls who were unable to respond to him in English.

I anchored myself on the warm bricks of the building while David rapped on a metal-sounding door. The bass inside the Strand was rumbling through my shoes, pricking the underside of my toes. It wasn't the Dead Eddies playing—not yet—just some semicurrent deejayed song mixed with another semicurrent deejayed song.

The door opened and music charged loud in my face. "Paulie!" David hollered over the noise. "So Marcus said I could slide in through the back door whenever I wanted." There was a pause in which I suspected Paulie—a bouncer?—looked unconvinced. David went on to say, "You can ask Marcus if you don't believe me."

"This is a big night, kid," Paulie said in a gravelly voice. "The kickoff for the Dead Eddies' reunion tour. There's a line clear down Sixth."

"Right, but the thing is that there are only three of us, so we won't even make a difference in the room capacity."

Paulie didn't say anything for several beats. He just stood there, smelling vaguely of body spray and spearmint gum and steroids. Finally he grunted, "Is the girl of age?"

David said, "Paulie, what do you take me for?"

Paulie exhaled a rather extreme burst of spearmint in my face. "Don't make me regret it, kid."

And then we were in.

The place was beyond packed. We took maybe five steps and were stopped by a wall of people. "YOU GOOD JUST STAYING HERE?" David hollered.

Like it mattered to me. "TOTALLY."

David took off to thank Marcus, leaving me alone with Mason, who, due to the number of people crammed in the place, was standing shoulder to shoulder with me. I'd never had a regular conversation with Mason, so I wasn't really sure how to behave.

Should I open with a joke? Small talk? Finally, I went with something honest.

"IT'S CRAZY IN HERE!" I hollered over the music, and he
said "I KNOW, RIGHT?" and I said "WHEN THEY PLAY 'THE
BEGINNING OF IT ALL' I MIGHT TOTALLY, LEGITI-
MATELY HAVE AN ANEURYSM," and he just laughed. This
marked the longest dialogue we'd ever had, and definitely the
most normal.

Just then, a cacophony of probably a half-dozen different per-
fumes floated up in front of us. I heard a chorus of squeals, and
then an awed female voice, clearly the spokesperson of the group,
yelled, "I CANNOT BELIEVE IT! IT'S REALLY YOU!"

"OH," Mason hollered back, "YOU GUYS THINK I'M—
RIGHT. I GET THAT ALL THE TIME. I JUST LOOK LIKE
THAT GUY."

I could hear the disappointment in the girl's tone as she said,
almost in a whine, "BUT YOU LOOK *EXACTLY* LIKE HIM.
YOU'RE REALLY NOT HIM? THE GUY YOU WALKED IN
WITH, HE LOOKS JUST LIKE—"

"NOPE," Mason shouted back. I felt his shoulder raise and
lower apologetically. "JUST A NORMAL GUY AT A CONCERT.
THANKS FOR THE COMPLIMENT, THOUGH."

Then the girls were gone.

I waited until the song ended, and then I leaned toward Mason
and said, "Smooth, by the way."

"Just wanted to enjoy the night, by the way."

I smiled in his general direction. I liked being with this Mason,
the one I couldn't see. He seemed more human somehow, more

real. I wasn't distracted by the hair and the eyes and the . . . everything. I wasn't trying to hide anything from him.

David made it back right as the Dead Eddies took the stage. The crowd went insane. Everyone was screaming, jostling into one another, dancing. I'd always loved to dance, but usually I was overly mindful of how my body was moving. But tonight I wasn't worried about what people thought of me. I wasn't uncomfortable. I wasn't self-conscious. I wasn't trying to prove anything to Mason. I wasn't anything but the music. My stomping feet were the downbeats and my hips were the chorus and my arms were the keyboard riffs.

When the band launched into "The Beginning of It All," we were jumping up and down, matching the beat. My hair had fallen out of its elastic band, and it undoubtedly stuck out in a tangled explosion, but I didn't even care. Due to Mason's close proximity and the fact that I actually, literally, could not help touching him, all at once we were dancing with each other without the formality of dancing with each other, complementing each other's movements perfectly. Every bend of his body seemed to seek out mine, every arch in mine fit perfectly in his. When the song ended, there was one fragile second when we didn't move, when we just stayed there, sort of smashed up against each other. And then we took a step apart.

David leaned into my ear and yelled, "I'M SWEATIN' BALLS"—which, incidentally, was not something I wanted to hear loudly—"GOING TO GET SOMETHING TO DRINK—WANT SOMETHING?" and I screamed, "YES, WATER, PLEASE," and he screamed something else, and I said, "WHAT?!" and he screamed it again, but I still didn't hear him, so I just nodded because it wasn't worth the hassle. Minutes later, David came back and shoved an overly sweet, overly aftertasty lemonade in my hand, which I chugged. I'd have preferred water, really, but I was hot and thirsty and frankly relieved to be drinking anything at all.

By the time the Dead Eddies wrapped up, I'd sort-of-danced with Mason for an hour and a half straight. Also, I'd downed several more lemonades, all of which had gotten surprisingly better as the night wore on, and all of which seemed to have descended to my bladder at exactly the same moment. "I have to pee," I announced grandly. "Which is a problem."

Man, I felt strange. Loose-jointed.

"Why is it a problem, Maggie?" Mason asked in an amused tone, as though he were talking to a child or a revered pet.

Which unglued me instantly.

After I recovered my voice, I said, "Because *someone* abducted me from the Milton estate without as much as a cane. So now I have to navigate inside the restroom sans cane, which is nearly impossible because I suck at navigation in general."

"Particularly when you're drunk," David added.

"I'm not *drunk*," I said indignantly. "I do not drink." Which was true on multiple levels. Even when I'd still had friends and gone to parties, I hadn't been a drinker. Seemed like I'd always had a big game or a big tryout or a big practice the next day. Besides that, the almighty keg always powered high school parties, and I was generally not fond of beer due to the fact that it tasted like an aluminum pole.

"Well." David sounded uncomfortable. "You drank tonight. I thought you said you were cool with hard lemonade?"

"I didn't actually hear that question." I'd meant to say this quite seriously, but the last part came out in a laugh. And when I tried to say something else, it also came out in a laugh, which then caused me to laugh harder and lose my balance, whacking into a wall.

Actually, not a wall: a rather large person who smelled strongly of spearmint gum and annoyance. "Paulie!" I said congenially, as though we'd served in Vietnam together or something. "You should try the lemonade—it'll change your life!"

Paulie steadied me and spoke over my head to David, "How many drinks did she have?"

"Like, four." After a long pause, David added, "Ish."

"Ish?"

"Okay, so possibly five."

I turned in Paulie's general direction and said, "By great error, I have had too much to drink and now I have to pee. Badly."

"Yes. That's generally how the plumbing works," Paulie said. "But I think you should take your pee elsewhere."

Probably the correct response to Paulie's request would have been "Yes, sir" with no sarcasm. The wrong response, evidently, was "Yes, sir" with sarcasm. And a salute.

....

"I have to pee."

"Right," Mason said. "You might've mentioned that already."

We were walking across a blessedly quiet parking lot to Mason's car. By walking, I mean that David had my legs and Mason had my arms. So technically, I was lying down and they were fulfilling all the walking obligations.

"When is your curfew, Maggie?" David asked.

"Don't have one tonight," I said loudly. "Parents are on an overnighter in the city."

They hoisted me into the backseat of Mason's car, where I curled up against the cool vinyl, suddenly exhausted. I shut my eyes and rolled over, forehead against the seat, not quite asleep, but not quite awake, either. I was straddling the obscure gray passageway that ran between the two.

After a couple minutes, I heard Mason mutter, "She passed out?"

"Yeah," David whispered back. For a moment there was just the steady hum of Mason's car. And then David's voice again: "You can thank me now."

The blinker clacked a couple times, and the car veered left. "For what?" Mason said.

"*I'm* not blind," David said lightly, a smile in his voice. "I saw you two dancing." He paused for a tick, probably waiting for Mason to respond. But he didn't. "Just wondering why it took the Dead Eddies to pull your heads out of your asses," David said.

Mason sighed. "It's a long story."

"It's a long drive."

Mason was quiet for several moments, and then, sounding slightly embarrassed, he said, "I thought she was a fan—that she faked her blindness so Ben would feel sorry for her. I thought she was stalking me, trying to find information about our concerts."

David whistled, long and low. "Damn," he said, "that's some bigheaded shit right there." When Mason didn't reply, David went on. "Is it that much of a stretch to see that Ben and Maggie might have something in common? I mean, life has basically handed them their asses. Maybe Maggie just needs a friend? Maybe she's going through a rough time?"

Big sigh from Mason's side of the car. "I know, I know," Mason said. "Mostly, I was worried about Ben—he's too trusting, and I didn't want him getting hurt. He really likes Maggie, you know?" He was silent for some time, and when he finally spoke, he seemed to be grasping for the right words. "And sometimes . . . sometimes I'd swear she can see. Sometimes it's like she's looking right *at* me."

"Yeah, jackass, it's called *adapting to your circumstances*. You should try it sometime."

....

"I have to pee" was the first thing I said to Ben. And then I cracked up.

Ben puffed out his cheeks and shot Mason the dirty eyeball. He gestured to the Miltons' living room, where we were currently standing—leaning, actually, in my case. To Mason, he said, "You stole her from here and got her *drunk*? I've been worried about her, you know. I mean, all you had to do was call and let me know she was all right."

Ben sounded so adorably old for his body that I started laughing again. "Aw. Ben? *Ben.* It was a spurred-moment thing." I shook my head. "A spur-moment." I sighed, let my head fall back, and shut my eyes. "A—spur—of—the—moment—thing, and I did not know I was drinking alcoholic beverages until they were all in my bladder. Can I go pee? I'm going pee." I stepped grandly into the tiny powder room to my immediate right, from where I could hear Ben and Mason arguing. It was about either what to do with me or what *not* to do with me. Definitely one of those. But when I made my way back into the living room, Ben was the only one standing there, still looking charmingly parental. "Where's Mason?" I asked.

"Went to find you some aspirin. Says you're gonna need it."

"Ah," I said, and I wove my way across the room, slamming into the piano and knocking a half-dozen or so pictures off the lid.

"Don't. wake. up. my. mother," Ben hissed. Ben had never been angry with me before, and I found it sort of endearing. I reached out and pinched his cheek between my thumb and index finger. He mashed his lips together and said, "My uncle would freak if he knew you've been drinking."

"Which is why you won't tell him. My probation officer would not understand what went down tonight."

"Yeah? Well, neither do I. What gives? You leave with my brother without even telling me?"

I collapsed on the couch, all sighs. "Ben. Ben, darling. You're only ten and I'm about to be a senior in high school and sometimes I need to hang out with people from my age group."

A small frown appeared between his brows. "I didn't know my age bothered you so much," he said quietly.

"Aw, c'mon, Ben. Your age doesn't matter to me. You know that. It's just, your brother is . . ." I heard a sigh escape my lips. I didn't know how it got there. My lips seemed to be sighing on their own. *"Mason Milton."*

Realization slid over Ben's features, and then he took a step backward. He looked as though he'd been slapped. "So Mason was right. You've been using me to get near him."

"Ack. That's not what I meant," I said, but Ben just shook his head—his eyes the deepest, darkest oceans of hurt and sadness—and spun around on his crutches and left.

Goddamn it. I tried to go after him, but the room was spinning, which was not something I thought actually happened in real life. Anchoring one foot on the floor, I shut my eyes. No dice. Still spinning. Next thing I knew, Mason was hovering over me—looking concerned and gorgeous and late-night tousled—tucking a stray curl behind my ear and letting his hand linger on my cheek, like it was fragile, like it was beautiful, the intensity of his eyes making my heart lurch. "Brought you some aspirin," he murmured.

The air between us was electric, the ions vibrating, unbalanced. I blinked up at him, achingly aware that his lips were only a few breaths from mine, and if I weren't so dizzy, so groggy, I'd close that distance and kiss him. Instead I reached up with my hand, found his mouth, and ran a clumsy index finger along his bottom lip. Suddenly—idiotically—I said, "Your lips feel a lot softer than they look."

The last thing I saw before I passed out was the stiff set of Mason's shoulders as he strode away.

21

"Cripes, Maggie. You're a late sleeper."

I winced and pulled the covers over my head. Clarissa was on the phone, shouting words into my skull.

"How come you're still in bed at one in the afternoon? Are you okay?" she asked.

Good question. I remembered going to Ben's last night. I remembered David asking me to tag along to the concert. I remembered the music, the dancing with Mason. The lemonade. Getting kicked out of the club. Arriving at the Miltons' and talking to Ben and Mason—

Oh shit.

Ben.

Mason.

I jerked upright. Clearly the wrong move, because—holy crap—my head was absolutely *screaming* at me. I lowered back down an inch at a time, holding it like any sudden movement might cause it to detonate right off my neck. Slowly letting go, I ran one trembling hand to the side.

My nightstand. My room. Had Mason brought me home last night? Yes. He must have, yes. I didn't actually remember it, but I could feel that it was true.

I was queasy and sweaty and smothered in blankets, and if I didn't stop thinking about my stupidity last night, I might throw up or explode or otherwise blink away from existence. *What have you done?* a voice whispered from some dark, regretful place in my chest.

I groaned quietly, a sound that banged agonizingly against my cranium.

"Anyway," Clarissa chirped, "Girl Scouts was canceled today, and I was wondering if maybe you wanted to work on our paper? Or else obsess and brainstorm on the Big Secret? Did you see the new comment on the last concert video? There's some guy called Cannon Dude who says that 'the secret lies with the singer' and that anyone who hasn't figured out the Big Secret by now doesn't deserve to listen to the Loose Cannons, let alone attend a concert. I know, right? Totally ridiculous. It cannot be that easy. It cannot. I may not be brilliant, but I am a huge fan and I know *every. stinking. thing* about the band. And I have spent hours investigating them, Maggie. Hours searching that website. Wouldn't I have figured it out by now? Yes. Of course I would, yes." She sighed loudly in my ear. "So. What do you say? Want to hang out today?"

I rolled onto my side and regretted it immediately. Something that smelled suspiciously like puke was crusted against my pillowcase. I swallowed and slid backward. "Actually, I think I have the flu or something."

"Want me to bring you some soup?"

My hand flew to my mouth. "No, thanks," I choked.

"Won't take no for an answer," she said lightly. "Fenstermacher soup is famous for its healing powers." And then she threw a bunch of words directly at my headache, telling me about all the things Fenstermacher soup had done for her—how last year, when she'd failed a math exam, she'd eaten it nonstop, and how it had helped soothe her after her dog had died, and so on and so forth.

In the end, I agreed to the soup, though I had no idea why. And when I stood up and staggered into the bathroom, the very thought of soup had me running to the toilet to dry heave. I stayed there for a moment, forehead resting on the cool toilet seat, before I crawled into the shower. Slumped under the faucet, I let the water massage my neck and tried to work out how to apologize to Ben, tried to decide what to say to Mason, tried to figure out how to clean up the gigantic mess I'd created.

I was still wrapped in a towel when I dialed the Miltons' number. It rang five times before someone picked up, and even then they didn't speak. I felt a cold trickle of water drip off my hair and slide down between my shoulder blades. "Hello? Ben?" I said after a few heartbeats. "Mason?"

Dial tone.

Something huge and sticky wedged itself into my throat.

Shortly after I got dressed, Clarissa appeared at my front door like an overly caffeinated jack-in-the-box. She passed me a Tupperware container of soup and some rather chirpy encouragement: "Eat this immediately" and "Call me tomorrow if you need more" and "I'm sorry you feel lousy." I nodded and um-hummed and thank-youed and said good-bye. And as I put the container in the fridge, I tried not to think about how Clarissa was acting like a real friend, even though I'd hardly said boo to her. I tried not to think about how she'd probably sooner shoot herself in the foot than hurt somebody's feelings. I tried not to think about how she'd basically dropped everything to come by and help me—something I hadn't done for a friend, not once in my life.

....

When I was twelve or thirteen—or however old you are when you're in the seventh grade—I decided quite suddenly and without sufficient thought that I should become a beekeeper. Back then I was terrified of bees. I found their little buzzing sounds and their little pointy stingers and their little fluttering wings absolutely frightening. Which was exactly why I found it necessary to conquer them.

Conquer them, conquer my fears.

Maggie Sanders: bee wrangler.

Looking for clear-cut beekeeping instructions, I went to the bookstore, where a bespectacled woman with pursed lips and a posture more erect than necessary led me to the *Idiots* and *Dummies* section of the store. She then spun around on one heel and stalked off, leaving me alone to decide which book to purchase. After some thought, I bought *The Complete Idiot's Guide to Beekeeping*, because if I had to classify myself, I'd be more of an idiot (somewhat ignorant) than a dummy (just plain stupid).

Anyhow, I learned that there were a couple of ways to start a bee

colony. Either I had to invest a significant amount of money in buying a colony of starter bees, or I needed to find a hive and collect
the starter bees myself. My being an idiot and all, I decided to go
with the cheaper route: scale the oak in my backyard and bag the
grapefruit-size hive that dangled from a thick, gnarled-up branch
about halfway up the tree.

So I was up in the tree—teetering on a fat branch with an extra-
large trash bag in one hand and a broom in the other—when I
remembered why I'd always sucked at softball. I had hideous aim
with a bat. I swiped at the hive with the business end of the broom,
trying to knock it into the bag. But I missed and nicked the thing
mid-hive, breaking off a large bee-filled chunk of honeycomb,
which flew straight up in the air, directly over my head, and then
straight back down into the floppy gap in the back waistband of
my shorts. Yes, I was stung about thirty times. And yes, on my ass.

On the positive side of things, I was no longer afraid of bees. I'd
seen the dark side of fear and, except for my backside, I'd made
it out unscathed. So I'd accomplished my goal. Sort of. But my
real takeaway that day had been this: the best way to tackle the
things that terrify you is to not overthink them—to just do them
quickly. So late that afternoon, I asked Gramps to drop me off
at the Miltons'.

Even from the porch, the place seemed excruciatingly bright.
The crystalline radiance bled out of the house and onto my feet.
And I wondered, as I stood there waiting for someone to answer
my knock, if Ben was getting even brighter or if my hangover had
made my eyes more sensitive to light. Whatever the reason, the
place seemed too vibrant, too intrusive, and it picked at the back
of my brain for some reason.

When nobody answered, I headed around to the back door, where I could hear Ben through an open bathroom window. He was giving Wally a bath, carrying on a conversation with him as though he were a person: "So next week, we'll go to the old-folks' home. The one across town? The Meadows? Granny has a roommate there who's been down in the dumps. I think we can cheer her up. I'll make armpit farts while you do that thing where you cock your head to the side. Everyone thinks that's hilarious." I probably shouldn't be so proud of someone whom I hadn't helped shape into a kind, decent human being, but I couldn't help myself.

How could I have ever hurt this kid's feelings? What sort of asshole *does* something like that?

The back door was unlocked. I swept inside, taking quick, purposeful steps to the bathroom, where I rapped on the door. "Ben. Open up."

For a moment, there was nothing but silence. I could feel him thinking of what to say, and as he did so, I sensed him pulling away from me, the space between us expanding and stretching from a few feet into several miles. When he did speak it was almost a whisper: "Go away, Maggie."

Maggie.

He'd called me Maggie. Not Thera.

My heart twisted. I hated the idea of fighting with Ben, of having caused him heartache, of screwing up our friendship. Not just because he'd gifted me with a portion of my eyesight, either. It was more than that. "Ben—"

"No," he said, more forcibly this time. "I need you to leave me alone. I'm sad right now, and I'm not going to be un-sad for a long time, and all I want is for you to get out of my house."

Guilt corkscrewed around me and twisted into my gut. I leaned against the door, sliding down until my butt hit the floor with an uncomfortable thud. I opened my mouth and then closed it again. I was afraid that if I tried to speak, more *stupid* would come out. "I'm sorry," I said finally.

"You might take that 'I'm sorry' and give it to Mason. You hurled all over his car last night when he drove you home. But don't worry about it. It only took him a few hours to clean it up. Probably the smell will go away in a month or so."

So Mason Milton had cleaned up my puke. Lovely. Add that to my list of offenses. "Is he home?"

"Nope," Ben said, popping the *P* to let me know just how little he cared to be speaking to me at this very moment.

I thunked the back of my head against the door, just once, and pianoed my fingers on the floor—a sad, lonely riff from one of Chopin's waltzes.

"Look," Ben said tiredly, "I'm not going to feel sorry for you, okay? You were using me to see, using me to get close to Mason." I folded my arms over my stomach. There was a vein of truth in his words; I couldn't refute them. After a beat, he went on. "Truth is, sometimes you do shitty things. Sometimes you say shitty things. Sometimes you're not a good friend. I'm not going to try to make you feel better about that."

. . . .

I thought about those words in Gramps's truck all the way home, and all the way up my porch steps, and all the way to my room. Flopping facedown on my bed, I recollected all those times I could have called Sophie to explain how I was feeling, to apologize for avoiding her, but didn't. I thought about how I'd let our friendship wither up and die because I was too ashamed to tell her I was scared and miserable, too focused on holing up in my house and hoping my blindness would just go away. It had been a decision I'd made months ago and every day after that—a decision I'd made to push her away.

And it had worked.

Right now my life was so broken, so mangled. I needed to glue something back together before my shaking frame fractured into a million different pieces. So I pulled my phone out of my pocket and dialed Sophie's number.

22

"Sophie. It's Maggie."

Her name sounded odd coming out of my mouth. Foreign. I wedged the phone between my shoulder and ear and then crossed my arms. Then I uncrossed them. Then I crossed them again. What did I usually do with my arms when I was on the phone?

I noticed a strange hiccup of silence before Sophie spoke, and when she did her voice sounded off: gluey and stuffy, like she was just getting over a cold. "Hey, Maggie."

I cleared my throat. Why was I so nervous? This was Sophie. We'd known each other practically all our lives, lost baby teeth together, gone through period trauma with each other. "Hey. Um. I was wondering if you want to come over? You know, like, to my house. In Bedford Estates." Oh my God. Did I just say that? I just said that. I cleared my throat again. "It would be cool if you bring Lauren, too."

"Okay." She sounded hesitant, dubious, and I guess she had every reason to be.

An hour later the doorbell rang. I padded into the entryway and stood there for a long moment, my heartbeat fluttering in my throat, before I took three unstable strides forward and grasped the knob. Sucking in a breath, I yanked the door open, hovering there for the space of several breaths before fundamental hospitality kicked in. I said hello and Sophie said hello. I asked if Lauren had come along, and Sophie said that she hadn't been able to make it. And then we just stood there, on opposite sides of the threshold, as silence wedged itself between us.

Finally I waved her inside and led her to the living room, which in and of itself was a little awkward. Back in the day, we'd always hung out in my room. But I was hesitant to take her to my new bedroom. I didn't want her asking questions I had no clue how to answer.

So: the living room, where I sat on the couch as though I had a javelin shoved straight up my spine. I waited for Sophie to start talking. She didn't. Even though the air-conditioning was set on glacial, I felt sweaty and feverish and short of breath. Wiping my palms on the couch, I opened with the brilliant "So. Um. Lauren's busy today?"

Sophie pulled air through her teeth, a nervous habit of hers. It used to drive our fourth-grade teacher, Mrs. Jones, completely out of her head. Finally she said, "I guess she had plans or something?"

In all honesty, I hadn't actually expected Lauren to come along today. Out of all the girls on the team, Lauren was the one who had seemed the most uncomfortable with my blindness. I waited for Sophie to say something else, but she didn't, so I let out a little cough and said, "So. How are you?"

Sophie sighed. It made me feel weird for some reason. Heavy-hearted. "I'm doing well," she said softly. I got the impression that she was trying to convince herself more than she was trying to convince me. "You?"

"Fantastico," I said. As an expert liar, my voice didn't waver one iota.

The quiet settled over us again.

Small talk. I needed more small talk.

"Are you still going out with that guy?" I said, sort of loudly. "The one with the hair?" Just before I'd lost my sight, she'd started dating some guy from Central—a wide-shouldered jock who looked as though he'd styled his hair by gelling it up and jumping backward out of a plane.

"Jason Salamone? Um. No," she said. Her *no* had two syllables, the first one for the *no* and the second one for the rest of the story.

I bit my thumbnail. God, this was excruciating. "What happened?"

"Jason moved to North Dakota."

I had the feeling she was still leaving out something huge—like maybe he'd dumped her or had treated her badly or something—but I wasn't going to press. Instead I said, "North Dakota? What the hell is in North Dakota?"

"A military base. Jason's dad got transferred there," she explained.

"Oh."

Silence.

I shifted on the couch. Folded one leg under my butt. Twisted my hands together. With every shift of position, I begged myself to apologize to her. To tell her how hard the past several months had been. But the truth was, I was terrified of what she might say. So instead I blurted, "Are you sick?" The question took her off guard for some reason, because she didn't answer right away. "You sound stuffy, is all. Like you have a cold."

"I—yeah. I mean, I don't feel well."

More silence.

This ranked as the most awkward conversation we'd ever had, even worse than the Target conversation, which was saying something. I never thought we could disintegrate this badly. Never thought we'd end up here, like this, sitting next to each other and groping for words that neither of us had. *Okay, fine,* I wanted to scream up at the sky. *Lessons learned. Payback noted. Hallmark moment not going to happen.* And I couldn't blame Sophie. It was exactly what I deserved.

. . . .

The next day I kept picking up my phone to call Ben for dumb, random stuff: to tell him that maybe chocolate Pop-Tarts were my Thing, and to ask him if he knew when the word *anniversary* was invented, because it seemed like one of those words we should be celebrating, oh, I don't know . . . say, once a year. But then I'd realize he wasn't speaking to me, so instead I'd just flop down on my bed and mope all the air out of my room. Once the evening rolled around and I was properly tired of moping, I checked out the post Clarissa had mentioned earlier.

They were still there, Cannon Dude's pompous, self-righteous ramblings, and listening to my screen reader shout them into my room irritated me to no end. I wasn't the only one annoyed. Several people had posted since, all telling him he was a complete, total, absolute raging jackass.

I dialed Clarissa's number. "Hey," I said when she picked up. "Cannon Dude is the douchiest of bags."

She snorted. "Right? After I got off the phone with you yesterday, I checked out his profile. Age: thirty-five. Sex: male. Occupation: computer scientist at Apple. He works at Apple, for Pete's sake! So—*hello!*—he's a supersmart techy guy who probably hacked into Mason's computer. Hence 'the secret lies with the singer.'"

As she paused to take a breath, I realized that I'd just spent the past several seconds tapping my fingers to the cadence of her speech. That weird, manic way she spoke, the stopping and starting and stopping again, had a chaotic rhythm, an almost-melody.

"Anyway," she went on, and I heard the rattle of her iced coffee and a pronounced swallow. "That flu! How are you feeling? Are you all right?"

I opened my mouth and then closed it again. Truth was, I wasn't all right. Not in the slightest. And part of me wanted to tell her everything: how my life had cracked down the middle when I'd lost my sight, how my mother had disappeared while I was in the hospital, how I'd walked away from my old friendships, how I'd shattered my new ones. And my sometimes-eyesight, I wanted to tell her about that, too. But I didn't trust my judgment or my mouth right then, so all I said was, "Couldn't be all righter."

"My soup! It helped, right? Was it good?"

I'd actually forgotten about her soup, and so after we got off the phone I took a bowl of it to the living room. It was a summer night, so Gramps and Dad were in their usual summer-night spot: in front of a baseball game, grousing about the Red Sox's current losing streak. This went on for several minutes, their complaining, and then Dad cleared his throat, which was my first indication that the conversation was about to go south.

He said, "So, Maggie. I was talking to your mother this morning, and she mentioned that Merchant's has a soccer team."

"Yeah. I know," I said, dubiously poking at the soup with a spoon. Brothy things were generally not my cup of tea. Mostly because I didn't like my tea served with wilty vegetables floating around in it.

"Have you thought about checking it out this fall?"

"Nope," I said, cramming some soup in my mouth so I didn't have to comment any further on the subject. My school counselor had mentioned the soccer team a couple months back. Five-a-side soccer: soccer adapted, so the blind can play.

I wanted no part of it.

"You ought to consider it," Dad said. "Keeping involved in soccer really helped your mom when she had to stop playing."

What I wanted to tell Dad was that it hadn't been soccer that had helped my mother. It had been me. *I* had been the one who had given her hope again. *I* had been the one who had given her a new dream to chase.

And I had been the one who had stripped everything away.

She hadn't forgiven me for it yet, that much was true. But then, neither had I.

Gramps saved me by changing the subject. "What the hell are you eating, kid?" he asked.

I shrugged. "Soup."

"That the crap your mom bought with all the fiber?" Gramps asked.

"Nope," I said. "It's homemade. And why is Mom buying you high-fiber soup?"

"Prostate is swollen. Fiber is supposed to shrink it."

Once you get as old as Gramps, no subject is particularly good or bad, so all of them can be freely discussed over chicken noodle soup. I made a little gesture in the air to him, like *Hello, I'm trying to eat here?* and in doing so, I managed to knock the bowl with my elbow and tip the soup into my lap. I lurched sideways, slamming my shoulder into the end table.

Dad was beside me in seconds. "Maggie! You okay?"

I jerked upright, irritated that my father was hovering over me like I was an invalid. The worst thing? I couldn't get angry with him about it. Not really. He was just trying to do *something*. Sure, he was gentle and rangy and awkward, but it had always been his job to make sure I didn't get hurt—a task he'd never failed to take seriously. It was difficult for him to accept that he hadn't been able to protect me from losing my sight. As though something like that is even possible. You can't stave off *life*. Sometimes life just happens, no matter how careful you are. "I'm fine," I mumbled, jerking to my feet.

"Let me just run down to the laundry room and grab a rag—"

"I've got it, Dad," I said, sort of loudly, spinning on one heel and hustling to the basement before he could protest. But in my haste I caught my foot on some unidentified object at the base of the

stairs, pitched forward, and—yes—spectacularly took out whatever was in my path, namely a waist-high object that thumped
hard on the carpet.

Perfect.

"Maggie?"

"I'm *fine*, Dad," I yelled, totally annoyed now. Groping for purchase of my second casualty of the day, my hands bumped against
familiar glassy plastic. An indefinable, complex emotion socked
me in the gut.

My old keyboard.

I sat down hard on the floor, resting a palm on the instrument's
cellar-cooled plastic, where stickers of my favorite bands had been
slapped every which way. Though it didn't look the part, the keyboard had been the top of its class and I'd practiced it thusly,
taking full advantage of all of its features. I'd thrust an arm into
Mr. Hawthorne's pieces, fishing around in the melody and then
jerking out what had interested me, marrying it with the various
synthesized effects that the keyboard offered.

I ran a finger along the stickers, seeing them vividly in my
mind. Phantom Keys. The Dead Eddies. Drift District. Operation
Scarce. A couple of Dad's bands, too: Led Zeppelin, the Eagles.
Feeling guilty for some reason, I pressed down on a key, which
protested momentarily before it gave way with a *tunk*.

I didn't know why I'd expected a note to sing out in the room.
Surely the keyboard was unplugged. I ran an index finger down
the flats and sharps until I found middle C. The pads of my fingers paused over the keys for only a moment, and then I played
the song I'd tapped out earlier to Clarissa's speech, my fingers

reacting automatically to the twisty, knotty little melody that had run through my head while we'd been on the phone.

"Maggie?" Dad's concern carried down the stairs.

I touched the stickers one last time, staggered to my feet, and then took off for the laundry room, leaving the keyboard exactly where it had fallen.

23

With Ben's sudden disappearance from my life, loneliness crept in. Which was oddly reminiscent of my first couple months without my eyesight. Technically, I *had* lost my sight again—the small sliver I'd recovered, at least. I felt abandoned in some strange way, like life had decided I wasn't worth the effort, and in all honesty, I sort of agreed. What's worse, my parents were hardly ever home. Dad was working on a big case that kept him in the city until late at night, and Mom, in addition to her regular job, started coaching an evening soccer clinic, which meant that she spent even less time at home. I stayed up late, my bedroom door cracked open, listening for her to return.

Wondering whether she would.

Then on Wednesday afternoon, Clarissa called. At the time, I was in the kitchen with Gramps, trying to locate a slice of leftover pizza. Gramps was giving me the complete lowdown on his prostate issues, and I was thinking that if I had three wishes, two of them would be for him to stop talking about his prostate and the other one would be for more wishes, and then my phone rang. Plucking it out of my back pocket, I said hello, and by means of a greeting, Clarissa said, "You're going to freak because I just found something out about the Big Secret and it's really reliable and there's only one other person out there who knows about it and cripes, Maggie, *cripes!*"

"Cripes!" I yelled, even though I'd never yelled that particular word once in my life. But in my defense, it was the only thing that seemed to fit.

"I have reason to believe there's a concert *tonight*," Clarissa said in a rush. "Right now I'm smack in the middle of cake-decorating class—worst timing ever—so I'm going to hang up and call Dad and ask him to pick me up early and bring me to your house because we have to figure out the Big Secret now. Maggie, we have to figure it out now now now." And then she hung up.

Clarissa didn't knock or anything when she arrived. She just burst through the front door, hollering my name. "Two things," she said as we hustled down the hallway to my room. "First off, tell me you've downloaded-and-or-made-accessible the video from the last Loose Cannons concert. Please tell me you've done this. Please. Time is of the essence here. Time is tick-tick-ticking."

"Yes," I said as we stepped in my room. "I mean, I keep it up on my computer, so yes."

"Oh thank God," she breathed. "So the other thing is that if we, by some great miracle, figure out the Big Secret today, we'll need a ride. To the concert. My dad will be busy sawing out someone's organs, so we are rideless unless you can get us a ride."

"My grandpa can take us."

"Perfect. Yes. That's absolutely perfect." All quiet and fast, she whispered, "Okay so here's the deal: Remember that kid I told you about? Jase? My friend who knows Mason? Well, I guess Mason butt-dialed Jase today during a rehearsal, and Jase overheard some awfully interesting things."

I swallowed. Butt-dialed by Mason Milton.

I would not think about Mason's butt.

I would not.

I would *not*.

Yet, because I was weak and pathetic and generally irresponsible, there it was: the image of Mason's butt. Followed by another image of Mason's butt. Followed by another image of Mason's butt. And so on and so forth.

I was completely out of control. I needed a padded cell or a straightjacket or some sort of medication that limited the amount of sheer idiocy that my mind produced.

Clarissa was still talking: "So at first the band is just playing, and then after a couple songs, Carlos starts complaining about how "singing the clue is lame" and about how "everyone is going to figure it out" and about how "tonight they have to be more careful." She grabbed me by both shoulders and shook me. "You understand what this means, right? They sneak their clues into their songs. It's genius."

. . . .

Three hours later we were side by side on my desk chair, squashed up against each other, listening to last week's concert for the third time in a row. We had yet to hear any sort of clue. Clarissa, too wound up to concentrate any longer, sat next to me and lorded over her wristwatch, yelping about our elapsed time.

"We're screwed," I basically whined, my leg spastically bouncing up and down to the music.

She bolted out of the chair. "We must be missing it somehow. Even Cannon Dude said 'the secret lies with the singer.'"

I massaged my temples. "Look—I know every Loose Cannons song in existence. Mason's lyrics are Mason's lyrics are Mason's lyrics, and none of them were altered during this concert. And anyway, Cannon Dude was just jerking everyone around when he said 'the secret lies with the singer.' He's a jackass."

"Okay, so he's a smidge over the top," Clarissa admitted, "but probably only because he's really passionate about the band." I exhaled, flapping my lips loudly, and she spoke over me. "No. For real. I've been thinking: Cannon Dude totally reminds me of this character in *Star-crossed Bermuda*. This superintense famous-actor guy who—"

"*Star-crossed Bermuda*?"

"A book I read," she said dismissively. "Anyway, he's exactly like this famous actor guy, who initially comes off all conceited and arrogant. The other characters in the book basically hate him. Especially his costar, Bianca, who—"

"Does this have a point?"

"It offends me that you have to ask," Clarissa said. She did not sound offended. "Anyway, so Bianca is forced to do this kissing scene with him. They're on the seashore, his lips are on hers, and she's trying to remember how much she hates him but her body is betraying her. She's realizing how sweet and tender his kisses are—"

"Hold up. Are you reading *beach trash*?"

"It's quality romance." Clarissa sniffed. "Anyway, my point here is that right after that scene, you find out that the guy is just misunderstood. Underneath it all, he's this passionate, intense performer who rose from the trenches by working as an understudy to—"

I slapped the desk with both hands. "That's it!" I screamed. The understudy. The guy hovering in the background, waiting for his chance to take the stage. The backup guy.

Mason wasn't the only person who sang. He had a backup singer: Gavin.

It took us only a couple minutes to find it: Gavin's splitting off from the lyrics, right in the middle of the very first song. So quiet and yet so unbelievably loud, he sang, "sunset on the twentieth in the park of Alexander" while Mason sang "all of the things I swear I still remember."

And I just froze, right there, leaning toward my computer with both palms flat on my desk, because I needed my entire body to process my shock. Finally I whispered, "We have a half hour to get to Alexander Park."

. . . .

The last time I actually saw Alexander Park was a couple years ago. It was fall, the air was crisp, and the place was lit up with leaves dying in brilliant bursts of red and yellow. Mom and I had been moping around the house all morning, both of us suffering from our own respective losses. I'd just lost a soccer game, and Mom's star goalie had unexpectedly dropped out of school. Dad had shooed us out of the house after lunch, preaching the benefits of fresh air and sunshine.

So for the better part of the afternoon, Mom and I strolled barefoot across the park's wide lawns, our long curls joining as one in the wind. Then we lounged in the open-air pavilion, watching a skinny towheaded girl celebrate her seventh birthday. By the time we left, we were laughing our heads off and poking fun at each other, our troubles insignificant. I'd always called the place Frito Park in honor of the nearby Frito-Lay factory that blanketed the park's entire five acres and three city blocks in a near-constant burnt smell. And now charcoal was all I smelled as Clarissa and I piled out of Gramps's truck.

Currently, I was incognito. Which was to say that I'd hijacked my dad's biggest, longest, grayest, homeliest sweatshirt and pulled the hood over my head, yanking the strings to effectively cover most of my face. Last thing I needed was for Mason to recognize me and cause a scene.

Or kick me out.

As I stepped onto the sidewalk, I forced in a breath and tilted my face to the wind. The afternoon was absolutely gorgeous: breezy and comfortable, without a trace of humidity. One of those perfect June days that Connecticut had coerced into feeling more like late September. The only sounds were the hum of the Frito factory, the muted traffic coming from the street, and the voices of two women, fighting like cats in a bag. Their argument was over some guy, naturally. I'd like to say that I wasn't the type of person to be entertained by the misery of others, but, well, it was pretty entertaining.

Clarissa clapped her hands once. "All right. We don't have a lot of time, so I figure we'll just head straight down the sidewalk until we hear the crowd. My guess is that the concert will be held at the pavilion. Or else by that big fountain that's just past the Fifth Street intersection. Okay? Okay." And I heard her tapping away from me.

I stood completely still.

She stopped. "Maggie? Tight schedule here. Heading toward the fruits of our labor. Let's *go*."

I chewed my bottom lip. "Well, the thing is?" I said finally. "I'm not so great with intersections. Or sidewalks, for that matter."

"For real?"

"For real."

"No worries," she said as she clinked her way back to me. "I've walked this route a thousand times. My O and M specialist brings me here for picnics all the time. Just sort of tuck up alongside me and stay half a step behind. And keep your cane in front of you." And just like that, we took off. The blind leading the blind.

I took wobbly, uncertain steps, clipped to her elbow like a miniature koala bear on a fourth-grade pencil. Trying to distract myself, I cleared my throat and said, "So. What's going on with Iced Coffee Guy?"

She snorted. "Nothing. Absolutely nothing. I mean, I don't even know what to say to him besides 'double caramel iced coffee, please.'" I barked a disbelieving laugh; she seemed to have no problem whatsoever cramming words into *my* ear. "No, for real," she said, halting for a moment and listening. Not hearing the crowd, we started walking again. "I'm actually quite shy with boys. A failure in the romance department, just like my dad."

"Meaning . . . ?"

"Meaning my mom left us when I was two," she explained in a forced perky tone, picking up the pace a little to yank me through an intersection. "I guess it was too much—having a blind daughter."

I swallowed. It had never occurred to me that Clarissa had any real issues or problems, that blindness had stolen something precious from her. "I'm sorry," I said quietly.

"'S okay," she said as she jolted to a stop again.

I could hear a hum of voices to my right. We were close.

We cut through a patch of grass and up a knoll, hanging back when our canes tapped ankles. This place had a vastly different vibe than the concert at the Strand. Here, it was all quiet anticipation and reverence, mixed with the indescribable scent of people gathered together in commonality. My nervousness dissolved into eagerness. *Who cares if Mason recognizes me underneath this hoodie? Who cares?* It wasn't as if he could think any less of me.

That wasn't even possible.

I'd already lied to him for weeks. Puked in his car. Crammed a live hand grenade in his brother's heart. What was left? And anyway, I could tell by the quiet buzz of conversation in front of me that there were enough people here to hide my slight frame. So for the first time since we'd arrived, I felt safe. Excited, even. There I was, standing in the middle of Alexander Park, among the few, waiting to hear the best emerging band of the decade. I just wanted to smile and smile and smile.

The microphone crackled and the crowd hushed. My head jerked up.

It was time.

For a couple heartbeats, it felt hard to breathe. Like maybe something had crept into my chest and taken up residence against my lungs.

I leaned toward Clarissa. "This is . . ."

"The best!" she squealed.

David gave the cymbals one quick hit, as though metaphorically clearing his throat, and then Mason's voice rang out—devastating and absolute and compelling—buckling my knees and stealing my breath in a single instant.

I'd heard "Lucidity" probably a thousand times over the past couple months. It was a ballad that began with just Mason's voice and nothing else, a ballad that ached and exhaled and bent and glowed, so intense and so earnest that it almost hurt to listen to it. It was as though this sort of emotion was what this park was made for, maybe even what Mason was made for—to sing here, where the modulations in his tone arched up to the sky, sank into the grass, and then vaulted back up again to twist through the trees. An instant later, the band fell in step alongside him and the music took off, all wheeling clouds and gossamer strands of wind.

There was a type of perfection I would always connect with that moment. Someday, I might forget a few of the details—how the pads of my fingers felt as they tapped the keyboard riffs on my thighs, or how Mason's voice dipped an octave lower than expected when he sang the third verse—but I would never, ever forget how I felt.

Clarissa grabbed my hand. I squeezed and didn't let go, smiling the most genuine smile I'd had in years. And just for that moment in time, I couldn't remember what it felt like to be unhappy or unfulfilled or unloved. This was my whole world, in this very moment, and for the first time since I'd lost my sight, I felt like I belonged.

24

"Reach your hands back a little more," said a fellow restroom patron who wore so much sweet-smelling perfume, she was giving me a candied headache.

Trying not to inhale, I nodded a thank-you in her direction and moved my hands backward in the sink. Nothing.

Ugh.

I wasn't in the mood for China Bistro Day, and I certainly wasn't in the mood for this restroom. Couldn't we go back to knobs? What was wrong with knobs? You grope around for them, find them, and turn them. One, two, three. But these days, you have to be a Hogwarts graduate to get all this automatic stuff to function properly.

I waved my hands under the sink again. And . . . nothing.

"Here—let me help you!" she yelled. She took my hands unexpectedly, attempting to move them to the right spot. Startled by her sudden touch, I sucked in my breath and twitched away from her, which must have triggered the automatic faucet, because water was abruptly flying everywhere, spattering my hands and face.

She stuffed a wad of paper towels in my hands and said sympathetically, "I'm sure it isn't easy being blind."

I fought the urge to sigh. She was using the Voice—the one people use that is saturated with pity. I said, "I'm fine, thanks," and I took off toward the door, suavely tripping on what sounded like a trash can on the way out.

China Bistro Day was a cornball holiday, a ridiculous celebration that Gran had fabricated years ago to persuade Gramps to eat Chinese food. Gramps, a picky eater who always claimed that "Chinese food has too many damn colors in it," would unfailingly grumble and grouse all the way to the restaurant, but when it was time to leave, his plate was always licked clean.

The tiny restaurant was out in the sticks, about twenty miles inland from our house. Which was sort of weird if I really thought about it. Why drive away from a perfectly decent midsize city to Podunk, Connecticut, to eat a meal? But the fact was, years ago Gran had claimed that this place was the best, so this place was where we came. Even now, years after Gran's death, we all piled into the car on this day and drove to the China Bistro for dinner.

I'd been coming here since I was a little girl, so I knew the place well. I knew it was owned by an ancient Chinese woman who shook a good-natured index finger at me when I used a fork instead of chopsticks. I knew that there were so many reds and yellows and oranges decorating the place that it looked as though a Starburst bag had burst all over the walls and then tracked its feet over the throw rugs. I knew that the fortune cookies tasted like pure heaven when dredged through plum sauce. And I knew that the side window overlooked a monstrous soccer field owned by a neighboring college. My mother always requested a table next to that particular window, which meant that we usually had to wait to be seated. Tonight had been no exception. We'd waited a full hour for our table. It was now creeping up on eight o'clock, and though our table was dotted with appetizers, Gramps was growing more and more irritable with every passing second.

"Where are the breadsticks?" he said in a surly voice.

"Dad," my father said to Gramps, "there are no breadsticks here. It's a Chinese restaurant."

Gramps was a big eater. I knew this because he spent a good deal of time in our kitchen, mooching food out of our fridge. He lived with us without technically living with us, in the garage we'd converted to a one-room apartment after Gran died. While he griped about his lack of privacy, he spent more time in our house than in his own place, swiping food from our refrigerator and watching TV on our big screen. Though he'd never actually said it, I knew why. He was lonely. He missed Gran.

Since my mother spent her days coaching and Dad spent his days lawyering, Gramps leveled out our lopsided house. He was the guy who was available to cart me around when I needed to go somewhere. He was the guy who sat with me at the counter to eat microwavable frozen dinners. He was the guy who'd taken me to the hospital when I'd come down with meningitis.

The morning I'd gotten really sick, I'd stumbled out of bed and into the kitchen. Though it was only five o'clock, my mother was already up and dressed in her usual attire: pleated khakis and a pressed oxford shirt. She was making a pot of coffee.

"Mom, I have a fever," I said, my voice slow and thick.

She frowned and touched my head with the back of her hand. "Oh, sweetheart," she said, her face crumpling. That was the thing about my mother: she hated seeing me sick. "You must have that flu that's going around."

"Yeah," I told her, so lethargic that the words felt heavy as I struggled to move them out of my mouth. "And my head is killing me. Plus, my neck? It's so stiff."

She held my face in her palms and kissed me on the forehead. "Go back to bed and rest. I'll call my boss and tell him I won't be in today."

"Don't you have a game this afternoon?"

She waved a dismissive hand and nudged me toward my room. "That's why I have an assistant coach."

Guilt clawed at my stomach. "I'll be fine, Mom. Promise. I just need to sleep. Go to work."

And so she did.

Four hours later, I called her to tell her I was getting worse, but she must've already headed to the field, because I got her voice mail. Six hours later, Gramps took me to the emergency room. Two hours after that, I'd nearly died—twice—from my fever. Three hours after that, I was blind.

But tonight at the China Bistro, my mother had absolutely no problem picking up her phone. It rang twice during dinner. Both times it was the university.

"Hey, kid," Gramps said to me as Mom took her second call. "Your friend just walked in."

My fork hovered over my plate. "What friend?"

"The blond one with the big mouth."

Lauren.

I swallowed. "Where is she?"

"Hostess station."

I probably should have stayed put, just sunk down in my seat and played dumb. I had the perfect excuse for not knowing she was there, after all. But something inside me tugged me upright, toward the hostess station. Maybe I wanted to find out why she hadn't come to my house with Sophie. Maybe I wanted to know where I stood with our friendship. Maybe I was just into self-torture.

I called out a general hello as I approached. And in the short, uncomfortable silence that followed, I almost spun around and hauled ass back to the table. But then Lauren descended on me in a cloud of her mother's perfume, hugging me quickly in one jerky motion and then pulling away. "Maggie!" she said, her voice overly resonant for such a tiny place. "Holy crap—I haven't seen you in *forever.*"

"Yeah," I said. "It's been a while. I thought maybe you'd come by with Sophie last week."

Awkward pause.

I crossed my arms. Shifted my weight. Trying to calm down, I tapped the little Chopin riff on my side. Then the Clarissa rhythm. Then both of them together.

It didn't help.

Finally Lauren cleared her throat and said, "Yeah, well, I had plans to hang out with Kirsten Richards. Remember her? Used to play middie for Southington? The girl who could hit the upper nineties without even trying? She's on our team now! She moved here after you..."

Another awkward pause.

"Lost my eyesight," I supplied.

"Right," Lauren said. "Anyway, we sort of lucked out because Kirsten's, like . . . well, you remember. She's so good. She's already bagged a full ride to UConn!"

"A full ride to UConn," I breathed, swaying on my feet as the enormous injustice sucked the wind right out of me. "Good for her."

And as I lugged myself back to the table, I realized that Lauren hadn't even bothered to ask how I was doing. I probably shouldn't have been surprised. Lauren had always been more interested in Maggie the Soccer God than just plain Maggie. Still, it didn't hurt as much as it should have. I just wondered why I'd set the friendship bar so low.

"How's Lauren?" Dad asked as I sat down.

"Great," I said with false cheer.

"Did she mention where she's applying to college?" he asked.

I propped my elbows on the table and jammed my fingers into my eyelids. "She didn't say."

Dad cleared his throat, segueing into interrogation mode. "What about you? What did you think about those DVDs?"

"I haven't had a chance to listen to them."

"Chop-chop," he said, his tone practiced-casual. "For the record, Cal Poly sounds amazing. They have some awesome programs for the visually impaired. Your mother is dead set on Missouri State."

I heard Mom's phone snap shut. "I'm not dead set on it, Steve," she interjected. "The choice is ultimately up to Maggie."

The way she spoke about me—it was like I wasn't even here. Maybe I wasn't.

I said, sort of loudly, "Why do I even have to think about college right now?"

My mother sighed tiredly, as though I was intentionally being difficult. "What is that supposed to mean?"

"It means that I've been blind for seven months and I still basically suck at it," I said. "What if I never really learn how to get around on my own? What if I never understand how to make it across a school campus without breaking my face? What if I can't go to college?"

"Maggie, we understand it's been a big adjustment for you," my mother said, her words forced and stilted, like she'd been practicing them. "But once you try, once you get out there, I'm sure you'll be surprised by how much you can do." This little spiel of hers was over the top, and frankly, over the top wasn't Mom's style. She sounded an awful lot like she was quoting some book like *How to Help Your Child Adjust to Blindness.* "Maybe you should schedule a couple extra sessions with Hilda?"

"No," I said.

"No?"

"No. I spend plenty of time with Hilda."

Her voice slightly wooden now, she said, "Well, your counselor at Merchant's said that some extra O and M sessions might help you."

Twisting my napkin in my hands, I said, "My counselor has spoken to me exactly twice, and one of those times it was to ream me out for the prank. He's hardly an authority on what I need."

She cleared her throat. "Well, maybe you'd benefit from talking to him a little. He could probably help you . . . you know, sort out some of your issues."

I felt my face flush. She somehow managed to forget that she was one of my biggest issues, that she was the fault line running underneath every small, uncertain step I'd made over the past several months. "I'm fine," I said, effectively ending the conversation.

By eight forty-five, all I wanted was to go to bed. Just curl up in a little knot under my covers and forget about this entire evening. Somewhere in a dark, dusty corner of my chest was the excitement I'd once had about applying to UConn. It crushed my lungs like the weight of a planet. I leaned back and tried to inhale, tried to force my lungs to expand, and in doing so I saw a flash of something green in the vicinity of the window beside our table. For a moment I thought I'd imagined it, just some strange hallucination of a troubled mind. Still, the shock must have shown in my face, because Dad said, "Mags? What's wrong?"

Before I could answer, an ancient, stooped man wearing a jade-colored polo shirt shuffled into the restaurant, lighting up a small, muddy radius around him.

There was a time when I'd anxiously awaited this moment. A time when I'd peeked around doorways and held my breath when I'd walked into stores, hoping I'd see something—anything—besides Ben. But now that it was actually happening, it made me desperately anxious.

The man looked normal enough. Sure, he was old, and yes, he moved wearily. But he looked like somebody's great-grandfather—the sort of guy who listens to AM channels and refuses to use a microwave, the sort of guy whose smile lines never actually smoothed out flat.

I collapsed back in my seat and covered my mouth. I have this bad habit of laughing when I get overwhelmed, which is unfortunate because laughter isn't appropriate in certain circumstances. Like during my fifth-grade school play, for instance, when I'd momentarily forgotten my lines. And just before I'd walked into the courtroom during sentencing for the school prank.

So now, as I looked at this man—at the sag in his skin and the gloomy light that cloaked his body—I started to laugh. There was something about him that resurrected the same unease I'd been feeling off and on for weeks now. And it terrified me.

25

Several months ago, my parents sent me to a shrink, probably because I was newly blind, easily agitated, belligerent to my teachers, and fantastically sarcastic. Oh, and also because I was suddenly jolting them awake at all hours of the night with my newest and grandest hobby—chronic sleepwalking.

The shrink's name was either Dr. Samuels or Dr. Smithton. It was some time ago, so I'm not exactly sure. What I do remember is slouching in her squeaky leather chair as she cheerfully grilled me about my school and my friends and my nonexistent eyesight until my butt went numb. In the end, she declared that I was a normal teenager adjusting to new and difficult circumstances. And the sleepwalking thing? Just a temporary side effect.

For the next month, though, my temporary side effect led me to wake up in the bathtub, on the stairs, and in the hall closet. I argued with lamps and raked invisible leaves off the living-room carpet. But it wasn't until a couple months ago that I actually wandered out of the house in the middle of the night. I awoke to find myself sitting in an unknown location on an unknown slab of concrete, wearing exactly what I'd gone to sleep in—a T-shirt and my very worst underwear—with no cell phone, no cane, no shoes, and no clue what to do.

Did I yell for help? No. Wait for assistance? Not exactly. What I did was listen to my inner jackass, who told me to stand up and start walking. So I stepped into the street, in front of a car, and immediately got hit. In the end, (a) I sprained my wrist, and (b) I vowed to never again set foot in the Outside World by myself, and (c) I stopped walking in my sleep, and (d) I realized that I was shitty at decision-making because I rarely thought things through.

So I was lying in bed the next morning, wondering what to do, which made me think about getting hit by a car, which made me think about the school prank, which made me think about the mess I'd created with Sophie, which made me think about what I'd said to Ben, which made me think about selling myself out to Mason, which made me come to the conclusion that I was probably one lousy decision away from having the National Society of Crappy Decision Makers put up a monument in my name.

Fact was, I'd waited and waited for something to happen with my eyesight—to see something besides Ben Milton and the landscape around him—and now that it had? Well. I had no idea what to do about it, other than tell Ben.

But Ben would not pick up the phone. Like, ever. None of the

Miltons would, for that matter. And I'd left so many messages on their landline that their voice mail was overflowing, screaming digital profanities in my ear every time my phone connected with theirs.

Maybe they're just busy, I reasoned, trying not to get overly paranoid. They couldn't all hate me. Not all of them. Not Mrs. Milton.

But three days became four, and four became six, and then all of a sudden a week had passed, and I wondered if maybe all of them *did* hate me.

"Fine," I muttered out loud, blinking back tears and chucking my phone on my bed. *Fine.*

I got to work researching. Holing up in my room on the computer, tabbing through articles of inexplicable science. Minds capable of incredible feats. People who achieve incomprehensible miracles. Brains that stretch beyond gray matter. But after hours of searching, I came up empty. I learned of a man who could lift a car on his own. A woman who was able to digest metal. Some guy who had the ability to move objects with his mind.

Even in a world of anomalies, I was an anomaly.

....

It struck me as kind of unfair that Clarissa had the type of O and M specialist who took her for picnic sessions at Alexander Park while I was stuck with Hilda, who, the very next day, dumped me in the middle of town and told me to cross Seventh Street on my own.

"Well, first off," I said to Hilda, "I'd have to find Bush Street in order to even get to Seventh Street. Which I can't do." I was leaning against a parking meter, arms crossed, laying out all the reasons why she couldn't trust me to navigate on my own.

"*Pfffft,*" Hilda said. "You have learned quickly, even though you don't wish to admit it." She waited a beat for me to respond to that particular morsel of bullshit. I did not. "Now: you try," she prompted.

"I'll get lost if I try," I pointed out as the wind changed direction. I caught a strong whiff of baked goods from Big Dough.

"You will not get lost. It is only a five-minute walk. Worst-case scenario, you will explore."

Why is it that whenever someone gives you a worst-case scenario, it really isn't the worst-case scenario? I remembered exactly what it had felt like to get hit by a car, and I wasn't keen on duplicating the experience. "I will explore my own death."

She snorted. "You are dramatic. It's a beautiful day, and plenty of others are outside enjoying the weather. You won't be alone."

"Well, that's a relief," I muttered. "Nothing alleviates the fear of doing something poorly like having a big audience."

No reply.

"Hilda?"

No reply.

She'd already gone.

What the *hell*?

For a second, I almost burst out laughing, but only to prevent myself from yelling out something wildly inappropriate. Because really. What was Hilda thinking? I drummed my fingers on the parking meter. I felt marginally manic, edgy, and jumpy, ready to scratch my way right out of my skin.

I threw both hands up in the air. Fine. *Fine.*

Spinning on one heel, I strode away. Only toward Big Dough instead. Judging by the potent, familiar smell of baked goods, the place had to be close.

Given that I'd probably paid attention to only a quarter of what Hilda had told me over the past several weeks, I didn't have a solid plan for navigating down the sidewalk. I just walked. Cane tapping, feet slapping defiantly on the pavement, nose pointed toward the distinguishable scent of Big Dough, I just walked.

It wasn't pretty.

I traveled in quick spurts and jerky, clumsy stops, my free hand running down the bumpy brick-faced storefronts as I searched for the bakery's entrance. Since I'd spent half a lifetime in Big Dough, you'd think I'd know the storefront when my hand passed across it. But I did not. I opened three glass doors—barreled into three random businesses—before I jerked open the fourth door, where a familiar bell signaled my entrance.

Big Dough: shining in front of me like a beacon of complex carbohydrates.

I stood there, half in and half out of the bakery, completely shocked. I'd actually made it here without killing myself.

I could hear my pulse hammering in my ears, and I could hear the traffic on the street behind me, and I could hear the radio crackling overhead, and, if I really listened, I could hear congratulatory, enthusiastic applause bursting from a sudden standing ovation in my brain.

Which made this either the corniest or the grandest moment of my training thus far.

I took one step inside and inhaled. Sure, I'd spent hours upon hours inside this campy, sixties-style bakery, but I hadn't put as much as a toe in here since I lost my sight.

It smelled the same, only different.

The strongest of scents—the sharp peppermint and the caramel, the bitter dark chocolate, the mocha, the cinnamon—those were still there. But now I could catch subtle hints of butter and brown sugar and cream. Of yeast and flour, and—*oh God*—mellow, smooth white chocolate.

Probably I looked like I was missing a few dials and knobs, standing there with my nose pointed up to the ceiling, a ridiculous smile on my face, but I didn't even care. So I took my time, savoring every victorious step as I made my way to the front counter.

The owner of the place, Sal, was an ancient cornball of a guy who had a beaky nose, a long gray braid that he'd always worn in a hairnet, and the very interesting habit of whistling every time he said his Ss. "Snickerdoodles are on sale," he told me from behind the counter—probably hailing a taxi, a couple of dogs, and a waitress.

"Great." I almost laughed instead of speaking, and I ordered a snickerdoodle, a double chocolate crinkle, and an oatmeal raisin.

"And a surprise," Sal added.

I smiled. "And a surprise." Sal always gave out a bonus cookie with every order—sort of a taste test for whatever new creation he'd recently conceived.

I found a seat and rustled through the bag for a cookie. Sliding it out, I held it to my nose. Holy mother of God: double chocolate crinkle. I took a bite, chewing leisurely and nodding along to an old Drift District song, its descending bass line winding its way out of the overhead speakers. I'd probably eaten only half the cookie when the door dinged. To my surprise, and in a giant *flump*, someone sat directly beside me. And then blew an unpleasant Romanian exhale in my face.

I swallowed, my cookie sticking somewhere in the middle of my throat.

Her breath all up in my face, Hilda said, "We have a saying in my country: *'Cum îți aşterni, asa te vei culca.'*"

Oh shit.

"The meaning is this," she said when I didn't reply. "'You must put up with the unpleasant results of a foolish action or decision.'"

"Hilda, I—"

"But this decision, which I observed from open to close," she said, plucking the cookie out of my hand, "was not foolish." She whistled, long and low, and then chortled. Chortled. I could practically feel her whole body rocking with it. "It was momentous. Yes?" She paused for a moment, chomping on my cookie. Through a full mouth, she said, "Congratulations."

Um.

"You're not mad?" were the three dazzling words I finally threw together after a significant delay.

"Mad? *Pish*," she said. "You think I am only . . . old battle ax? You chose a destination, traveled independently, and arrived safely. I am pleased. Today, we celebrate." She rustled around in my bag and shoved a cookie in my hand.

"For real?"

"For real," she said, and the words sounded so hilariously odd coming out of Hilda's mouth that I cracked up laughing. Breaking off a piece of cookie, I popped it in my mouth.

Sal's surprise cookie.

It was all salt and all caramel and all chocolate, completely different from anything else I'd ever had here, yet absolutely perfect.

26

Back when I could see, I dreamed in vivid Technicolor: light, color, texture, and sound, all synchronized into movies in my head. But when my world disappeared, the visual quality of my dreams began to fade with each passing night. The emptiness from my waking hours crept in, and my once-bright images blurred, became nebulous, and then finally blinked away, leaving nothing but random voices, thoughts, and ideas.

But tonight, I *dreamed.*

Aware in some corner of my consciousness that I was dreaming, I recognized the closed wooden door in front of me, the smell of mothballs escaping from the hall closet, the family portrait on the wall beside me. I was standing in the upstairs hallway, in front of the door to my old bedroom. I could hear frantic whispering behind the door.

I placed a hand on the doorknob but didn't turn it. "Hello?" I called out, my voice shaking.

The whispering stopped. It was dead quiet. Too quiet.

"Hello?" I called out again.

Nothing.

Ben appeared beside me. I'd never been so relieved. "Ben," I said in an exhale. "There's somebody in my room."

He shrugged. The motion caused his crutches to groan. It sounded off. Wrong. "Go see who it is, Thera."

I bit my lip so hard that, though I was dreaming, I swore I could taste blood. Taking a deep breath, I slowly twisted the knob. The whispering started again. Louder.

My hand sprang away from the door. "I don't think that's a good idea," I said, turning toward Ben. His facial features had changed. There were deep hollows beneath his cheekbones, black smudges under his eyes. His lips were cracked, bleeding.

He sighed. His breath smelled rancid. Decayed. "I'll open it," he said. Balancing with one side of his body, he peeled off a crutch and reached for the doorknob.

"Wait!" I screamed, terrified.

But he'd already pushed open the door, taken a step into the doorway, jerked to a teetering, unstable stop at the entrance to my room.

I gasped. There was no room. No walls. No floor. Nothing but a massive, whispering void. And Ben was lurching forward, falling into it.

Screaming, I groped for him, narrowly missing his arm. Our eyes locked for a fraction of a second, his sending mine a silent plea: *Help me.*

And then he plunged into the nothingness.

I jolted awake, my heart clubbing in my ears. Panic surged in my chest, sharp and visceral. Trying to quiet my gulping breaths, I listened for a sound that told me I wasn't alone—my parents chatting, the cat padding down the hallway, a rustle, a footstep . . . *anything*—but the house was horribly, desperately silent. Soaked in sweat, I slipped out of bed and into my parents' bedroom. From the doorway, I could just barely hear the TV. Turned almost all the way down, a familiar scene from *Romeo and Juliet* whispered into the room.

A closet sentimentalist, my mother had always been a sucker for heartbreaking romantic movies. I'd spent more nights than I could count curled up beside her on the couch while she sniffled unabashedly over some on-screen heartbreak. It had made me feel special in some small way, like she was sharing a faraway part of herself that she'd never shared with anyone else.

Now, though, the only things she was sharing were her soft snores, deep in an Ambien stupor. I ghosted toward her and knelt beside the bed, my fingers walking across the sheets until I found the curve of her spine. I laid my head carefully, silently on her back, wishing I could wake her, wishing I could fold into her lap like I used to when I was little. But instead, I just stayed on my knees, listening to the steady thrum of her heartbeat and her soft inhalations until I felt steady enough to walk away.

27

The next morning I woke to the sounds of my parents getting ready for work: the shuffling of feet into the kitchen, the
clinking of a spoon in a coffee cup, the low-voiced chattering, the
jingling of keys. After they left, I sprang out of bed.

I felt antsy, restless, like I'd been plugged into an electrical
socket, so I paced the house: down the hallway, up the stairs,
back down the stairs, and then down the hallway again. Rinse
and repeat. During one of my trips upstairs, I hitched to a stop
in front of my old bedroom and just stood there in the silence,
palm flat on the closed wooden door.

There were a thousand ghosts living in that room.

Outside, a car door slammed and a pitiful yowl sliced through
the morning like a gunshot. Completely spooked now, I crept
downstairs, pausing in the entryway. Someone pounded on the

front door, and I squawked and jumped out of my skin. "Who's there?" I hollered.

"Maggie? It's Lauren."

Lauren?

I folded my arms across my chest.

"Maggie?" Lauren repeated.

I knuckled my forehead. "What's going on, Lauren?" I said. I was aiming for snarky, but my mouth betrayed me. The words came out wobbly.

"Can you open up? I'm having a bit of a . . . situation with Sophie and I need your help."

I crossed the entryway in three steps and flung open the door. "What's wrong with her?" I practically yelled.

There was a long pause in which I wondered whether Lauren was still there. Then she said, "Um, I think Sophie should be the one to tell you." Lauren led me to her car, where Sophie was having some sort of wild breakdown. As we came to a stop by the open driver's side door, Lauren said, "I thought maybe since you . . . um . . . have been through some difficult times, you could help her."

What I really wanted to ask Lauren was how she'd known I'd even gone through difficult times. I wanted to ask her why she thought I'd actually *made it through* those difficult times. I wanted to inform her that if Sophie weren't bawling in my driveway, I wouldn't have bothered to open my front door for her. But I didn't have time to give Lauren a speech on loyalties, because she half pushed, half guided me into the driver's seat.

I fell into Lauren's car with an *oomph* and then sat there for a moment, chewing on my bottom lip. I'd always been a little awkward with this sort of thing. The rough waters of the Estrogen Ocean were not easily navigable. Besides, the last time Sophie and I had spoken had been miserably uncomfortable. Finally, and so Sophie could hear me over her crying, I basically shouted, "So. Having a crappy day?"

"Shut. Up." The words sounded odd coming from her mouth—about as natural as Mother Teresa calling Gandhi a dumbass—and I couldn't take them seriously.

"I don't shut up well," I informed her. "Mind telling me what's going on?"

She just sobbed harder.

"Aw, come on, Soph. It can't be all that bad."

I could hear her breathing, all quick and jerky, like hysterical people in the movies. I tried to reach for her hand, to pat it or something—or whatever girls do in situations like these—but when I finally found her fingers, she flinched away from me and basically yelled, "Remember the other day? When I came to your house?"

How could I forget? "Yes," I said.

"And you asked if I had a cold?" she went on, her voice screechy. "Because I sounded stuffy?"

"Yes."

"Well, I'd been crying all morning. My period had been two and a half months late and I'd just taken a pregnancy test."

Given everything that had been happening in my life lately, I thought nothing could shock me. But when I realized what she was saying? I was shocked. "You're . . ." I began, but then stopped. The two words I was going to end my sentence with were *knocked up*, but I figured they were probably a little inappropriate. Nevertheless, they were the only words that seemed to fit. Forty-year-old schoolmarms could be "expecting," and thirty-five-year-old women could be "pregnant," but high school girls? Well. They were "knocked up." Which was something I'd expect from Lauren, not Sophie.

"WHAT AM I GOING TO DO?" Sophie wailed.

I jerked out of the car, slamming immediately into Lauren. "She's knocked up," I said brilliantly.

"Yeah," Lauren whispered, "and I just . . . I mean, I'm supposed to be at practice in, like, fifteen minutes and I don't know what to do. Could you . . . ?"

"Could I *what*, Lauren?" I hissed.

"I don't know. Keep her here with you for a while? Talk to her? I mean, this is just . . . I don't really know what to *say*."

I stood there for a moment, trying to process her words. Trying to process the fact that she'd brought Sophie here just to get rid of her. Then I pursed my lips together and made a little gesture in the air, like, *Just go.*

Sophie and I went to the backyard and sat side by side on a pair of cracked plastic seats that dangled from an old swing set, stiff grass poking at our ankles. When we were little, we used to spend hours upon hours out here, just dreaming and talking and hanging upside down. Back then I never would've imagined we'd be sitting here like this. Different in so many ways.

We didn't talk at first. Not because we had nothing to say, but because we had so much to say. So for the longest time, we stayed there and sorted through our thoughts—Sophie's tears drying and my shock ebbing. I curled my little finger around the warm metal chain, listening to a pair of blue jays squawk at each other in the far corner of the yard, listening to Gramps bang around in his apartment, listening to my neighbor's sprinkler. Finally Sophie took a shuddering breath and said, "I never told you this before. I just didn't know how to bring it up, and I didn't want it to change the way you saw me, but..." She stopped, cleared her throat, and started again. "I was adopted. My birth mother was sixteen when she had me, Maggie. *Sixteen.* I wouldn't be here if she'd, you know..."

I nodded, understanding the subtext. "How does Jason feel about you not having an abortion?"

"I haven't told him that I'm pregnant yet," she admitted quietly, "haven't even told my parents. I—I guess I kept hoping that maybe it would all go away if I ignored it. I guess I'm just terrified, you know? I mean, I have to tell my *dad.*"

I nodded. Sophie's dad was a hardass, had been for all her life. Sophie had forever been the one with the early curfew, the one not allowed to wear miniskirts, the one with all the rules.

Sophie went on. "And besides that, things are already stressed at home."

"What do you mean?"

She paused for several beats. There was still this hesitation between us—this sharp, broken shard of glass that neither of us knew how to touch without getting sliced open. Finally she said, "My parents have been fighting a lot."

"Sophie, I'm so sorry," I breathed. "You should've told me."

"Yeah. Well, the arguments didn't get really bad until right around the time you lost your eyesight. I figured you had enough going on."

"I wouldn't have minded. It's not like my family is perfect," I muttered. "Do you think they'll work it out? Your parents?"

A little bit of air shot out of Sophie's nose, and she said, "Well, I can tell Mom is trying, but Dad has been so distant. I'm terrified that this will be the thing that finally breaks them up."

"Sophie, you can't worry about that right now. Like it or not, this is happening. You have to tell them."

"I know," she murmured. "I just don't know if I can do it."

"Sure you can," I said. "When you get home, just barrel in and tell them—before you can talk yourself out of it. You know, tear off the Band-Aid as fast as possible."

She sniffled. "That's not me, Maggie. That's you. I wish you could just . . . do it for me."

My response was timid and weak and flimsy, but it was a response all the same. "Why don't I go with you?"

....

The night was properly silent by the time Gramps dropped us off at Sophie's, too silent for the two of us to be walking knowingly into a shitstorm. I took her porch steps slowly, soundlessly, and when I stepped into the house, I paused. I'd spent half my life bursting through these doors. I'd enjoyed Fourth of Julys eating watermelon on Sophie's back porch, banked hundreds of hours under blanket forts in her mother's sewing room. I knew the squeaky spots on their floor, the garlicky scent in the kitchen. Now, though, the house seemed different. It smelled like too much take-out food and caked-up dust. And as we walked into the living room and sat on the couch, I turned to Sophie, cleared my throat, and whispered, "Where is everyone?"

Beside me, Sophie unloaded a sigh. "Mom is probably upstairs reading. And I guess Dad is working late, as usual."

"Ah." I pianoed the Chopin-Clarissa jig on my leg for a couple minutes. Which, I came to find out, is a really long time when nobody's talking.

"Distract me," Sophie blurted suddenly. "Tell me something unrelated to parents and babies. Please."

I didn't even hesitate. "Well, I went to a Loose Cannons concert a few days ago."

For a moment I got the impression that she was gaping at me. "Are you freaking kidding me?" she said in a choked whisper. "Did you just . . . stumble on it? The concert?"

"Something like that," I muttered, not wanting to get into the specifics. "Anyway, it was amazing."

"I'm sure it was," Sophie said. "I mean, Mason Milton's voice is like . . ."

I swallowed. "Yeah. It's perfect." And it was. *He* was. And now he hated me.

Sophie went on. "I heard he started dating Hannah Jorgensen, like, a couple months ago."

"Who's Hannah Jorgensen?" I asked, my voice an octave or two higher than normal.

"Mags. What rock have you been living under? The model? From New York City?"

My mouth formed the word *oh* but I didn't actually say it. I just tried it out on my lips. Not liking the way it felt, I left it somewhere in the middle of my throat.

I wrapped my arms over my stomach and sank into the couch. Had I imagined the sparks between Mason and me the night of the Dead Eddies concert? Yes. I must have, yes. I'd been drunk. He was dating a model. End of story.

Outside, a car door closed. Heavy footsteps clomped up the porch.

"It's showtime," Sophie said, and then she laughed, an uncertain invention that sounded more like a bark. I could feel the hairs on her arms brushing against mine as we sat side by side on the couch and waited for her father to open the door. I tried to think of what to say, tried to dredge up one of the huddle speeches I'd given the team over the years. But my past seemed irrelevant right now, and so I did the only thing I knew to do: I stayed beside her and reached for her hand.

. . . .

Sophie's father was drunk.

He hadn't started out drunk. He'd breezed into the house, all briskness and aftershave, shot us a hasty greeting, and then immediately retired to his den. I'd felt Sophie starting to have second thoughts, so I'd nudged her with my elbow. "You can do this," I'd said, and she'd sighed resolutely and stood. And now, in the kitchen, her mother speaking in a voice laced with the sort of hurt and disappointment that I knew was absolutely killing Sophie, and her father screaming—holy *crap* he was screaming—I was beginning to wonder whether I'd given Sophie the wrong advice.

Sophie was crying.

Her mother was crying.

Her father was yelling horrible things. Sophie was a disappointment. A tramp. An embarrassment. A failure.

When I couldn't stand it anymore, I lurched toward him. I didn't know what I was going to do—take a swing at him, maybe?—but in the end it didn't really matter, because Sophie pulled me back, wordlessly reminding me that I was there for only moral support.

Her father paced in front of us, his shoes like gunshots firing off on the tile floor. And then he stopped. Everything went dead still. His voice suddenly disturbingly even, he told Sophie that she wasn't his daughter anymore. Told her to pack her things and get out.

Sophie said nothing.

Why the hell wasn't she defending herself?

But as it happened, she didn't have to, because her mother— loudly, clearly, fiercely—stepped in and screamed that if he was kicking their daughter out of the house, he'd have to kick his wife out as well.

Nobody spoke. Nobody breathed. I could almost hear the walls lean in to hear her father's reply: "Fine then. Go."

And so it happened, that terrifying thing that Sophie had known was coming. Her dad stormed out of the room, slamming doors in his wake. Her mom called a relative in Ohio and asked if she and Sophie could come stay. And as I stood there in the kitchen that night, arms wrapped around myself with Sophie's silence ringing loudly in my ears, I knew with absolute certainty that I'd just lost Sophie for good.

28

What sort of feeling came over me when I heard Mom's car pull up at Sophie's instead of Gramps's, I wasn't sure. But whatever it was, it warped my exhale into a long, quaking sigh. Stepping off Sophie's porch, I walked across the driveway and fumbled to find the latch on Mom's passenger-side door. Collapsing into the seat, I asked, "What happened to Gramps?"

"Stuck at a poker tournament," Mom said in the half-mocking, half-affectionate tone that she always used when she spoke about Gramps, an inflection that was as familiar to me as my own hand. "I was surprised you were here. I didn't know you and Sophie were hanging out again."

I picked at the frayed hem on my shorts. I didn't want to tell her about Sophie's pregnancy or the confrontation with her parents or the way Sophie's mom had stepped in to support Sophie. I didn't want to tell her that the scene in Sophie's kitchen had made me wish like hell my own mother had come to my rescue when I'd needed her most.

"We aren't really hanging out," I said, swallowing over the clog in my throat.

"Oh. I'm sorry to hear that."

"Are you?" I said, the words coming out so quickly that I hadn't even had time to filter them. "I mean, I didn't know you cared about my friendships." I felt a lone, fat tear fall down my face, and I turned away from her.

"Of course I do," she said quietly. She paused. "Maggie? Are you okay?"

Still facing the window, I wiped my cheek with the heel of my palm. "I just wish," I said slowly, thinking about my string of failed friendships, "that I'd done some things differently, is all." Ambiguous as they were, my words were imploring, reaching for her, invisible fingers trying to stretch across the gap between us.

"Don't we all," she said softly.

Though the moment was awkward, this was the closest we'd been since I'd lost my sight, so both of us latched on to it like it was a single life jacket that we'd each crammed one arm into—it wasn't enough to save either one of us, but it was enough to keep our heads above water for the time being.

For a few minutes, there were only familiar sounds. The way Mom's car squeaked as it came to a stop. The tick of her blinker. Finally she cleared her throat and said, "Mind if I run in to the dry cleaner's to pick up Dad's suit?"

"No," I said, a little too loudly. And then I wiped my palms on my shorts. "No, go ahead."

When she came to a stop in front of the dry cleaner's, I stayed put, just shut my eyes and let my head fall back against the seat. It had felt odd, extending myself to my mother. All my life, I'd always followed her lead: she was tough, and I was tough. She played soccer, and I played soccer.

She deserted me, and I deserted her.

A car horn blasted. Startled, I flinched and jerked open my eyes. Then I covered my mouth with my hand.

Because I could see again.

A woman was trudging in front of the car in a massive puddle of brilliant white light, so dazzling that the air itself almost sparkled around her, millions of tiny diamonds. It was in stark contrast to her appearance. She was aggressively thin and wispy-looking, her bony shoulder blades jutting out beneath her blouse. Wrapped loosely around her head was a flowered scarf, which failed to conceal a thin line of bald scalp above her forehead. There was a rustle of movement to my right, and I saw my mom walking toward her, smiling, saying something to the woman that I could not hear. I sucked in my breath as I saw my mother for the first time in seven months.

Mom's normally cherubic curls were unkempt, bordering on frizzy. She had lines all over her face—creases wedged around her eyes and furrows pitting the corners of her lips—all pointing in the wrong direction. She looked defeated, from the slope of her shoulders to the way her mouth turned downward as she spoke. Her eyes flickered toward me and I looked away guiltily. By the time I turned back, the woman had walked away, taking her impossibly bright light with her, and my mother was starting toward the car, disappearing into my non-eyesight before she opened the door.

"Were you talking to someone?" I asked as Mom started the car.

Mom sighed, a sound that stole the oxygen from my lungs. "Yes. I was talking to Kelly Downs. The mother of one of the girls on my team? She has breast cancer. She's been sick. Real sick. And—"

"And what?" I said. They were only two words, but they barely worked their way past my throat.

"Well, she's dying, you know? And her doctors can't do anything about it."

For a moment everything went perfectly still and I heard the world around me with flawless precision: the sharp click of heels hustling down the sidewalk, the sleepy jazz music drifting out of a passing car, the sound of a loose wheel on a shopping cart rattling through the parking lot. But mostly, I heard the one word that had jogged loose from my mother's sentence, tumbling around some cog in my brain.

Dying

dying

dying

Awareness started filtering through me, ice slipping through my veins. I was shaking. Had to be. My knees were rattling against each other. I'd been denying it all along, of course. I'd denied it every time I'd hung out with Ben. I'd denied it when I'd seen that old man in the China Bistro. I'd denied it when I'd had that dream. Everything had pointed to it, but I'd been looking in another direction, terrified. But now I couldn't look away. I couldn't run or hide. Now I knew, with absolute chilling certainty, why I was seeing Ben Milton.

He was dying.

29

I fell into bed that night with my clothes on, praying for sleep that took forever to come. And when it did, I dreamed in random, sharply colored images. They flashed through my mind like jagged pieces of a stained glass window that were too splintered and confusing to assemble: a burgundy sunrise, a bright yellow rose, tired hazel eyes, a dove taking flight into a cerulean sky, jade sand slipping through an hourglass.

I woke up early, even before my parents left for work, and sat on the edge of my bed, trying to figure out what to do to help Ben, trying to figure out how to *find* Ben.

I swallowed. What if I was too late? What if the Miltons were gone because Ben had already di—

My trembling hand covered my mouth. I couldn't even think it. Not that. Not about Ben.

I stayed in my room until late that morning, when I walked purposefully to the kitchen and did the only thing that made sense: I made lasagna. Lasagna-making was a skill I'd learned from my mother. Fantastic lasagna snob that she was, she refused to buy the pasta frozen or use ready-made ingredients. She made the whole dish from scratch. It was a long, drawn-out affair, a ritual of sorts, in which the majority of the day was spent leaning over simmering pots of pureed tomatoes, garlic, and spices. For whatever reason the process seemed to set things straight in my head, so I padded through the empty house and got started.

It took me longer than expected. Back when I could see, I had the system down perfectly: run the tomatoes through the food processor, simmer the onions and garlic, slowly add the spices, et cetera. But now I had to cook with my fingers, my nose, my ears. And even though our kitchen had been organized to the point of nausea, every move I made had to be slow, deliberate, and then checked and double-checked. Had I turned on the correct burner? Was this tomato bruised or just overripe? Where the hell was the oregano?

By late afternoon I knew what to do: I had to call Mason. Sure, the two of us had a checkered past, but he loved his brother and he was a man of action. He would know what to do.

I dialed Clarissa's number, speaking right over her hello. "Clarissa, it's Maggie. Sorry to interrupt, but it's sort of an emergency. Any chance you could ask that friend of yours for Mason Milton's cell phone number? I need to get in touch with him."

Thirty minutes later, I had Mason's number punched into my phone. The line was ringing. And panic was settling in. What the hell was I going to say? My thumb was hovering over the END button when a hello finally boomed over the line. It wasn't Mason, though. It was Mrs. Milton.

I held the phone to my ear with an unsteady hand and said, "Hi! It's Maggie!" Was I yelling? I was yelling. I sucked in a breath and exhaled slowly. Like a human person, I went on. "I was calling for Mason. I thought this was his number?"

"Hello, love," Mrs. Milton breathed into the receiver. "Actually, this *is* his number. I'm just playing secretary for him right now while he takes a turn driving." When I failed to reply, she went on to explain. "We're on our way home from my sister's house in Georgia. We go there every year for the first week of July. Anyway, we should be home in about an hour?"

I staggered into the wall. They were on vacation. That was all. Ben was okay. I said, "Could you have Mason call me back when you guys get home, please? At this number?"

"Sure," she chirped.

"And Mrs. Milton?"

"Yes?"

"Tell him it's important."

....

An hour later, Gramps came banging into the kitchen. My arms were elbow-deep in the soapy waters of the sink, and the lasagna was doing something magical in the oven.

"What smells in here?" Gramps asked.

"Lasagna," I said, rinsing the last of the pots and pans.

"Heh," he said, and I heard him clomping to the oven. "You gonna eat all that yourself, kid?"

"Nope. *We* are."

He harrumphed. "Don't like casseroles."

"Gramps. It's not a casserole. It's lasagna."

"Looks like casserole to me."

I blew a loose curl off my forehead, lifting a pot from the sink and groping around for a towel to dry it off. "Mom and Dad will eat some."

"Nope," said Gramps. "Your parents have that banquet tonight. Remember?"

"Oh. Right," I said, although I did not, in fact, remember. Not in the slightest. All I knew was that by the time we sat down to dinner, Mason still hadn't bothered to return my call. The longer I waited, the more anxious I became, and the more I second-guessed myself for calling him in the first place. My mouth was dry from nerves, so I chugged my milk and then refilled my glass, sticking my index finger inside so I could tell when it was full—slightly unsanitary, but necessary.

Gramps's fork *tink*ed on his plate as he stabbed at his lasagna. "Don't see any meat in here," he said.

"That's because Mom's lasagna recipe is vegetarian," I pointed out.

"I should cram some bologna in it," Gramps mused.

The ring of my cell phone interrupted my reply. I swallowed the mouthful of lasagna I'd been chewing. It stuck somewhere halfway down my throat. Two rings. Three rings.

I didn't move.

Gramps's chair ground on the tile as he stood up. Seconds later he said, "Hello?"

He'd answered my goddamn phone.

"Uh-huh," he said after a moment. "She's right here. Eating dinner. No, no, it's fine. It's just a casserole." Then he stuffed the phone in my hands.

I glared in his general direction and put the phone to my ear. I felt like a tiny, wounded bird trapped in a cast-iron cage. Finally I took a deep breath and squeaked, "Hello?"

"Maggie." Mason's voice was clipped and annoyed, but damned if it wasn't dead sexy.

My palms started to sweat. A lot. I lurched out of my seat and paced into the living room. "Um. Hi, Mason. Is there any way you could come over tonight? There's something important I need to tell you."

He was quiet for several long moments, and then, still sounding not at all amused, he said, "Well, I have to drop Ben at swim practice. And later on, I have rehearsal."

This was going better than I'd expected. He had actually spoken to me. With words. "How about after you drop him off?" I asked, unable to keep desperation out of my voice. "Can you swing by my house for a little bit?"

He exhaled loudly into the phone. "Yeah. Okay. Whatever."

30

Mason pulled up to my house thirty-five minutes later. All he
said to me when I opened the front door was hello. I didn't
know what I'd been expecting from him—concern or curiosity,
maybe?—but I was taken slightly aback by his curt tone.

He was still furious with me. That much was clear. I could sense
his annoyance radiating off him like acrid damp heat on summer
pavement as he followed me to the living room. He sat on the
couch while I stood stiffly, several paces away, my back to him and
my arms crossed. Silence pressed hard on my eardrums. Finally I
opened my mouth and started talking. Since I didn't know where
to start, I started at the beginning.

"I haven't been completely honest with you," I said, my voice
shaking, "but I guess you already know that. The truth is, I've
been blind for several months now, since I came down with bacterial meningitis." I paused. *Hold it together.* I took in a breath,

and in my exhale, I said, "When I first met Ben, I'd just fallen and hit my head. I was lying on the floor with my eyes closed, trying to shake it off. When I finally opened my eyes, Ben was standing over me."

As I told the story, I could still picture Ben's wide smile that day. I could still hear him bellowing that I was his girlfriend. It made my chest ache. "I could see him and a little bit around him, like he was a lightbulb or something. I was shocked and amazed and so freaking happy. It was the first time I'd felt normal in months." I paused for a moment, waiting for Mason to say something. But he didn't. He just sat there and judged me with his silence. "At first, I thought I'd gone crazy," I went on. "I mean, hitting my head and seeing someone?" I exhaled loudly, shaking my head. "Life just doesn't work like that, you know? But the thing is, I wasn't crazy—I'm *not* crazy." I spun around to face Mason, my entire body shaking as I grappled with the words I knew I had to say.

There was no sound from the couch. No movement. No words. Nothing. Just the musky smell that was Mason.

"I've seen two other people since then," I said. "The first time was in a Chinese restaurant. The man I saw was so old. He looked...well, *wrong*, I guess? But I couldn't put my finger on it. When I look back on it now, I can see that he was probably sick. And yesterday, I saw another person. A woman. My mother happens to know her. She's—" My sentence stopped abruptly. The word *dying* had fallen from my mouth before I could speak it. It would be so much easier if Mason would just say it for me. I wanted him to. Needed him to. To take the weight off my shoulders for me. So I silently stood there as the living room clock marked off the seconds. We stayed like that for exactly fifty-two ticks: me, standing in front of him, a single word frozen on my lips, and Mason, sitting noiselessly on the couch.

The gravity of the situation would become desperately, crushingly real to me when I finished that sentence. It would not be a theory I'd pieced together in my head, but a conclusion. There was too much finality in that. I didn't know whether I could take it. Tears pricked at my eyes. I blinked them away.

"The woman I saw is dying," I said finally, my voice cracking. "And the man I saw in the restaurant? I'm sure he is dying as well."

Mason wasn't stupid. He knew what I was insinuating. But he still remained silent and unreadable. And it infuriated me.

"Has Ben gone to the doctor lately?" I practically screamed. "Has he seemed sick at all?"

Mason didn't answer me. He just huffed disbelievingly.

Where the hell was the guy from the night at the Strand? Had he been a mirage? A fake? Hurt and anger thundered out of me as I said, "Goddamn it, Mason. Ben could be—Can you *say something*?"

I heard him stand up and head for the door.

"ARE YOU FREAKING KIDDING ME?" I bellowed, stomping after him. "Where are you going?"

Silence.

"Do you just leave when things get uncomfortable?" I yelled furiously. "Is that how you cope?"

Nothing. Not an answer. Not an utterance. Not a word. Just the *swuff swuff swuff* of his gigantic boots on the carpet as he made his way out of the house.

There was a bomb inside me now, ticking off seconds. Stomping after him, I answered on his behalf, sarcasm coating my every word. "Why yes, Maggie. That's what I do. Because I'm an egotistical, self-centered jerk who only cares about myself."

His footsteps came to an abrupt halt. We were close to the front door now. I would be willing to bet he'd turned around and was glaring at me. I could feel his anger all around me, a sharp electrical current quaking in the air between us. I ignored the alarms blaring in my head. The ones that were telling me to shut up. Not long ago, Mason had beaten the crap out of some kid for almost no reason whatsoever.

And I couldn't care less.

I said derisively, "You know, you sort of remind me of someone. He's been assuming the worst in me for weeks now." I paused for half a second, waiting for him to say something. But he didn't, so I plowed on. I was on a roll now. Somewhere in the back of my mind, the theme song from *Rocky* was playing. "You might know the guy. Lives in Chester Beach? Sings with the Loose Cannons? What's his name again?" I tapped an index finger on my chin, in a sarcastic parody of thought. "I'm terrible with names, but I'm pretty sure it's something like . . . Asshole."

I heard the front door jerk open and his footsteps stride outside, and that was when I completely snapped. I stomped after him, weeks of frustration and hurt pouring out of me all at once, too big and too wide and too explosive to be contained anymore. I reached out for him and snatched him by what felt like his upper arm. It was flexed. Tense. Ready to fight.

The air crackled between us.

We were too close. My emotions were detonating. I wanted to

melt into an ocean of tears and I wanted to shake the hell out of him and I wanted to fling myself into his arms.

My hand sprang free. "WHAT THE HELL IS YOUR PROB-LEM?" I screamed. "Would it kill you to talk to me? Listen to me? Consider what I have to say? What makes you think that you are entitled to treat other people like complete crap? Because you're in the Loose Cannons? Do you seriously—*seriously*— think that I would go through the trouble of faking my blindness just to get *near* you? What do you think, that you're some sort of goddamn gift to the world?"

He was maybe a foot or two away from me. Too close. I could feel his breath. It was hot, choppy, enraged. But I didn't step back. I leaned forward, taunting him.

A phone started ringing—some electronic ringtone I didn't rec-ognize. Mason's, no doubt.

"Are you planning on answering that?" I said through my teeth.

He growled, and a second later, I heard him say in a tight voice, "Hey, Mom. . . . At Maggie's." He said my name as though he were naming the dog crap stuck on the bottom of his shoe. Silence as he listened some more, then he exhaled heavily. When he spoke again, his voice was softer. Sad, almost. "Where?" he asked. "Okay. Of course. Leaving now." His phone snapped shut, and then it was dead quiet. "I need to run an errand for my mom," he said finally, almost more to himself than to me. I heard his boots slap against the concrete walkway as he clomped away.

I followed him, fury and desperation in my every footfall, mis-judging my steps and slamming into a landscape boulder that had been in our front yard since the day we'd moved in. I growled and cursed under my breath, rubbing the sting out of my shin. I heard a sharp intake of breath from Mason that might have been concern. But he didn't say anything.

"I'm going with you," I informed him. "I'm not finished with this conversation."

He didn't answer me, but he didn't stop me from getting into his car.

31

I sat unmoving in the passenger seat, my arms crossed tightly on my chest. Silence squeezed on me from all sides, heavy and thick. I was so far beyond mad that I could hardly breathe. I'd never met anyone as difficult as Mason. I had a handful of personas that generally worked on everyone, but none of them had worked on him. Not Deep Maggie. Not Sarcastic Maggie. Not Self-deprecating Maggie. Not even Funny Maggie. I was fresh out of Maggies.

And I was running out of time. Correction: Ben was running out of time. His life was falling away from him, and there was nothing I could do about it.

I rubbed my temples with my index fingers and leaned against the headrest, heaving out a massive gust of air. *Think.* I was so unprepared to hear Mason speak that I flinched in my seat as he said, "Somebody reported that a stray dog has been struck by a car off of Second Avenue. Mom wants me to bring it to the vet hospital for treatment."

All I could do was nod. Then I counted. Twenty-eight words. The most he'd ever said to me. Realizing my mouth was hanging open in shock, I promptly shut it. Then, pitifully enough, I analyzed his tone. As always, his words had been smooth and buttery as they'd slid from his mouth. But unlike the other times I'd heard his voice, a dozen different emotions fought for control over his tone.

We drove in silence for several minutes. I tried to organize my thoughts. Mason obviously hadn't believed me, so I needed to find another tactic. But what? I'd given him the truth. He'd rejected it. I didn't have anything else to give him.

We finally slowed on a quiet road, the car crunching to a stop on a graveled shoulder. Mason climbed out and hustled off, but I stayed planted in my seat, my eyes shut and my head leaning back. I didn't know where Mason had gone. His footsteps had gotten fainter and fainter until they had faded away completely. What felt like hours later, I heard him hurrying back to the car. To my surprise, he opened my door. My eyes jerked open as he placed a tiny, shaking dog in my lap.

I could see it.

It was one of those miniature dogs that women carry in their purses and decorate with bows. The kind that yips instead of barks. It lit up a small puddle of light inside the car. I could now see the dog, my lap, a crunched-up napkin in the console, a blue guitar pick that said FENDER, and, as Mason started the car, a snatch of his tanned fingers gripping the keys.

Suddenly, I didn't know what to do with my hands. "Is it . . . is it going to be all right?" I whispered as Mason pulled back onto the road.

He sighed and said, "She. It's a she. And I hope so." I could hear something different in his tone. I wondered whether he'd noticed that I'd gone from completely blind to semisighted once he'd placed the dog in my lap, whether he saw something different in my expression now, whether he was starting to believe me. I had no way of knowing.

The dog shifted in my lap. I went to catch her, to keep her from sliding to the floorboard, and my fingers found her soft muzzle. Long, tangled fur. Skinny legs. She nudged my hand with her wet nose, saying, *Comfort me, please.*

I swallowed and then ran a tentative hand down her torso, afraid to touch something that might cause her pain. She felt small, ribby, unloved. I swallowed again, this time pushing a huge lump down my throat. "Where does your mom work? Is it close?" I asked.

"Chester Beach."

The ride to Chester Beach dragged on forever. I didn't notice any bloody, twisted limbs or obvious signs of trauma on the dog. But I knew they were there. I could see them hiding in the labor of her breath and her too-slow heartbeat on my thigh.

The vet hospital was crowded for some reason. Full of people and chatter and healthy animals that didn't need to be there. Mason's mom had gone on break, so she wasn't there as I stood stiffly at the front desk in a tiny pool of light, the dog cradled in my arms. Mason spoke in a low voice to the people at the front counter. He seemed to know everybody who worked there—his name floated over my head in a half-dozen different voices, all friendly and appreciative.

A nurse took us back to a room that smelled of rubbing alcohol and bleach. As the vet inspected the dog, I gripped the exam table, my stomach twisted in knots.

"Mason," the vet said as he worked, "we appreciate your helping us out again." I couldn't see the vet's face. It was just past that dim area where the light dwindled away. But he had a low, kind voice, the sort of voice that generally doesn't have the title "Doctor" stapled to it. His hands were wide and freckled, with fat veins crawling from wrist to knuckle. There was a thin scratch on his thumb. A battle wound, presumably, from working with animals.

The dog looked up at me, and our eyes locked for a terribly long moment. *You're going to be all right,* I mouthed. Her tail twitched as though she wanted to wag it but she had no energy left to do so.

Something in my throat was strangling me, so I groped for a chair and then collapsed into it, pulling my legs up to my chest and balancing my chin on my knees. I squeezed my eyes shut. If I could just make myself small enough, maybe I'd stop hurting.

Seconds dragged into minutes. Minutes felt like hours. I wondered why such a tiny dog had been wandering around by herself. I wondered whether we were the only ones who had ever really cared about her. I wondered why life was so ridiculously unkind.

I couldn't deal with this.

I had to deal with this.

Finally, the vet exhaled slowly. I felt the hair rise up on my forearms. "I'm sorry," he said, his voice soft, almost a whisper, "but there's nothing we can do to save her."

. . . .

Back in Mason's car, my arms were crossed again. This time, for a different reason. I was trying to hold myself together. I felt as though I'd been turned inside out, all my emotions scattered across the state of Connecticut.

I'd stood frozen in place in the vet's exam room as the dog had died quietly in my arms, her tiny bright light blinking away into nothingness. When I'd handed her to the vet, my hands shaking uncontrollably, I'd felt as though I'd failed her. Which was asinine. I couldn't have done anything for her. And besides, I didn't even *like* dogs.

"Can you . . . can you get me home quickly, please?" I asked Mason, my voice breaking. I closed my eyes and pressed my thumbs into my eyelids, angry with myself for being so emotional again in front of him.

"Sure," Mason said, his voice pensive.

I nodded a thank-you but said nothing. *Breathe,* I told myself. The tears were coming regardless, running in huge, fat trails down my cheeks. I could hear Mason's concern long before I heard his voice.

"Are you . . . are you okay?" he asked, touching my hand lightly for the briefest of seconds and then pulling away.

Nothing was okay. Things were so not-okay that my *no* would seem inadequate, flimsy, so I didn't even bother to say it. And anyway, I was crying hard now in huge, fractured sobs, so he had his answer.

Neither of us spoke when we arrived at my house. We just sat there for several moments in the uncomfortable silence. I didn't know what to say to him—*Good-bye* or *Please believe me about Ben* or *Help me, Mason Milton.* Nothing seemed to fit. For once in my life, I had no words. Just a firestorm of emotions raging through me. A volcano.

Silently, I opened the door, slid out of Mason's car, and walked slowly into my house.

32

My feet felt as though they weighed a thousand pounds as I climbed the stairs to my old room. Oddly enough, it was the only place I wanted to be tonight, even though I hadn't set foot in there in months.

The door stuck a little as I opened it, as though it had been hastily sealed shut with flimsy Scotch tape. The room sighed out in front of me. I stood there in the dead silence, my hand still on the doorknob, hovering at the entry but not walking through it.

The place smelled stale. Dusty. Like old, musty body spray and sweat-encrusted cleats and forgotten dreams. But even so, it was familiar. A part of me nearly as much as my hand or my nose.

I knew this room. I knew the books crammed into every corner. I knew the glow-in-the-dark stars that speckled the ceiling. I knew the half-dozen soccer balls jammed in the closet. I knew that memories—full and sharp and colorful—breathed freely in this space. I could feel them there. Even see them there.

I crossed the room and sat on the very corner of my bed, running my hand along the worn blue and green quilt Gran had sewn for me years ago. When I was eight, she'd presented it to me for my birthday. I'd wondered why she had given me a quilt when all I'd wanted was a handheld video game. But after she died, I treasured that quilt.

I didn't know why I'd moved into the boxy, functional room downstairs after meningitis took my sight, and I didn't know why I hadn't touched this room ever since. All I knew was that this was the only place I wanted to be tonight. So I fell asleep there, underneath Gran's blue and green quilt and the slanted ceilings dotted with glow-in-the-dark stars.

33

The next day I felt foggy, sluggish, like I was trapped in some-body else's dream—some pitiful girl who had lost more than she ever thought she'd had to begin with, who was about to lose even more. Surely I wasn't the indomitable Maggie Sanders, that much was true. And yet here I was in that other girl's body, woe-fully tapping out the Chopin-Clarissa tune on my sheets. And then on my desk. And then on the shower stall. And then on the kitchen counter.

It was unrelenting, that melody.

Finally I crept to the basement, an extension cord in hand. My old keyboard—still on the floor, right where I'd left it—kicked to life with a hum of chaotic energy when I plugged it in. I sat on my knees in front of it, uncertain, and then leaned over and ran my fingers along the sharps and flats until I found middle C.

I pressed down with my thumb. The note sounded rusty, old, like it had been imprisoned in the keyboard for centuries.

I was shocked, actually, that I'd managed to produce real sound. So I stayed like that, hunched over the instrument with my thumb on the key, until the room swallowed up the note. Then I placed my hands in position.

The basement held its breath.

Originally I'd planned to just tinker with the tune so I could get it out of my head. But my fingers had different ideas. They ripped into the piece as though I'd been playing it forever—quick, clean, flawless.

I jerked my hands away and twisted them in my lap. It had sounded strange to me. Not like my song. But exactly like my song. It was a hodgepodge of everything that had been stamped-ing through my head the past couple weeks. It was something that would make my old piano instructor bleed from the ears. Placing my fingers back on the keys, I pounded out the song once, twice, three times, ten times, sometimes adding synthesized effects, and sometimes letting the music stand on its own.

Then I sat back on my heels.

The music seemed to hang over me, slightly unfinished—a sentence without an ending. And it picked at me in an indescribable way. Leaning over the keyboard again, I tacked on the descending base line I'd admired the other day in Big Dough. The conversion was clunky as hell, and I stumbled over it again and again.

"I didn't know you played."

I jumped like a startled cat and shrieked.

Mason.

I resolutely turned toward him—like I was trying to prove something. What that *something* was, I didn't know. That I wasn't backing down, maybe. That I'd told him the truth. I said, "It's been a long time since I've played." It was embarrassing that he'd heard me, but I wasn't going to let him know that.

Neither of us spoke for the space of several breaths. Finally I lifted my chin and said, "How did you get in my house?"

I heard his boot kicking against the wall. *Lunk lunk lunk. Lunk-lunk-lunk-lunk-lunk.* "The door was unlocked," he said. "I let myself in. Heard you playing down here." He cleared his throat and said, "Listen, can I talk to you about your sight?"

....

Mason had done some digging. Knowing that Merchant's would never admit someone who wasn't visually impaired, he'd called the school to confirm I was a student. He'd stewed on the information for a few hours before he'd come over, but even so he seemed confused, disconcerted, like he had a lightbulb in his hand but no idea where to screw it in.

"You have to admit," Mason said, "you can understand why it was so hard for me to believe at first—your hitting your head and then suddenly you can see people who are . . ." He swallowed loudly and shifted a little, his leg so close to mine that I could feel the heat coming off of it. We were sitting on the steps of my back porch, where we'd been for the past hour. He'd probably asked me a hundred questions so far, about my blindness, about my eyesight around Ben, about the others I'd seen.

Having our relationship switch gears so completely and so

abruptly was bewildering. What had caused him to confirm my story, I didn't know—whether he'd noticed my expression change when he'd placed the dying dog in my lap, or whether he'd seen some sort of truth in me when I'd fallen apart in his car, or whether he'd simply taken some time to really consider what I'd told him. All I knew was that the huge boulder between us had shifted a little, and I could finally squeeze past. I said, "Yeah. Believe me, I know."

Was his leg drifting closer to mine? It felt like it. Somewhere in my body was a miniature fire truck, speeding desperately to the three-alarm on the side of my leg.

"It could be something else, though—the reason you're seeing these people," Mason said. "It could be a million different things."

I nodded a wordless assent, not to tell him I agreed with him, but to show him I was listening. I knew I was right. I just couldn't explain how. The truth was like a cold palm pressed on the nape of my neck.

"Have you told anyone besides me?" Mason asked.

"An online doctor. And it didn't go well. He suggested I was crazy," I said.

As he blew out a sympathetic breath, his leg, just barely, rested against mine. My heart stuttered.

He didn't move.

Neither did I.

There's something about a light, hesitant touch. It makes you ache for more.

I shook my head, attempting to reclaim my brain. Mason had a girlfriend. Probably didn't even know he was touching me.

Still, though. The heat on the side of my leg was reaching

nuclear. I was going to explode right here, combust all over my backyard. I shifted positions a little, moving away from him to lean against the deck railing, equal parts relief and regret.

He let out a little sigh.

A sigh.

What did that even mean?

Finally he cleared his throat and said, "Have you considered telling anyone else?"

"Like who? My parents?" I scoffed. "They'd never believe me. But—what about your mom?"

I heard him take in a deep, shaky breath. "I think we should wait on telling Mom until we know for sure. Losing Dad was so hard on her. If your theory is wrong, we'd put her through an awful lot for nothing."

He was probably right. If I had a little more proof, something convincing, maybe my story wouldn't be so far-fetched. "What about Ben?" I asked. "Are you going to tell him?"

"He's *ten*." I nodded, feeling relieved. After a short pause, Mason said, "It's just hard for me to swallow because Ben had a routine checkup a couple months ago and he was fine. And he hasn't been sick, hasn't even had a cold. I mean, he's been a little tired and grumpy, but that's it."

I cocked an eyebrow at him. "Ya think?"

"He'll forgive you, Maggie," he said, a half smile hiding somewhere in his tone. "It's not in his nature to stay angry."

34

The next morning I told my parents I had a stomachache. It wasn't a complete lie—indecision and stress had fused into a roiling lump in my stomach, and I couldn't seem to digest it no matter how hard I tried. And anyway, it was the only way to get out of my session with Hilda, who was due to show up at noon.

After my parents left for work, I agonized for a while. Cried for a while. Fidgeted for a while. And then I called Sophie. She'd been hovering in the back of my mind for the past couple days, but with everything that had been going on, I'd put off calling her.

"Hey, Sophie. How're you holding up?" I asked her as soon as she picked up.

A couple heartbeats' worth of a pause on her end of the line. Finally she said, "Well, just about everything I own is getting carted into a moving van right now, I threw up five times this morning, and I'm craving squid. So there's that."

I didn't know whether to laugh or bawl.

Silence spread between us, so bulky and dense I could feel it weighing down the phone.

"So you're really moving?" I whispered.

"Yeah."

My throat felt tight, like someone was jamming a fist into my windpipe. "When?"

"Tomorrow."

Sitting on the very edge of my bed, I wrapped my arms around myself. I hated that she was pregnant. Hated that her parents were splitting up. Hated that she was moving to Ohio. Hated that I'd hurt her.

"I'm sorry," I blurted suddenly. It was all hurried and all shouty and all wrong, but I kept going anyway. I had to try to make this right. After all these years of friendship, I owed Sophie that much. "For avoiding you when I first lost my sight. It was just so . . . awkward." I twisted my hands together, gripped my toes down on my flip-flops, like maybe I was getting ready to bolt, just run away from this conversation.

Sophie waited a moment before she spoke, and when she did, her voice was soft. "It was my fault, too. I've been busy fighting my own battles. I've been sort of avoiding everyone—keeping people away from my house. I didn't want everyone to know how bad it was at home. It was so embarrassing."

"Well, maybe with a little distance, your parents will decide they want to stay together?" Even as it came out of my mouth, I knew it would never happen. That house had been a time bomb that had detonated the night Sophie told her parents she was pregnant.

"Right," she muttered. "And maybe my dad will offer to knit the baby some booties."

Baby booties.

Wow.

That was when it really hit me: Sophie was actually going to have a baby. I'd always been a little leery of babies, what with their big heads and their inconsolable crying and their jerky movements. I'd once seen a baby laugh and puke at the exact same time. It had been like something out of a horror movie. But if anyone could make it through this, it was Sophie. She just didn't know it yet.

Sophie cleared her throat. "Maggie?"

"Yeah?"

"I have to go."

I knew she'd meant that she was just busy, that she had to finish packing and whatever, but it felt more like a final good-bye. A decade of friendship and laughter and familiarity slid through my fingers, wisping away into nothingness. I whispered, "Bye, Soph."

....

I was sitting on the back deck when the doorbell rang that afternoon. I made no move toward the front door, just stayed right where I was: butt on the edge of the chair, eyes closed, hands gripping both sides of my head.

But when the doorbell sounded off a relentless couple thousand times in a row, I staggered to my feet and opened my eyes. Then I froze. I was standing in the murky outer ring of my sight. My eyes traced slowly along a wooden deck slat toward the house, my vision becoming clearer with every foot. Trancelike, I walked to the slider and put one palm on the glass.

I could see inside my house.

There it was, just like it had always been, only . . . different. Furniture was lined up in a square, uniform manner. Mom's vases, which used to live on the shelf just inside the door, were gone, replaced by a line of books. *Independence Without Sight* and *Adjusting to Blindness* and *How to Cope with Loss*. There were no stray shoes on the floor, nothing that made the space appear lived-in or homey or cozy. It was a page inside a catalog. A model home.

The house of a blind girl.

I flinched as the doorbell kicked in again.

Opening the slider and stepping inside, I felt guilty for some reason, like a trespasser or an unwelcome houseguest. I walked through the house in a daze, hitching to a stop in the hallway in front of a huge picture of Mom and me after regionals last year. I was beaming, one hand holding a soccer ball and the other raised high above my head, knotted together with Mom's.

My mother's expression was triumphant.

Suddenly I felt like the hallway was caving in on me, and I took off, hurrying toward the door. Everything around me was hospital-bright, and my insides were in revolt, churning and twisting as I stepped to the door and swung it open.

Ben.

It was Ben.

There he was, wearing a scowl and a blue baseball-style hat that said THINKING CAP. At his feet was a fabric shopping bag. Like a nocturnal animal emerging into the daylight, I squinted at Ben, then at the red-flowered cushion on our porch swing, then at the ancient maple in the front yard, then at Mason's car idling in the driveway, and then back at Ben again.

Ben used his crutches to propel the bag toward me. It crashed into my shins. "New flavor of Doritos," he said tersely. "Thought you might want to try them."

"Thanks," I said, shocked.

"Why are you wearing pajamas?" he blurted. "It's, like, three in the afternoon."

I glanced at Mason, who beamed a gorgeous, white-toothed smile at me from the driver's seat of his car. I'd seen him so many times in my own head lately that it was weird to *see him*, see him. No, not weird: overwhelming. I glanced away, but I could feel him watching me regardless, could feel his eyes on my face, my shoulders, my pajamas, my everything.

I took in a deep breath. *Focus, Maggie. Focus.* I looked down at Ben. "I don't know," I answered honestly.

For a moment, Ben and I just stared at each other, then Ben said tightly, "So Mason told me that you told him that you can see when I'm around."

I nodded robotically.

Ben let his head fall backward and he sighed heavily. "Okay, fine. Fine: Mason said I should come over to hear you out. So here I am. To hear you out."

All I could think was that he was giving me another chance, and this time I was going to do it right. With complete honesty. Looking down at my feet, I said, "You were right. In some ways, I did use you for my eyesight. I mean, when I first met you, my life was just . . . I was just . . ." My voice sounded loud and hurried, and I told myself to take a breath. "I was completely off the rails." I swallowed. The sound seemed loud in my ears. I glanced up at Ben for a moment. His lips were still tight, but there was a loosening in his eyes that encouraged me to go on. "But you were always my friend. You were always the person who helped me realize that somewhere inside me, there's still a *me*. I've been a crap friend, and I'm truly sorry. I shouldn't have left your house without saying good-bye the night of the Dead Eddies concert." I cleared my throat. "And about Mason..." Instinctively, and before I could stop myself, my eyes shot up to where Mason sat in his car.

He was still staring at me.

Heat crept up my chest and into my face.

"I didn't—" I began, but cut myself off. Christ, this was degrading. My cheeks felt like they were purple now. They literally ached from the heat. Praying that Mason couldn't read lips, I whispered, "I promise you, I didn't know Mason was your brother at first, not until you told me. And even after that, I didn't hang out with you to get near him." I folded my arms over my stomach and shifted my weight, and then I went on. "But over the past few weeks I've... I've discovered that I have feelings for him." Ben's brows were pulled together, and I couldn't tell whether he was considering my admission or considering throttling me for crushing on his brother. My eyes shot to my feet again. "And it isn't because he's ridiculously talented. It's more than that. He..." I let out a breath. Did I really have to do this with Mason here? "He stands up for what he believes in. He's ferociously protective of the people he loves. He isn't okay with doing things half-assed and he isn't okay with insincerity, and... and I guess I find that compelling." I cleared my throat. "But he doesn't know how I feel, and I would absolutely die—*die*—if you told him."

I couldn't look at Ben, couldn't look at Mason. And for several miserable seconds, all I could hear was the squawk of birds overhead and a car starting up in a neighbor's driveway. Then, Ben's voice: "Fine."

My eyes jerked to his. "Fine?"

"Yes, fine. To all of it," he said. His tone was indicating I was being extremely dense, but his mouth was starting to turn up at the corners. "Just don't make me regret it, Thera."

Thera.

I felt a strong, visceral tug in my heart. I didn't know what I'd done to deserve him. "I won't."

. . . .

Ben had been gone for about a half hour when my mom breezed through the front door and into the living room, where I was distracting myself from my problems by means of Ben's Doritos and a movie. Mom placed a palm on my forehead and said, "Are you feeling any better?" I wanted to lean into her touch, keep it there forever. But a second later her hand was gone, my forehead cold.

"Maybe a little," I said, which was true. Ben's forgiveness had loosened the knot in my chest, just a little.

She collapsed on the couch beside me, all sighs, dropping what sounded like her coaching equipment bag on the floor. Then she cleared her throat. "*Titanic*, huh?"

"Yeah."

"I love this movie," she said quietly.

"I know."

Silence spread between us.

A handful of months ago I would've been thrilled to curl up on the couch with my mother and watch this movie. But now her presence felt threatening, suffocating—like she was vacuuming up all the air in the house. She wasn't exactly saying anything to me, but she wasn't going away, either, so finally I grabbed my chips and stood. Taking a step forward, I said, "So I think I'll go work on my research paper until dinner? Clarissa and I are almost finished and—" My sentence came to a halt as my foot thumped into her equipment bag.

An achingly familiar noise filled the room.

It seemed so loud, the sound of a soccer ball skipping across the floor, banging into a wall and then rolling back toward me. I heard the couch creak sharply as Mom jerked to her feet, heard the ball come to a stop somewhere between the two of us.

I didn't move.

"I'm sorry," I blurted, and I didn't even know why. What was I apologizing for? Everything, I guessed. Knocking the ball out of her bag. Ruining her dream. Screwing up our relationship. I thought about that picture I'd seen on the wall. I thought about everything we'd had, everything we'd lost, and it all came down to this.

A ball between us.

"It's okay," Mom said quietly. "I didn't mean to leave it so close to your feet. It's just—*Titanic* was on when I walked in and I got distracted." There was an ache in her voice that I'd never heard before.

"It's fine," I said loudly. And before she could reply, I hurried to my room.

35

Mason and I were sitting on the metal bleachers of North Bay Aquatic Club, where we'd sat for the past several nights while Ben had his swim lesson. It was our meeting time, our hour to sit and brainstorm and stress out, and it was part of the cycle of my life lately. Morning: research terminal illnesses that present no symptoms. Afternoon: hang out with Ben while doing my best to pretend that nothing is wrong. Evening: tag along to swim practice so Mason and I could talk without Ben getting too suspicious.

Mason had taken Ben to the doctor that morning—a massive waste of time. According to the doctor, Ben was the picture of health.

Except he wasn't.

I sighed tiredly and looked around. The entire swim club was clinically bright. My eyesight spread past the big picture window on the far wall of the pool room, past the well-kept lawn outside, and past a little knoll dotted in shrubs before it petered away into the void.

Yet whatever was killing Ben was gray, amorphous, ducking into the shadows, just out of reach.

Mason looked strangely out of place beside me on the bleachers. Sure, he was simply dressed in his standard plain black T-shirt and jeans. Nothing rockstarish. Nothing bold. But his presence was too big for his body. Too big for the swim club, actually. Like Ben's light, it spilled out of the building and onto the lawn.

A handful of other people were here, a few moms flipping through magazines, watching the swimmers, mashing buttons on their phones. Samantha—the smart-alecky young girl I'd encountered when I'd arrived at the swim meet several weeks ago—was sitting on the bottommost bleacher, glaring at me and muttering mildly entertaining curse words under her breath. I'd discovered recently that she was Teddy's little sister, which hadn't been good news or bad news, just news. It was obvious that she had a crush on Ben. Her eyes got drifty when she watched him swim.

Samantha and I had been getting along famously. Moments ago, we'd had a little run-in in the swim club's restroom. I was standing at the sink, getting ready to wash my hands, when she barreled in. She scowled when she saw me, which I completely ignored. Tromping up to me, she jabbed an index finger at my forearm and said, "I don't like you."

I snorted. Clearly, she didn't know what she was up against. I'd been practicing the fine art of insolence for seventeen years. I was practically a professional. "You're such a charming child," I said lightly, soaping up my hands and rinsing them off. "Why hasn't your mother left you at a gas station?"

Ignoring the gas-station crack, Samantha scratched herself indiscreetly—the sort of scratch that only little kids and old people can get away with—and said, "I don't like you," yet again.

"Yes, Attitudy Judy, I heard you the first time," I said, shaking my hands off so they spackled her with water.

Her eyes narrowed. The little wiseass had so many freckles that they were practically touching one another. She put one hand on her hip and said accusingly, "If you're blind, then how come you are looking in my eyes right now? Huh?"

I shrugged at Samantha, tapped my temple with an index finger, and said, "Must be psychic."

"Liar," Samantha grumbled under her breath.

"Now, that's not a nice way to talk to your brother's friend's friend," I said cheerfully. And then I made a point to smile. A big smile. Not because I was "turning the other cheek" or "attracting more bees with honey than vinegar" or "being the bigger person," but because I wanted to tick her off. And I did.

She crossed her arms, jammed her fists into her armpits, and said, "Go screw yourself."

Wow. The kid had a mouth. I was mildly impressed. "Go play in traffic," I said under my breath.

From inside a stall, some woman cleared her throat. My cue to walk out. Head held high and shoulders back, I strode out of the restroom. And now, Samantha was sitting on the bleachers, swinging her feet and doing that frosty *I'm watching you* thing out of the corner of her eye, which was mildly annoying. But more annoying were three girls—all around my age and all nauseatingly pretty—who were standing just inside the pool room, openly staring at Mason. Whether they had recognized him as the lead singer of the Loose Cannons or they just thought he was good-looking, I wasn't sure. The tallest of them was the perfect sort of girl you'd see in magazines—thin, blond, and gorgeous. The other two were pretty in subtle ways. They had smooth hair and smooth skin and smooth smiles.

Evidently Mason was accustomed to beautiful girls gawking at him. He didn't even glance their way as he gestured in the direction of Ben's coach and scrubbed a hand through his hair, rendering it fascinatingly messy. "Coach called Mom this morning. He said Ben's swim times are dropping. He was wondering whether there are problems at home." His eyes trailed to Ben, who was bobbing in the water next to Teddy, and then back to me. "You think it means something?"

"I think it *all* means something," I told him, pressing my fingers to my forehead. "Take Ben for a second opinion. His swim times aren't much of a symptom, but they're still a sign of something."

Mason shook his head. "They'll tell me the same thing, Maggie—that he's perfectly healthy."

I threw my hands up in frustration. "Then take him to the hospital."

"For what? A problem that hasn't even appeared yet? They'll think I'm crazy. They'll send us away."

"I'll go with you to the hospital, and I'll tell them everything."

"And they will send you away in a straightjacket."

I squeezed my eyes shut and let out a heavy gust of air. Mason was probably right. And what good would I do Ben if they threw me in the psych ward? I had a gut feeling that if I walked away right now, I'd be leaving Ben to die.

Suddenly Mason squirmed on the bench and muttered under his breath, "Crap. Incoming."

My head snapped up. One of the girls who'd been watching Mason—the perfect blond one—had stepped inside the gate and was heading in our direction. She had a stiff sort of gait that seemed to advertise *I have a potato chip that I don't want to break wedged between my butt cheeks.*

"Hi! Mason?" she said breathlessly when she came to a stop in front of him, fluttering eyelashes that were long enough to make a breeze. "My name's Lacey. I'm, like, totally your biggest fan." She swiveled her head around as though searching for something Mason had hidden in the bleachers. "Are you going to have a concert here?"

Mason tipped his head to the side, considering her words. "Here? Not a bad idea. But no. Not today. Have to rest my voice for next week's concert." I had to hand it to him. He sure played it cool, even when beauty was smacking him in the face.

"*Ooooo.* Can you tell me where it will be?" Lacey asked. Just by the way she stood she was flirting with him.

"Nope," Mason said. "You'll have to figure it out like everyone else."

She stuck her bottom lip out in a pout, and then she said, "Well, then . . . um, can I have your autograph?"

"Sure. You have a pen?"

She produced a Sharpie from her tacky rhinestone purse and handed it to him. Then she bent outrageously close to him and offered the back of her hand for him to sign. I'd like to say that this did not make me jealous. But it did. I drummed my fingers on the bench.

"Thanks!" she said, and she giggled her way back to her friends, who were jumping up and down like a couple twelve-year-olds.

After I fumed for a few minutes, and after Lacey McChipbutt and her friends left, Mason sighed and said, "Sometimes I wish we had a regular concert schedule and regular fans."

"Why?"

"I don't know," he said, shrugging. "I just wonder whether people are building up the concerts too much, making them into something bigger than what they are."

I shook my head. "Don't shortchange yourself. I went to one of your concerts, and it was off the hook—absolutely amazing."

Mason's eyes fluttered down and he bit his lower lip. My compliment had affected him somehow, though I couldn't imagine why. Clearly he received that sort of praise all the time. Why would it be any different coming from me?

I didn't know.

What I *did* know was that the way he was biting his lip made me ache in a million different ways.

"Thanks," he said finally. "Which concert did you go to?"

"Alexander Park."

His eyes focusing on mine, unblinking and intense, he said, "But I didn't see you there."

I gulped. Because gulping is attractive. "I was in the back."

He scratched the back of his neck, his gaze drifting back down to his boots. "So did you just stumble on the concert, or . . . ?"

"Um," I said, stalling. I didn't want to get Jase in trouble for telling Clarissa what he'd overheard, but I didn't want to lie, either. So I told Mason only part of the story. "Some guy posted a comment on one of your videos, hinting that the clue was in the music. I figured it out from there."

Mason let out a big sigh. "Cannon Dude?" he said, and I nodded. "That guy is a complete..."

"Dickbag," I supplied.

Mason laughed once and beamed a smile at me. "Well said." I bowed, just a little, swooping one arm out to the side. "Seriously, though," he went on, "do you think the clue is too easy to figure out?"

"No way—it's tough as hell."

"Gavin was the one who came up with the idea," Mason explained, running a finger across the edge of the bleachers. "He's obsessed with puzzles, mysteries, that sort of thing. Carlos has been arguing with him about it since day one. But then, Carlos has been arguing about *everything* since day one." I shot him a questioning look, and Mason held up his hand and, one by one, used his fingers to count off the reasons. "He doesn't get enough solos. Our newest songs suck. He'd rather not rehearse on Mondays, Thursdays, Fridays, or the weekend. And he thinks Gavin's singing the clue is both 'lame and sophomoric.'"

I blinked. "Whoa."

"Yeah." He sighed, glanced at Ben, and then looked down again. His voice suddenly soft, he said, "Anyway, that's just band stuff. It's not important right now."

I nodded, gnawed on my thumbnail for a minute, and then asked the question that had been weighing on my mind for days. "Do you think this thing with Ben could be hereditary? I mean, your dad...?"

"Dad died of a freak thing," Mason explained. "He came down with a cold he couldn't shake and ended up with a blood infection. He was hospitalized, and within a week he was gone. It's totally unrelated to Ben. Besides, *look* at him," he said, gesturing to Ben, who was now sitting on the edge of the pool, dangling his legs into the water. He looked healthy. Relaxed. Carefree. "Does he appear sick to you?"

Mason was hoping we were way off base, that there was some other crazy reason that explained why I was seeing these people. But I felt the truth in my gut. It twisted my insides and made nausea curl in my stomach.

Ben was dying. And I was his only symptom.

. . . .

When you are really young, you take everything that adults say as gospel. All that bullcrap about Santa Claus and the Easter Bunny. All the ridiculousness about babies being delivered by storks. When you get a little older, there are *Listen to me—I know what I'm talking about* speeches that are overflowing in wisdom. And then, usually sometime around puberty, some random grown-up says something so outrageously idiotic that you finally figure out that half the adult population is pretty freaking clueless. So you just stop paying attention to them.

At this point in my life, I knew what was right for me. I happened to be an expert in the field of Maggie because, after all, I was Maggie. Which was exactly why I didn't take it kindly when Dad poked his head into my upstairs room that night and said, "What are you *doing*?"

I couldn't answer him on account of the stack of grade-school artwork I was carrying with my teeth. So I dropped the box I was lugging across the room, plucked the artwork from my mouth, and said, "I'm moving back up here. So I'm sorting through my old crap."

After I'd gotten home from the pool that night, I'd walked my fingers over every dusty inch of this bedroom. The place was stuffed full of years and years of near-constant motion: mud-caked soccer cleats, two snowboards, a pair of ice skates, piles of drawings from art classes, a bee costume from a school play, books, books, and more books.

I could feel Dad's anxiety buzzing in the room like a high-tension wire. "Why?" he asked.

Because the boxy room felt like it was pressing on me from all sides. Because I could breathe up here. Because I'd left too much of myself here for far too long. "Because it suits me better," I said, hand-inspecting an ancient bra. I grumbled under my breath. Christ. Had I not grown a cup size since I was twelve? I chucked it in the garbage can beside me.

"Do you think that's smart, with the stairs and all? And the sleepwalking?" he asked.

"I haven't walked in my sleep for months," I pointed out. "So technically, I'm more of a menace to myself when I'm awake."

After a long moment, Dad said, "Just be careful, okay?" His voice sounded light, but I could sense the thin river of unease snaking through his words.

My chest knotted up reflexively. "Dad?"

"Yes?"

I opened my mouth to tell him I missed him, but then promptly shut it. Irrational as that declaration would be, it was true. I missed what we used to be, what had been. I wanted to backpedal through the past seven months and become invincible to him once again, wanted to hang out with him first thing on Saturday mornings, one hand holding a to-go coffee and the other flipping through a dusty box of timeworn records. But in the end all I said was, "Mind taking my snowboards down to the basement for me?"

It took me a full two hours to weed out my upstairs room. But after I finished, I'd created a home for the things I wanted to move up with me, namely my computer, my CDs, and my clothes. Since my clothes were all color-coded, they took the longest to move. I lugged them in sections: blue, then white, then green, then red, then black. When I got everything put away, I hesitated in the middle of my room, all too aware that it wasn't a sighted girl's room anymore, but it didn't quite feel like a blind girl's room, either.

With a loud sigh, I collapsed on my bed, thinking about Ben, thinking about my parents, thinking about Sophie, thinking about Clarissa, thinking about Mason—feeling oddly as though I had one foot stretched out in front of me, planted in a new world, and the other behind me, rooted in the past. Straddling two worlds, but not fully belonging in either one.

36

I don't know what it's like to get shot by a hit man, but I'd venture to guess it's not unlike having Ben sneak up behind you and blast a party horn in your ear. At the time, I was sitting in the Miltons' living room, hate-watching a fishing show while mentally running through my descending bass line. And so the horn-in-the-ear thing took me by absolute surprise. With a loud screech, I jerked upright, clutching my chest. "Ben, what the—"

Ben blew the horn again and then let it dangle out the side of his mouth like a cigar, supporting it with his smirk. I rolled my eyes. It wasn't Ben's birthday, and it wasn't even his half birthday. It was his quarter birthday—which, evidently, was a big deal.

From the floor, Mason smiled at me with one side of his mouth. He'd been sitting on the carpet with his legs crossed and his guitar in his lap, brows knotted together while he'd plucked a major D chord again and again.

"Ben," I said, "you need to stop doing that because you're going to give me a—"

Another blast from the horn and, grinning maniacally, Ben swung off to the kitchen, where his mother was making a cake. Wally trotted off behind him.

I watched Ben leave the room, wishing I couldn't see so well. My eyesight was everywhere now, refrigerator-bright light blasting brutally through the Miltons' house and halfway across the street. A few weeks ago that would have thrilled me. Now it made me want to puke.

With a loud sigh, I paced across the room and unloaded on the Miltons' piano bench. It creaked and shifted precariously underneath me. I stared at the lid, where Mrs. Milton's photos were strung in a jumble of mismatched frames and blurry faces and dust. I found Ben and Mason in dozens of them—Mr. Milton, too. The pictures were a reel of film, where the boys aged in each frame. They looked happy and relaxed, even after the notable absence of their father. I wondered how they'd done it. How they'd made the best of their lopsided lives. How they'd stood up and kept walking.

And how I hadn't.

I stared at the most recent picture of Ben—at a swim meet, looking young and outrageous with his wet hair sticking up in a fauxhawk. A swell of emotion rising in me, I let my eyes fall down to the piano keys and slowly plunked out the Chopin-Clarissa tune, marrying it with the descending base line. The three of them slid together now, connected by some invisible notch.

"What was that?" Mason asked, standing up.

"One of Chopin's waltzes," I muttered.

"No, it wasn't," he said, sitting down beside me. "It was something . . . else."

"Right. So I just pieced a bunch of stuff together that's been running through my head. Was it that bad? God, it was bad. Just tell me it was bad and get it over with."

"Actually, I liked it. You're really good. Like, a natural."

I glanced over at him. Mistake. He was *right there*, a breath away, staring at me with those soulful eyes—the sort of eyes that were almost painful to gaze into, and equally painful to look away from. My lungs felt like they were folding up, collapsing in on themselves. "Um," I said, sort of breathlessly, "I took ten years of piano lessons, so I spent a lot of time bent over the keys. You can't just unlearn something like that, you know? It sticks with you." Clearing my throat, I gestured to the keys. "What about you? Do you play?"

He shook his head. "Dad used to play. Piano never interested me like the guitar does, like lyrics do."

"So you always wanted to be in a band?"

He shrugged with one shoulder. "My head has always been stuffed full with songs, so being in a band wasn't something I wanted to do, it was something I had to do."

"It's your Thing," I surmised.

He nodded and then glanced toward the kitchen. "It's my Thing," he agreed quietly. His eyes flickered back to me. "Music wasn't ever a choice for me. It just *was*." The way he spoke made music seem so simple, so elemental, so magical. I felt oddly as though he were disclosing one of life's great mysteries to me—as though he were weaving creationism and the big bang theory together as one—and I held my breath as he went on.

"When I was Ben's age," he said, "I mowed lawns for an entire summer to earn the money for my first guitar. It was a gaudy, piece-of-shit red electric, and it came with an amp that cranked up loud as hell. My parents despised it." His mouth twisted into a half smile, half frown. "But I was shy—sort of a loner—and music was just a way to be me, you know? So they let it slide. Until I was fourteen, that is," he said, his Adam's apple sticking out a little as he spoke, "when I was in my room, banging out this alternative chord progression at seven in the morning. Dad came marching in, and without a word he plucked the guitar from my hands, not giving it back no matter how much I begged. Looking back, I can understand why: it was the weekend and the entire world was asleep. But at the time? I was pissed. I told him I hated him, then refused to talk to him." He took in a slow breath, and in his exhale he added softly, "He died a couple days later."

I let out a little gasp—just a small, inhaling sound. But Mason heard it anyway and he turned toward me, his eyes tired and world-worn. "Yeah," he said. Just the one word: *yeah*. But I understood the subtext. "Anyway," he said, "when Dad died, I couldn't even think about music. I refused to talk to my family, my grades were a train wreck, I was just . . . messed up. I spent my days mouthing off to teachers, my afternoons in detention, my evenings holed up in my room, my weekends playing video games."

"So what pulled you out of it?" I whispered.

"My principal."

"Your principal," I repeated blankly.

Mason nodded. "Yeah. Principal Morris. I spent a lot of time in his office. Particularly at the end of sophomore year, when I got into a fight at school."

"Ah. Right," I said.

"You heard about it? The fight?" Mason said.

I waved a palm at him. "Ben might have mentioned it."

The corners of Mason's mouth tugged up. "Right. So I was sitting across from Principal Morris, and he was informing me that I was a loser and that my grades were absolute crap and that I would never amount to anything—" He abruptly stopped, evidently noticing the shocked look on my face. "Yes, he actually said that I would never amount to anything." Mason ran an index finger slowly over the edge of the piano lid. "I was just so angry. Angry at life, angry at myself, angry at Dad, angry at Principal Morris for being right. Nothing—*nothing*—is more infuriating than having some holier-than-thou asshole call you out on your bullshit, you know? So it was when Principal Morris was telling me what a piece of crap I was that I made a vow to myself: I would become so goddamn successful that I would force him to choke on his words."

I just stared at him.

Mason nodded as if I'd spoken, and he said, "The way he looked down on me that day? It made me want to bust my ass, practice every night—become someone."

"I imagine you've succeeded," I said in a whisper.

He shrugged, an unassuming little jerk of his shoulder. "I'm not there yet," he said.

Neither of us spoke for several minutes. I closed my eyes, placed my fingers back on the keys, and replayed my song. Everything in my life was a mess and I felt completely overwhelmed, but for once in my life I was just…there—on that piano bench with Mason and nowhere else. And when I played the last note, I left my fingers on the keys for several seconds, keeping the music hanging in the air, and then I inhaled, as if drawing the moment deep into my lungs, where I could keep it safe.

....

My mother was eating dinner at the kitchen counter when I got home. We spoke, but not really. As I sat down with a plate of leftovers, I said, "Hey, Mom. How was your day?" and she said, "Not bad. Yours?" and I said, "Pretty good. It was Ben's quarter birthday, so we had cake," and she said, "What kind?" and I said, "Marble fudge," and she said, "Sounds yummy," and then we were silent.

I had thousands of things I wanted to say to her. Real, genuine things. But that soccer ball from the other day—I could still feel it between us. So I just picked at my food until she got up and rinsed off her plate. While she banged around at the sink, I thought about how she'd silently stood there when that ball had rolled to a stop at our feet. And I thought about how Dad had lied to me so he could slip off on his own to the garage sales. My parents had hardly tried to connect with me since I'd lost my sight.

I remembered all the smiling pictures I'd seen on the Miltons' piano lid. Mrs. Milton was involved in her kids' lives; she loved them unconditionally. The three of them were a family.

My parents and I had been sleeping under the same roof and that was it.

Could blindness make you invisible to your parents?

I blinked a couple times, took a deep breath, and, plate in hand, went to my room to finish my dinner.

37

I woke up to Mason singing in my ear. I rolled over and yawned, figuring it had to be morning because there were little splinters of light shooting through the cracks in my eyelids.

Wait. What?

My eyes flew open and I sat straight up in bed. Bold light was blasting through my room. I didn't know whether to answer the phone—which was blaring out my latest ringtone, the Loose Cannons' "Eternal Implosion"—or run to the window, so I did both.

"Hello," I said, staggering out of bed.

"Thera!" Ben said.

I looked out the window. Mason's car was parked on the street, and he was leaning against it, looking almost unjustly gorgeous. He gave me a little wave—the kind where only your fingers move. Next to him, holding a phone and wearing both cowboy pajamas and a fuzzy hat with earflaps—as though he were braving the Alaskan tundra instead of a summer night in New England—was Ben.

I looked around my room, drinking it in for a moment. It was a strange melding of past and present that somehow felt like me. I sat on the window's ledge and made a little gesture in the air like, *What are you doing here?* Into the phone, I said in a rush, "What's going on? What time is it? Is everything okay?"

"Duh. Of course everything's okay. It is four-oh-seven in the morning, and I'm taking you on a date," Ben said.

Oh, Christ. "Seriously? Where?" I said, searching for some cleanish clothes and running a hand through my bedhead.

"Surprise."

"Didn't I tell you? I don't like surprises," I told him.

"Too bad." I could hear the smile in his voice without even looking out the window.

I exhaled into the phone. "Okay. Give me a minute to get dressed. And Ben? Nice jammies." I hung up before he could answer me.

It was so much easier to get dressed when I could see what I was doing. I pulled on shorts and a T-shirt and padded downstairs, slipping out the front door and running soundlessly across the driveway. My troubles were still there, churning somewhere under the surface, but for now I was skipping over them—a rock dancing across the top of a lake.

"*Hola!*" Ben said loudly as I came to a stop in front of him.

I clamped my hand over his mouth. "Shhh. Gramps can hear like a bat. And jeesh, aren't you warm in that getup? It's, like, seventy-five degrees."

"I'm waaaay hawt, Thera," he said against my palm.

I couldn't help but smile. Looking up at Mason, I said, "It's only fair to warn you: I'm not exactly a morning person. And it's so early that it's practically yesterday."

Mason held both palms up toward me in innocence. "Not my idea, Maggie. Blame my brother."

Wally was in the back of the car. Head hanging through the open window and tongue lolling out of his mouth, he was wearing one of those monstrous dog-smiles. I shot him a look that said *If you stick your nose in my crotch, you're dead.*

We climbed into Mason's car and headed out of my neighborhood. Ben said from the front seat, "So. Thera. The thing is? I have to blindfold you."

I snorted. "Seriously?"

"Serious as a heart attack," said Ben.

I looked back and forth at the profiles of the two boys. "Am I the only one here to see the hilarity of blindfolding the blind girl?" Neither of them answered me. They both gave me identical sidelong looks of impatience. "Just saying," I mumbled. "Fine. Whatever. Blindfold me."

Ben handed me an obnoxiously orange bandanna and instructed me to put it on. We drove for what felt like hours, although it was probably only fifteen or twenty minutes. When I couldn't take it anymore, I said, "Where—"

"Patience, Thera," Ben said to me, sounding like some sort of guru.

After bumping down a dirt road, we finally came to a stop. Everyone was quiet. Even the morning seemed hushed, as though it didn't want us to know it was there.

"We're here," Ben announced.

"By 'here' you mean . . . ?"

"Richardson's Cove."

I'd never heard of the place. "Oh, well, of course. That explains everything," I said.

When Ben cracked open his door, a scent washed over me—all briny and seaweedy and thick. In the not-too-far distance, I could hear waves crashing against the beach. I slid out of the car. My flip-flops sank into sand. "Okay," I said. "So we're at the beach. Can I take off the blindfold now?"

"Nope."

I rolled my eyes. My lashes brushed against the blindfold.

"Mason. Take her hand so she doesn't fall," Ben said. "I've seen her fall, and it isn't pretty."

I'd just opened my mouth to spew out a retort when Mason took my left hand. My snappy comeback flew off into the sea breeze.

We walked over a course of sand-covered mounds before heading up a steep incline. My feet slid out of my flip-flops, so I plucked them off and carried them up the hill. I could hear Ben struggling along in his crutches. Mason slowed me to a stop and let go of my hand. Suddenly, I felt untethered. "Can I take off the—"

Ben huffed. "You're so impatient, Thera. Okay. Fine. Take it off."

I took it off.

"Ta-da!" he said with a flourish.

I was standing on top of a sand dune, looking over a tiny cove. It was probably dead dark there, but, thanks to Ben, I could see the area as though a spotlight were blasting over it. The place was small—Wally could race from one side of the cove to the other in about fifteen seconds, tops—and it was private, protected by an army of sky-high trees on one side and the ocean on the other. It was perfect.

"Wow," I said. "It's really beautiful here."

Ben shot Mason a pointed look. "Told you she'd love it." To me he said, "Dad used to take us here when we were little. We fished off that point over there. Off the rocks? So anyway. This isn't actually the surprise." He nodded at Mason.

For the first time, I noticed that Mason was carrying a dark-colored backpack. He swung it off his shoulder and unzipped it, producing a checkered blanket. He spread it on the sand.

"Lie down and shut your eyes," Ben instructed.

I growled and said, "You sure are bossy at zero dark thirty." When he pursed his lips and pointed with his eyes to the blanket, I heaved a sigh and lay down, promptly shutting my eyes. "Okay. Fine. They're closed."

There were some rustling noises, the sound of a zipper, the clink of Ben's crutches as he took them off and collapsed to my right, an enormous *swoof* as Mason sat on the other side of me, the clearing of Ben's throat, and then—

"Okay. Open your eyes," Ben said.

I didn't know what I was expecting. I guess I wasn't expecting anything in particular, which was why I was so surprised when I saw ... stars.

Ben was holding a mirror in front of my face. He had it pointing up to the sky at just the right angle, so the glittering reflections of dozens of stars were scattered across it. I hadn't seen stars in so long, it was as though they had stopped existing for me. Emotions crowded in my head. They were joy, sorrow, and wonder, all crushed into one. It took me a minute to find my voice. "Ben, I—"

"Shhh. Wait. There's more." He was still sitting beside me, holding the mirror, his expression bright and elated with whatever he saw in mine.

I lay there in silence—Mason on one side of me and Ben on the other—and watched as dawn crept across the sky, snuffing out the stars, one by one, and replacing them with fine, wispy clouds and the magentas and oranges of sunrise. *Hi, Gran,* I thought, reminded of all those sunrises I'd seen on the beach with Gran. I could almost feel her quiet presence.

Weeks ago, I'd told Ben that I missed the sky. The stars. The colors of sunrise. He'd remembered. It was so sweet and so touching and so *Ben* that I had to shut my eyes for a moment. I felt as if I were too big for my body, as if I might split somewhere in the middle and leak out all over the sand.

"Mason," Ben whispered. "Um. Is Thera crying?"

I didn't hear Mason's response, but he must've nodded.

"Is that good or bad?" Ben said in a low, concerned voice.

His voice rich and goose bump–inducing, Mason said, "Good, I think."

I felt a finger poke against my shoulder. I opened my eyes. Ben was hovering over me, worry etched into his features. "Thera," he said, "you look funny when you cry."

I laughed, sending tears scuttling down my cheeks, and then I wiped them off with the back of my hand and smiled up at him.

38

I stayed on my back, watching the sky until the yellows took it over. Ben had gone to sleep beside me. He looked several years younger in his cowboy pajamas, his mouth cracked open and his limbs spread indelicately across the blanket. Wally—caked with wet, course sand—was lying dutifully beside Ben, watching him as though standing guard, his muzzle supported by Ben's leg and his nostrils working. Mason sat on the other side of me, resting his elbow on his propped-up knee while he stared at some unknown point on the horizon. He looked as if he were in a photo shoot for *Rolling Stone* magazine. The thing I was discovering about Mason was that he didn't try to be larger than life, and this was what actually made him larger than life. He was so understated and so simple that he was grandiose.

All around us were signs of morning, seagull cries and golden light glinting off the sand and horns of nearby boats. But I felt lazy, peaceful, as though I'd just collapsed into my bed after arriving home from a long trip.

"It must've been difficult to lose your sight," Mason said. There was something about the way his words slid out of his mouth, not with pity but with understanding. The sort of understanding you only get from people who have suffered in life.

I didn't bother trying to lighten up the moment. "Yeah, it's been tough," I said. "I've had to change an awful lot of things about my life that I never thought I'd have to change."

He sat up, leaned toward me, and, suddenly looking rather boyish, said, "Are your other senses, like, supersharp now?"

I swallowed.

Jesus.

I should have told him that blindness doesn't sharpen your other senses as much as it makes you use them more, and I should have told him that my hearing was still a little sketchy compared to my sense of smell, and I should have told him that I was still lousy at telling the time of day from the way the sun felt on my skin, and I should have told him thousands upon thousands of things. But there were only a few inches between us right now, and I seemed to have lost my ability to pull a sentence from wherever sentences come from.

Realizing that I was sitting there with what I assumed was an extremely enchanting look of idiocy on my face, I finally snorted and choked out, "It doesn't exactly work like that. I just pay more attention to my other senses now."

Our eyes met for a moment and then twitched away. Needing something to do with my hands, I adjusted the mirror on my lap. And that was when I saw myself for the first time in seven months.

Sure, I'd seen my passing reflection here and there since meeting Ben. But I'd never taken the time to actually look at myself. Not like this. I barely recognized the girl blinking back at me. My hair was darker and longer than it had been the last time I'd seen it. It fell in shiny ringlets. My nose was dusted with tiny freckles. Had I always had freckles? I wasn't sure. I was struck by how much I resembled Teddy's little sister, Samantha. She was just a young me—stubborn and obnoxious and fiery. But what shocked me most were my eyes. There was a realness there that I'd never seen before, something honest and naked. Unnerved, I placed the mirror beside me.

After a space of several breaths, Mason gestured to the mirror and said, "I understand why you love the sky so much. There's something about it that gives me the impression that there's more out there. Stuff I can't see. Stuff I can't understand. It's as though the universe has a huge secret, and if I look at the sky long enough, I'll figure it out." He turned to me. "Have you ever gone skydiving?"

"Skydiving?" I repeated blankly. He was sitting so close to me that I could practically fold into his scent.

Mason laughed. "Yeah, you know," he said, "jumping out of a plane and free-falling at a hundred and twenty miles per hour?"

Suddenly I remembered the skydiving pamphlets I'd seen in his room. At the time, they hadn't fit the image of Mason I'd formed in my mind. But now I could see how he'd appreciate the absolute freedom the sky offered, if only for a minute or two. "No. Never," I said, finally answering his question. Back when I could see, I probably would have pounced on the chance to skydive. But now? It felt unnatural to even consider it.

"You'd love it," he said. "People who really love the sky? They love to skydive."

"What does it feel like?" I asked.

His face lit up. "Like nothing else. At first, your stomach completely leaves you. Then you hit terminal velocity and you're weightless. There's this tremendous wind hitting you in the face and you're just . . . there, you know? For forty-five seconds or so, you are nothing, but you are everything."

"Wow. That sounds . . ."

"Perfect," he supplied. His eyes slid down my face, clear to my lips. Suddenly I got the impression that he wasn't talking about skydiving anymore.

We looked at each other for longer than the acceptable amount of time, and then I jammed my toes into the sand and blurted, "Were you scared? The first time you jumped out of a plane?"

He blinked. Cleared his throat. "No. I did it for Dad," he said. When he saw the question mark in my expression, he went on. "Dad always wanted to go skydiving, but he died before he had the chance."

I felt as though I should say something to him like *I'm sorry for your loss* or *My condolences* or something, but those responses seemed cheesy and canned. After a substantial pause, I said quietly, "It must've been really difficult."

"Yeah. It sucked," Mason said, his voice wavering a little. "The worst thing? Watching my mom go through losing him. It sort of made me crazy, you know? I knew she was hurting, but there was nothing I could do. Nothing. And Ben . . ." His words trailed away and he shook his head. The pain in his expression was so intense that I felt as though I should turn away. But I couldn't. So I just nodded.

Mason fidgeted for a moment, glanced at his watch, and then gave Ben a little poke. "We should probably start heading home, buddy."

Ben's eyes opened to slits. "Yup. Home," he repeated, his voice gummy from sleep.

Mason helped Ben to his feet. He was right in the middle of saying, "Ben? Why don't I just carry you—" when a terrible cracking sound punctured the morning. Ben's eyes slowly, horrifically, rolled back into his skull. And he collapsed face-first into the sand.

39

I couldn't move or blink or process my thoughts. All I could do was stand there, gaping at Ben, whose right leg was twisted away from his body at an unnatural angle.

I was only partially aware of a god-awful sound—a horrible, raspy sound that I would later come to find out was Wally's barking. And there were voices. No. One voice: Mason's.

"Richardson's Cove," he said into his phone. He was talking quickly. So quickly I could hardly make out what he was saying. "One mile north of Chester Beach. It's on a gravel road off Ocean Drive. In the dunes." There was a pause in which I could swear that I heard Mason's heartbeat crashing in my ears, but it was probably mine. "How long?" Another pause. He raked a hand through his hair. "Tell them to hurry, for Christ's sake. He's only *ten*," he said, his voice pleading. He nodded as though the person on the other end of the line could see the motion, and he snapped his phone shut.

A fierce, biting sense of panic climbed up my chest and out of my mouth. "What the hell is happening?" I asked Mason, my head jerking back and forth from him to Ben. "He was just lying here, and he was fine. He was *fine*. How could he just..." My mouth wasn't working anymore. I was shaking too badly to form words.

"Maggie," Mason said, grabbing me by both shoulders. "I don't know what's wrong with him. But listen to me: you need to focus. I need your help. You have to watch Ben. Don't let him move. That's very important. I need to go to the road and wave the ambulance down. They'll be here in a few minutes." Then he was gone, his massive frame rocketing over the dunes and disappearing from sight.

Terror surged in. This could not be happening. Not to Ben. I stared down at his broken-looking frame. He looked small, crooked in all the wrong places. Mangled. I tried to swallow, but it was an incomplete motion. A choke. Crashing on my knees beside him, I cleared the sand under his face.

Tears ran down my cheeks. They plunked on the sand beside him. I leaned down so my mouth was beside his ear, and I said, "Benjamin Milton. I don't know what's going on right now, but you will not die on me. I haven't beaten you yet in Twenty-one Stones."

I didn't know what I had expected. For him to jump up and say *Gotcha*? For him to roll over and tell me that I look stupid when I cry? For him to call me Thera one more time?

Nothing happened, of course. Nothing at all.

I smoothed his hair away from his face. Against my will, I was memorizing everything about this morning—the sound of Mason's disappearing footsteps, the color fading from Ben's cheeks, the heat of the sun dying behind an unseen cloud, the low, lonely blast of a passing boat.

Everything was slipping away from me.

I prayed that Ben wouldn't.

Sirens approached, screaming their way through the morning, their sounds foreign alongside the crashing waves and seagull cries. I leaned down again. "Ben? You're going to be okay. They're coming to help you."

But even as I said it, I didn't believe it.

....

They left me there. At Richardson's Cove. I'd watched the paramedics as they'd loaded Ben onto a stretcher. I'd followed them as they'd hurried to the ambulance. I'd listened as they'd informed me that there was room for only one extra person. I'd seen Mason hesitate before climbing into the ambulance, and then he'd said, "Can you get a ride to the hospital?"

I'd just nodded.

Then they were gone. They stole Ben's light as they sped away from me.

And I was alone.

I walked my hands down the length of Mason's car until I found the door handle. It was unlocked. Legs shaking horribly, I collapsed into the backseat, leaving the door wide open.

I yanked my cell phone from my purse, intending to call Sophie, but I couldn't remember her number. I didn't know how to find it in my phone. I couldn't even recall how to use my phone.

I wasn't sure how long I sat there before I felt a breath on my leg. A paw on my foot. Wally leapt into the car and sat beside me. I didn't know where he was going with this, but I didn't move. I wanted him there. He might be the only thing holding me up. Taking a shaky breath, I used voice commands to call Sophie, but then hung up before it even started to ring, suddenly remembering that Sophie had moved.

I tried Gramps, who picked up almost immediately. Not even giving me a chance to speak, he said, "Would you people stop bothering me so goddamn early? I'm on the no-call list." And then he hung up.

Shit.

Clarissa picked up after only one ring, her voice overly chirpy and energetic. "Hi, Maggie! Wow, you're up early. I've been meaning to call you to—"

My phone made a telltale click that signified its battery had gone dead.

No no no *NO*.

I threw it and screamed a four-letter obscenity.

What the hell was I going to do? *Walk* to the hospital? I barked a derisive laugh. I could barely get down a sidewalk on my own. And besides that, I had no clue where I was. I'd worn a blindfold on the way here, so I hadn't even seen a road sign or the edge of a yard, let alone the hospital.

I buried my face in my hands and rocked back and forth, tears leaking through my fingers, my brain stuffed full of the image of Ben's broken frame, facedown in the sand. How had he gone from looking so normal, so healthy, to collapsing into a lifeless heap?

What had happened?

My hands fell to my sides and I stared off into the nothingness, wishing I hadn't dodged my last session with Hilda, wishing I'd figured out what was wrong with Ben, wishing I'd insisted on riding in the ambulance.

Wishing

I wasn't

blind.

A seagull cawed, and I swiped the wetness from my cheeks, furious with the circumstances, the morning, and, most of all, myself. For never pushing past the uncomfortable. For always taking the easy way out. For never *trying*.

Bullshit.

I slid jerkily out of the car and did the only thing left to do: I yanked my cane out of my back pocket, fished around in the backseat for Wally's leash, and started walking.

I let Wally lead, let him yank me down one quiet street after another, hoping he had an inner compass that would direct us to his family. He wasn't a guide dog by any stretch of the imagination, and he sure as hell wasn't going to protect me—he'd just as soon lick his balls as ward off an attacker—but he was tugging me persistently and that gave me hope on some obscure level.

But when I heard the familiar smack of the cove's waves, I realized we'd somehow ended up back where we'd started. I lurched to a stop and leaned over, hands on my knees, my breaths coming out in great heaves. Then I stood up and screamed, "IS ANY-BODY THERE?!!"

Nobody answered.

I held perfectly still, quieting my breathing and doing my best to gather clues from my surroundings. There was only wave after wave. A sharp, briny smell. Warm pavement on the soles of my flip-flops.

Yet.

If I really listened, I could barely make out a hum of inland traffic. Whether I was just imagining it I had no clue, but it was better than anything else I had right now, so I started walking. This time I took the lead.

The thing about walking with a cane is that you have to walk quickly if you want to stay in a straight line. And the other thing about walking with a cane is that a brisk pace tends to lead you into trouble at warp speed. So after a dozen or so steps, I turned my ankle on a wrinkle in the street and stumbled, my hands catching my weight on rough asphalt. I could've stayed down there—God, I wanted to stay down there—but I jerked back up and kept going, wiping sand and blood and chunks of pavement on my shorts and leaving the ocean behind me.

It took one hundred and twenty-three steps until a sidewalk lifted under my feet, three hundred and forty steps until a car passed by, five hundred and eleven steps until I heard the click of high heels approaching. "Excuse me," I said when the woman got close. And then I realized I had no clue what to even say. Finally I opened my mouth and asked the only question that mattered. "Can you help me get to Memorial Hospital?"

....

Probably climbing into an unknown car with an unknown woman to travel to an unknown address was the stupidest thing I'd ever done. Still, when the woman had offered to take me to the hospital, I'd climbed into her backseat with Wally without a moment's hesitation. And anyway, she'd had a kind, soft voice—a mother's voice—and so when she'd asked if I wanted a ride, my knees had gone doughy and I'd blinked away tears. All I'd done was nod.

And now, as I stood frozen in front of Memorial Hospital, I was all too aware that the place was lit up like a Christmas tree that had been decorated by a four-year-old. All the lights were jammed up in clumps. The places where patients were dying, I presumed. The ICU and the ER, et cetera. A siren shrieked in the distance—getting louder and louder as it approached. Beside me, Wally whined.

How long had it been since Ben had arrived? Two hours? Five? Did the doctors know what was wrong with him?

Was he alive?

The ambulance sped past, lit up by whatever tragedy it carried, and I followed it to the emergency room, tying Wally's leash to a pole outside the building and walking inside. The burnished light of heartbreak illuminated the place perfectly. Mason was not in the waiting room. Whether that was good or bad, I didn't know.

"Can I help you?" the receptionist asked as I approached the desk.

I ran a shaky hand along my forehead. "I'm looking for Ben Milton," I said, a gale of emotion crashing into my chest as I said his name. My next words tumbled out as part of my breath. "He came in by ambulance and he was really sick and I need to know how he is."

She blinked at me for a moment and then asked whether I was a relative, and I—stupidly—replied by saying, "I'm a friend," to

which she replied by saying, "Then I cannot give you any information on his status," to which I replied by saying, "Well, that's
complete horseshit," to which she replied by telling me to sit down
and wait.

And that was that.

I collapsed into a plastic chair next to a little girl—a couple years
old, maybe?—who stared at me with blatant shock. I looked like
I'd just gotten out of an exorcism, no doubt. Rangy, frizzed-out
hair. Puffy eyes. Banged-up knees. Bloody palms. I smiled weakly
at her. She scrambled into her mother's lap, casting uncertain looks
at me over her shoulder.

Seconds turned into minutes. Minutes into days.

Finally, when I couldn't take it anymore, I walked back to
the receptionist and said in an apologetic tone, "Um. Could you
maybe send out a family member to tell me what's going on?"

She gave me a curt nod and picked up her phone.

This time I didn't sit down. I literally couldn't. My feet were
cinder blocks on the floor as I stood in place and stared at the
double doors that led to the ward.

My breath hitched when Mason came out. His lips were drawn
in a tight line, tension in every slope of his body. His eyes met
mine for only a fraction of a second, and then they shot to the
floor. He said, "I have bad news."

40

Mason led me to a quiet corner of the waiting room. I didn't know how I managed to walk, only that I did. He opened his mouth and then let it drift shut. Then he opened it again and said, "You were right. Ben's . . ." He swallowed. Looked at the floor again. I groped for the wall. *You aren't going to throw up,* I told myself, and because I'd always been an ace liar, even to myself, I didn't hurl. Finally Mason blurted, "Ben's leg broke spontaneously because he has a rare form of bone cancer."

My throat was closing up. Getting sucked into my chest. "Bone cancer?" I breathed. "Wouldn't someone have known that by now? Wouldn't he be sick?"

Mason sighed. "Doc said that most people would've known. Patients with bone cancer usually have pain around the tumor. But remember, Ben has spina bifida, and his legs—"

"Aren't normal," I murmured.

He nodded and glanced out the window. His frowning reflection stared back at him.

"How bad?" I said shrilly. "How bad is it?"

"They need to amputate his leg," Mason said without looking at me. He kicked the wall with the toe of his boot a couple times. "But his fracture caused a fatty clot to travel to his lungs, and they can't take his leg until his lungs are stabilized. It's too risky. Mom is—Mom is not doing well. She's in the restroom trying to get herself back together."

"That doesn't answer my question, Mason."

His eyes finally met mine. I stared into them, to where Mason's emotion was a silent film. Heartbreak. Misery. Guilt. Despair. He whispered, "It doesn't look good."

I collapsed into a chair, realization coiling around me, squeezing my throat, stealing my breath. I should have known. It was so goddamn simple that I'd missed it completely. All the signs were right in front of me this entire time, and I'd been too distracted to see them.

I traced my memory back a couple years, to when I was sitting beside Gramps at our kitchen table, the contents of a bag of cookies from Big Dough scattered in front of us. It was as though my favorite aisle of the grocery store had coughed up everything worth a crap, and it had all landed on our table: double chocolate crinkle, oatmeal raisin, snickerdoodle, and brownie crinkle. All of them smelled amazing. But then, cookies are like massages—even the lousy ones are good.

Gramps had just come from some old woman's funeral, and to my irritation he was describing it in detail—the color of the casket, the ridiculous sushi at the wake, and the brown dress the dead woman had worn. And then he started talking about the woman's dog.

"Her mutt knew she had cancer," he told me. "Sniffed it out."

"C'mon, Gramps. That's ridiculous. Dogs aren't that smart," I said, shoving half a cookie in my mouth.

"Didn't say they were smart. Said they could smell cancer. Eloise's dog followed her everywhere. Even to the bathroom. Kept sticking his nose in her hair. Staring at her. Turned out, the old bat had brain cancer. But she didn't go to the doctor till it was too late." When I gave him a disbelieving sigh, he said, "Saw a documentary on it once. Science channel. Even a wiener dog has twenty-five times more scent receptors than a human. If something is wrong, they can smell it."

Now, as I sat on that cold plastic chair in the emergency room, I knew that I should have figured it out long ago. Ever since I'd known Ben, Wally had been following him around, staring at him, his nose always near Ben's leg—the one that was currently broken. Wally's behavior had seemed off to me, yet I could never quite put a finger on it.

Correction: I'd never *tried* to put a finger on it.

A continent's worth of guilt crushed my chest.

Mason squatted down in front of me, concerned. "Maggie?"

I squeezed my eyes shut. I couldn't let him see it in me—all my mistakes, all my secrets, all my fears.

He waited for me to say something, and when I didn't, he unloaded beside me, wrapping an arm over my shoulder and pulling me toward him.

. . . .

As I walked down the main corridor in the emergency room, I could see a tall male nurse bent over a computer, and I could see the stiff set of Mason's shoulders as he gestured to Ben's room and then took off to find his mother, and I could see the sickly yellow color on the walls, and I could see a massive whiteboard scrawled with patients' last names and bed numbers.

But I wasn't ready to see Ben.

I hitched to a stop just inside Ben's room, facing an olive-green curtain that had been yanked closed. The place reeked of medicines, fake clean, and sickness. Behind the curtain, a machine counted off heartbeats in a series of beeps. Twelve of them blared into the room before a passing nurse lightly touched my elbow and said, "Miss? Are you okay?" I swallowed and moved my head in a vague way. She took it as a yes. She was wrong.

Taking in a breath and letting it out slowly through my nose, I stepped forward and pulled the curtain aside.

I swayed on my feet.

Ben's skinny frame was splayed immodestly upon the bed. He looked broken, his parts slightly askew, as though he'd been dropped onto the bed all the way from the tenth floor.

His skin was shiny and mannequin-like against his pale blue hospital gown, and his mouth was lolled open in a sideways position that advertised complete and utter unconsciousness. He drew air into his lungs in long, rattling gasps.

"Ben," I whispered. Or at least I'd meant to whisper. The word was just a movement on my lips, a sound that never made it past my throat.

The room was perversely vivid—like I was viewing the scene through a camera lens that emphasized every detail, every fingerprint on the bed railing, every minute skid on the floor, every speck of dust on the window. If Ben weren't lying in the middle of it all, looking so damaged, it would be desperately, achingly beautiful.

Clamping my hands in my armpits to keep them from shaking, I took a small step forward and said, "Ben? Can you hear me?"

Ben didn't stir. There was no sound except his labored breathing.

"You were wrong, you know," I told him. "Swimming isn't your Thing. It never was. Not really. Your Thing isn't just one Thing, but a lot of Things—being part of a bigger whole, letting others have the glory, proving you're capable and strong and intelligent."

I looked up at the ceiling and blinked several times, trying to clear my vision. "Your Thing is treading carefully through life, refusing to hurt anyone or anything." My voice cracked horribly. I brushed away a tear that was scuttling down my cheek before going on. "Somewhere inside of you, you notice *this is good*. And so, you swim. You swim to show everyone that, although you don't always get to choose your circumstances, you can always choose what you notice in them."

I'd been doing a lot of thinking about my Thing. What Ben had really been asking me all this time was not *What is your Thing?* but instead *How do you connect with this world?* And I hadn't had an answer for him because I'd been steamrolling through life, moving too hastily and too indignantly and too . . . well, blindly, to notice anything of value.

Swaying, I collapsed in the chair beside the bed. Ben's eyes opened and focused on me. "Thera," he breathed. His voice was weak. Raspy. All wrong. I couldn't help but compare him to the tiny dog that Mason and I had picked up on the side of the road. Both of them put off the same quiet air of death.

I wiped my hands on my shorts. "Hey, kid," I said, trying to answer as if things were perfectly normal. But my words sounded as though they had come from someone else's mouth.

"Come closer," he said. At first, I thought he was going to ask me to kiss him again, but then I realized he was trying to tell me a secret. "I overheard Mom talking to the doctor. He thinks I might not make it." Everything inside me collapsed, and I fell back in my chair, unable to speak. Ben's eyes drifted shut. For a moment, I thought he'd gone to sleep, but then, his eyes still closed, he said, "But I think it's bullshit."

"You're too young to cuss," I told him, just like I'd been telling him for weeks now. Except now it felt as though I were getting run over by a freight train as I said it.

True to form, he ignored my words. He opened his eyes and pulled his brows together for a long stretch of time. "I don't feel like I'm dying," he whispered finally. "I just feel like I'm fading away."

I started to crumble. My chin was doing that wobbling thing it does right before I totally lose it. "Ben, I—"

Ben breathed out, a hot, sticky breath that curled around my nose and left me feeling paralyzed in the chair. In a small voice that skirted sleep, he said, "If I die, I'm okay with you and Mason hanging out. I can tell he likes you. His eyes smile whenever you're around."

I wiped a solitary tear from my cheek and said, "Well, that's mighty generous of you." But he didn't hear me. He was already slipping away into unconsciousness.

. . . .

I'd never been a particularly religious person, but if there was ever a time to become an armchair spiritualist, this was it. I was sort of desperate. So I walked purposefully to the front desk and asked for directions to the hospital's chapel.

I could see every step on the way there, a fact I tried to ignore as I took the stairs up one floor and lumbered down the white-tiled hallway to the chapel. For the past seven and a half months, all I'd wanted was to have my sight back. It had been an itch that I'd scratched and scratched until it bled all over my life. But now, having my eyesight was nothing but a constant reminder of loss, heartache, and crappy decisions. Now, it felt like a curse.

I rested one palm on the chapel door and closed my eyes. Standing in the familiar absence of light, I inhaled slowly, trying to collect myself. Eyes still closed, I pushed open the door and stepped inside. All I could smell was carpet cleaner and candle wax and broken dreams. I brushed the back of my hand over my eyes and then opened them. The place looked like a miniature church, almost too scaled down to be real.

Still, I felt strangely humbled as the door clicked shut behind me and I stood there in the silence. Chewing on the side of my lip, I shifted my weight several times, not sure what I should be doing. Did I really belong here? Seriously? I certainly wasn't fooling the Big Man Upstairs. By now, He had to be on to me. In fact, I was half-surprised I hadn't burst into flames the second I'd walked in.

Taking several steps forward, I collapsed in the backmost pew and dropped my head in my hands. My choppy breaths echoed off the walls. I felt as though my past had been chasing me and chasing me, and it had finally caught up.

"Thera, I don't think church is your Thing" was what Ben would say if he were sitting beside me right now.

A single tear slid down my cheek, all the way to my chin. Swiping it away with the back of my hand, I choked back a sob. I'd experienced pain in my life. Plenty of it. But never anything like this.

Months ago, when Gramps took me to the ER, my head rupturing with a meningitis headache, the nurse asked me whether I needed pain medication. I hadn't known how to answer her. I was tough, for Pete's sake. A Sanders. Sanders women got the wind knocked out of them, broke their bones, won games at all costs, and laughed in the face of pain. So my answer had been no, which had been an all-out lie.

But what I'd felt then was nothing. A paper cut. A stomachache after eating too much. A stubbed toe.

Now I was in agony.

Now I was an open wound.

I could not stop seeing Ben's face. I could not stop thinking that I was to blame for what was happening to him. I could not move. I could not breathe. I felt terrified, like I'd just been yanked into a dark alley and there was a knife at my throat.

Squeezing my eyes together, I started to pray. Plead, actually. I'd been there for probably close to a half hour when the door creaked open and Mason's loud, heavy-booted footsteps clunked toward me. Neither of us looked at each other as he sat down silently beside me.

Heat and indignation flared inside of me. "You want to know what I was doing today?" I screeched. "I was at the hospital! Ben Milton is dying. *Dying*. So, yeah, I was gone all day. And yeah, I forgot to let you guys know where I was." I knew that I should stop right here, that I was stepping into a place that would hold me hostage, but I went on anyway, my voice loud and accusing. "I'm surprised you two even realized I was gone."

"*Of course* we realized you were gone," Mom sputtered. "We're always looking out for you."

"Are you, Mom?" I said shrilly. "Are you *really*?" I could feel my eyes starting to well up. I didn't want to start crying, but there was too much hurt and resentment inside me, and I couldn't hold it in anymore. So I let the tears come, and I said it. I said the thing that had been eating at me for months on end. "What about when I was in that hospital bed? Were you looking out for me then?" I screamed. My breathing was rasping, choppy. I worked hard to get my next words to sound angry and loud and accusing, but they came out as nothing but a whispered, pitiful sob. "What sort of mother does that? What sort of mother just takes off when her kid is half-dead in the hospital?"

For several heartbeats, there was no sound but the hum of the air-conditioning. Then I heard Mom's voice, barely even a shocked whisper: "How do you know about that?"

"God, Mom, does it really matter?" I said, slapping the tears away from my cheeks. I groped for the wall to steady myself as I yanked off my flip-flops, one at a time, throwing them on the floor. Then I spun on one heel and stalked toward the stairs.

Dad bellowed in protest and my mother snatched my arm. I could sense her outrage filling the room clear to the ceiling. "You

41

It was almost midnight and Ben's condition hadn't changed, so Mason dropped me off at home for a couple hours of sleep. As I hauled myself through the front door, where my parents were waiting, Mom gasped, and Dad, his anger louder than his words, said, "Maggie, we were about to call the police. Where have you been?"

I ran an exhausted hand through my hair. I hadn't thought about my parents the entire day, hadn't even considered calling them before my phone had died. "I'm sorry," I said. "A friend of mine came by early this morning and—"

"Do you know how your father spent his day?" Mom said, her voice unsteady. "Driving the streets, looking for you. You could have at least *called*, Maggie."

I was too tired for this. "My phone died again, and—"

"Right. Your phone died," Mom said, not even giving me the chance to explain.

are not leaving this room, young lady," she snapped, and I could tell by her tone that I'd gone too far, that I'd tripped over some invisible line, and now she was furious. Sternly, with terse enunciation, she said, "In fact, you are not leaving this house at all—not tomorrow, not the next day, and not the day after that."

I twisted my arm free. "You've got to be kidding me," I said, shaking my head. "You're *grounding* me because I was at the hospital today with a dying ten-year-old?" I laughed without humor. "This is great. You two have finally found something I don't want to lose, something you can take away from me."

"Oh, come off it," Dad scoffed.

I whirled toward him. "No, I won't *come off it*. It's true and you know it. Until now, you've had nothing to ground me from."

"As parents," my mother cut in, her voice still sharp, "our job is to protect you from yourself. And that is what we are doing. You need to work on yourself. You need to start moving on with *your* life. You need to deal with your own problems instead of obsessing over a sick child."

I barked a derisive laugh. "*You're* preaching to me about moving on?" I threw my hands up in the air like I was giving up, and in a certain way, I was. And maybe they were as well, because they said nothing to me as I stomped up the stairs and slammed the door to my room.

....

When I climbed into bed that night I felt dirty, like I'd committed several unspeakable crimes. All I wanted to do was crawl into the shower and scrub myself until my skin was raw, to wash the memories and the hurt and the damage off my body. But I was too exhausted to stand, too exhausted to move, really, so instead I fell into bed, tumbling into a deep, empty sleep—the sort of sleep you have when you need protection from your own thoughts. When I woke the next morning I found myself dressed and sitting in a full bathtub. Apparently, I'd taken up sleepwalking again.

I toweled off and padded downstairs to the laundry room. Leaning against the dryer as my water-heavy clothes flopped around inside it, I debated whether I should go back to bed. I wasn't going back to sleep, so what was the use? I felt as though I'd arrived at a dentist appointment two hours early and I had nothing to do but plant my ass in one of their uncomfortable, fake-leather chairs and wait for my root canal.

I slipped into my room before my parents got up. I didn't want to run into them, and I didn't want to listen to their voices, and I didn't want to think about the things I'd said to them.

I spent the next three days either in my room or in the basement, avoiding my parents, playing my song again and again until my fingers were chafed and sore, and sagging over my cell phone as I waited for Mason to call with updates on Ben.

The first day: Ben's doctor amputated his leg.

The second day: Ben spiked a fever.

The third day: they were still awaiting the lab results to learn how far Ben's cancer had spread.

The fourth day: Ben was getting transferred to another hospital.

"Why is he getting transferred?" I asked Mason when he told me, jerking ramrod straight on the edge of my bed.

"I'm not really sure," Mason said, and I heard his car door slam. "I'm walking in there now, so if I cut out just know that the reception sucks here." He sighed heavily, not speaking for several long moments. I could hear his boots clunking down a tile floor. "He seems in such terrible shape to be transferred right now. I mean, he's so weak and sick, barely hanging on, and now they've put him—"

The line crackled.

"Mason? Are you there?"

Nothing.

He'd lost reception.

My hand shook as I hit the END button on my phone. All I could think about were the last words he'd said. Ben was in terrible shape. He was weak. Sick. Barely hanging on.

And it was my fault.

I collapsed on my bed, curling up in a tight ball and letting the guilt come. Weeks of it, hurricanes of it, slammed against me in staggering waves of nausea and remorse and shame. Fact was, I'd known all along that something was off, known there was a reason I was seeing Ben, and I hadn't bothered to find out what it was.

I hadn't even *tried*.

It was the same thing I'd done with my friendships, the same thing I'd done with my piano lessons, the same thing I'd done with practically everything I'd struggled with in life. It was half-assed and it was lazy, and the realization of it pinned me to the bed until I could hardly breathe.

All I could see was Ben, his skin pallid and plastic-looking, asking just one question: *Wasn't I worth the effort?*

Choking for air, I staggered upright and across the room. With shaking hands I grappled with the screen and shoved it outside, letting it tumble to the ground. Then I thrust my head out and gulped in the air. The evening was cool and breezy. Somewhere up there were billions of stars, whirling in a celestial merry-go-round. Maybe if I could see them right now I wouldn't feel so forgotten, so alone. I shut my eyes, trying to replicate the feeling of absolute belonging I'd had at the beach when I'd seen the stars, but I knew I couldn't. Perfect moments like that couldn't be duplicated. They could only be remembered. I sat down hard on the windowsill as my breathing slowed.

I needed a friend.

Sliding my phone from my pocket, I did the one thing I hadn't done since I lost my sight: I reached out for help.

42

Ben was fighting for his life, I'd been avoiding my parents for days on end, I'd gotten about fifteen hours of sleep over the course of a week, and yet here I was with Clarissa at my kitchen counter, in front of a couple dozen cupcakes. Just beyond these walls, the sky was dark and churning, gaining the strength of a category-five hurricane, but right now I was safeguarded by frosting and butter and chocolate.

I'd never called Clarissa for anything other than to discuss schoolwork or the Loose Cannons, and it had felt strange doing it today. I'd nearly hung up when her line had started ringing. But then I'd realized: backing away from the uncomfortable, the difficult, was the exact reason my life was such a catastrophe. So I'd taken a deep breath and invited her over.

"Absolutely," she'd bellowed into the receiver. "I'm totally free.

Cupcakes! I'll bring cupcakes for brain food." She paused for a moment. "Um. We're finishing up our research paper, right?"

"Nah. Not really. I mean, only as far as my parents are concerned, seeing that I'm grounded."

"Yuh-oh," she breathed. "What happened?"

It had felt right, telling Clarissa. I'd let it tumble out of me in a knotty, trembling mess. Not all of it. God, not all of it. If I'd told her I could see the dying, she'd likely think I'd gone straightjacket. I'd told her only the parts that mattered: Ben's illness, my crappy relationship with my parents, my wrecked friendships.

And now, a sea of cupcakes in front of me, I was surprised to discover that I felt slightly better, that I'd talked my way into a place where I could breathe again. I could almost ignore the sharp, insistent poke of my phone in my back pocket, awaiting Mason's update.

Almost.

All the same, Clarissa was doing a pretty good job sidetracking me. "Here, try this," Clarissa said through a full mouth, stuffing a cupcake in my hand. "Turtle brownie with cheesecake buttercream: the wind beneath the wings of many a grounded girl."

"Clarissa," I said, running my hand around the side of the cupcake, "did you take a bite out of this before you gave it to me?"

"They say that the first bite is the best," Clarissa said by means of answering. "That you get ninety-nine-point-something percent of your enjoyment out of that one mouthful, and then everything after that is just *eating*, not *enjoying*. I know, right? It's so true!" Her palms slapped down on the counter. "And so: yes. I will take a bite out of every cupcake on this table, and then I will pass them along to you. I will spend this entire time savoring, while you . . ."

"Eat your leftovers," I finished.

She snorted and bumped me with her shoulder. "But you have to admit: best leftovers *ever.*"

I laughed. She had me there.

We ate in silence for a minute or two. There was something peaceful about it, that silence—just the two of us hunkering down in a sea of sugar, an uncertain world swirling outside.

Clarissa handed me another one-bite cupcake. "So," she said. "Mason Milton, huh?"

The proverbial record scratched.

I cleared my throat, working to keep my voice even. "Yeah. I mean, like I said—he's Ben's brother. So, yeah." I shoved nearly the entire cupcake in my mouth so I didn't have to say anything else.

"Hum," she said after a tick or two, and I squirmed like someone had just dropped a pinecone down the back of my shorts. "By the way you talk about Mason, I can tell you really like him."

I swallowed, opened my mouth to lie to her, but then stopped. "Yeah. I do," I said, surprising myself a little. This was the first time I'd admitted it out loud, and the relief was immediate, a heaviness tumbling off my chest.

"Maybe you need to step up your game?" Clarissa said.

I snorted, swiped my index finger across the top of a cupcake, and tried the frosting. "He has a girlfriend," I said around my finger.

A model.

From New York City.

Whom I despised out of principle.

"All the more reason," Clarissa chirped. "Let him know he's wasting his time with that harlot."

I barked out a laugh. I was really starting to like this girl. "Maybe I will," I said. "What about you? Any luck with Iced Coffee Guy?"

She paused for a moment and then said, "Well, I talked to him. Like, for real talked to him."

"*And?*"

Her voice overly loud and forced-chipper, she said, "Turns out that he's twenty-nine. And married."

"Oh God."

She cleared her throat. "Yeah. It's . . . yeah. I mean, it's totally fine. It isn't the first time I made a crap decision based on erroneal information."

I smirked. "Erroneous. Erroneous information."

"Right. That's what I said, isn't it? Anyway. It's just . . . It would be so much easier sometimes if I could see, you know? Even a little bit. Or maybe . . ." She sucked in a breath and let it out loudly. "Maybe see everything, just once, so I could always remember how beautiful it is. So I could understand *what* it is. You know what I mean?"

All this time I'd thought life had been easier for her. But the truth was, she'd never see a color or a tree or even her own face. And yet, she was still happy. Borderline crazy, yes, but happy. "Yeah," I whispered. "I do know what you mean. You want your one bite of the cupcake."

She sighed. "Exactly."

Just then, my phone vibrated sharply in my back pocket, rattling against the stool like automatic gunfire.

"Maggie," Clarissa said, "is that your phone?"

I swallowed. "Yeah," I said, pulling it out of my pocket. It shook in my palm, insistent.

"Um. Aren't you going to answer it?"

Realizing I'd been holding my breath, I exhaled. "Right. Of course." I fumbled for the TALK button and squawked a hello.

A female voice, unfamiliar and detached: "Is this Maggie Sanders?"

Dread pooled in my chest, black and thick and endless. "Yes?" I breathed.

"This is Saint Jude's, calling on behalf of the Milton family. They need you here immediately."

43

My entire world caught in my throat.

"Is . . . is something wrong?" I whispered through unmoving lips.

Silence swallowed up the line. Finally the woman said, "I'm sorry, but since you aren't a relative, I'm not at liberty to give you that information. I'll let the family know you've received their message. Good-bye."

"Wait!" I yelled. "Ben Milton—is he okay?"

No answer.

"Hello?"

She was gone. The line was dead.

My fingers went cold. I couldn't release my grip on the phone. Seconds ticked by. I knew I had to think, knew I had to do something, but the woman's words were still ringing shrilly inside my skull, a terrifying echo. Finally, I forced my fingers to bend, to find Mason's number in my phone. My call went straight to voice mail.

Slowly, and with sharp articulation, I said to Clarissa, "We have to get to Saint Jude's."

And then slowly, and with sharp articulation, I thought, *Ben is dying.*

"Saint Jude's," Clarissa repeated woodenly.

I fell to my knees and swept my hands back and forth on the tile, frantically searching for my shoes. "Yes, it's a hospital."

Clarissa cleared her throat. "Right. That's what I thought. I'm pretty sure I've heard Dad mention it before. And every time I ride the bus, I—"

"Can you call him? Your dad? And see if he can give us a ride?"

"He's in surgery this afternoon," Clarissa said. The cadence and tone of her speech were all wrong. Flat and uniform. "Can you call your parents?"

"No," I said quickly, finally finding one shoe. I crawled forward, searching for the other one, banging my head into the kitchen cabinet. "No. I'm grounded, remember?"

"Your grandpa?"

"Out of town. At the horse races."

"Okay," Clarissa said in that same foreign tone. "Then we'll take the bus. You live in Bedford Estates, right? Do you know how to get to the bus stop on Sycamore? Bus Seven routes through there every twenty minutes."

I used to play soccer at a park on Sycamore when I was little. I'd seen that bus stop probably a thousand times in my life. It was two blocks from my house. "Yeah. I can find it," I said as I found my other shoe. I lurched up and jammed it on my foot.

"Okay, I'm pretty sure Bus Seven stops at Saint Jude's."

"You're *pretty sure*?" I screeched.

I heard Clarissa swallow. "Yeah. I mean, I've heard the bus driver call out the stop before, and there can't be two Saint Jude's, right?"

"Right. Let's go." Pushing back my anxiety as much as possible, I concentrated on each step—getting out of the house, making my way down the driveway, finding the sidewalk, crossing the first intersection, rounding the corner to Sycamore.

The bus stop was eerily quiet. Standing by the curb, I listened desperately for an approaching bus and punched in Mason's number again and again.

Voice mail. Voice mail. Voice mail. Voice mail.

I stuffed my phone back in my shorts and pressed the round button on the face of my watch. Two fifteen.

Stay alive, Ben.

"How do you know Bus Seven even comes through here?" I blurted, starting to panic.

"O and M," Clarissa said, and I wanted to shake her and tell her to speak normally. "I've had heaps of sessions here. Wait—I think the bus is coming."

The bus's brakes shrieked as it halted at the curb. Clarissa snatched my hand and dragged me along the length of the bus, presumably looking for the door. Coming to a quick halt, she said, "Excuse me, this is Bus Seven, right?" When a rumbly-voiced male made an affirmative noise, she yanked me on board, paid the driver, and moved skillfully down the aisle, apologizing occasionally to the other passengers as she tapped her way down the walkway and found two empty seats.

Say what you would about Clarissa, but she knew what she was doing.

"How'd you learn to do all this?" I asked as we sat down.

Her leg bounced up and down beside mine. "O and M taught me the basics. But that only takes you so far. So once I got out on my own, I mostly learned by screwing up." Her hyper, manic tone was back, just a little, and I exhaled at the sound of it. "I mean, you take the wrong bus, go the wrong direction a few times, look idiotic once in a while, but you figure it out. Kind of like life, I guess?"

Yeah. Kind of like life.

I exhaled loudly. I might've been getting around on my own now, too, had I put any effort into it. I'd spent so much time fighting Hilda, fighting being blind.

As if that were the worst thing out there.

I rubbed my forehead with my fist. I couldn't just stand still anymore and let everything steamroll over me. There were people relying on me right now, things I needed to do, a life I needed to live.

The bus lurched to a stop and the doors coughed open. "Merriweather Mall," the bus driver drawled. In the aisle, passengers bumped slowly past me. I dialed Mason again. Voice mail. Wiping the sweat from my forehead, I checked my watch. Two forty-five.

Time seemed to be speeding up.

"We should be there soon," Clarissa said.

"Right," I said, twisting my hands together in my lap and keeping them that way. There was no music in my head right now, nothing to keep my hands occupied.

"Civic Center," the bus driver called out lazily as we slowed to a stop again. Someone wearing flowery cologne moseyed past me. I heard the door wheeze shut, but we sat there for a painfully long time before we crept forward, seemingly one car length at a time. I tightened my grip on my cane.

Stay alive, Ben.

The thought was weak now, a guilty whisper, and I reached in my pocket and turned off my phone, suddenly terrified that Mason would call and tell me otherwise.

"Saint Jude's," the bus driver said, and it had no sooner come out of his mouth than I jerked to my feet and scrambled down the aisle. Clarissa called out in my wake as I lurched down the steps and took off, leaving her behind.

....

I couldn't see Saint Jude's, but I stumbled forward anyway, snatching a passerby and pleading for help to find the lobby. Once inside, I twisted around in staggering circles, praying for a speck of eyesight.

I saw nothing.

"Welcome to Saint Jude's. Can I help you?" said a pleasant female voice from somewhere in front of me.

I scrambled forward, slamming hard into a counter. "Imlooking-forBenMiltonsroom," I said, my words all coming out in one breath.

"Excuse me?"

I put my palms flat on the counter. Leaned forward. "I am

looking"—I paused, trying to control my inhalations, trying to calm down—"for Ben Milton's room."

"Let me check," she said haltingly. For a moment, the only sound was the snapping of computer keys. Then: "First floor. Room one-oh-two, straight past this counter, second door on the left. Would you like some—"

I lurched away. My feet felt slow, like I was trying to trudge through deep, damp sand. People were everywhere, it seemed, wandering slowly down the corridor. Bumping into them, I apologized and then wedged myself past. I found the wall with my left hand and kept walking, images of Ben blurring together in my mind.

Stay alive, Ben.

It wasn't even a thought anymore. It was a prayer.

My fingers skipped over the first doorjamb. I jerked to a stop. Took a wobbly step backward. Slid a flat palm up the wall until I found the number plate for the room. My fingers skimmed over the braille. Room 101.

Ben's room was next door. And I still couldn't see.

Something was clawing at my stomach, my chest, my heart. I couldn't breathe. Tears tumbled down my cheeks. I pitched forward, running my hand along the wall until I found the next doorjamb, the next number plate.

Room 102.

I froze. Someone was crying in the room. It was Mrs. Milton, her muffled sobs drifting out of the room and floating around me.

The moment was hopelessly huge, and it seized me so quickly, so severely, so unlike anything else I'd ever known, I felt like I'd flatten beneath the weight of it. My cane fell to the floor. It rolled away, a long, drawn-out tinny sound trailing off behind me. I stood completely still, rooted in the emptiness, feeling as if something were crushing me, squeezing the air from my lungs. Something massive and unyielding.

Ben was dead.

44

My knees buckled and I collapsed to the floor.

No.

I thought this as forcibly as I could, so I could make it true. Ben couldn't be gone because I could still feel his kindness, and I could still feel his smile, and I could still feel all the beautiful things he'd done for me. I could still feel *him*.

I wasn't in a hospital, unable to see. I was stuck in some horrific dream. I'd wake up any second now, roll out of bed, take a shower, have breakfast, and ask Gramps to drop me off at Ben's. Ben would be home and I'd see him, because he'd be alive.

A speaker system blared overhead—a page for an X-ray tech. "No," I whispered. I felt my chin wobble, felt my lungs closing up, felt hopelessness surging in. I wrapped my arms around my stomach and rocked back and forth on the hallway floor. If I had any sense about me, I would've known I was in shock. I couldn't grasp any thoughts. They were all slippery, dark, transient, sliding through my fingers before I could get purchase of them.

My head jerked up as I heard footsteps coming down the corridor. A gurney's wheels on tile floor. Chatter. Banter. Laughter. Staggering slightly, I lurched to my feet, wiping the wetness from my cheeks and glaring into the void. There were only three cards in my verbal Rolodex right now, and all of them were printed with four-letter words.

That was when I heard one voice.

One familiar voice that brought back memories of laughter and video games and Doritos and stars.

"Thera?"

The voice was horribly weak and slurred, but it was Ben's.

I sucked in the sort of breath you take when you're swimming and come up to the water's surface in dire need of air. Ben was *alive*?

The gurney bumped past me and into the room. Groping for the doorjamb, I teetered there for the length of several heartbeats, confused. Dizzy. Inside the room were scuffles and grunts. More chatter. More laughter. The nurses were doing something. Transferring Ben to his bed? Then they breezed past me in a sea of babble, taking off down the hall. Mrs. Milton captured me in a quick hug. "Isn't it wonderful?" she blubbered.

But she was still crying.

Nothing was making sense.

Mrs. Milton let go of me, blew her nose in one loud honk, and then announced that since Ben was so groggy she was heading to the cafeteria for a quick bite.

As the hallway swallowed up her footsteps, I lurched into the room, slamming into Mason, who grunted his surprise. Taking a fistful of his shirt for balance, I hissed, "Mason, what the hell is going on?"

"Didn't the nurse tell you everything when she called?" Mason said, sounding confused.

My words started coming out quickly, separated by sharp breaths. "All she told me was that I needed to come to the hospital—and she wouldn't tell me why because I'm not family—and I couldn't get a hold of you because your cell coverage is lousy here—and I had to find the bus stop—and then when I got here the halls were so crowded and I couldn't see anything—Mason, *I can't see anything—*"

"Oh God," he breathed. "You thought..." He was supporting my weight now. Muttering a low oath under his breath, he went on. "I *knew* I should've just gone outside and called you myself instead of asking the nurse to do it. Mom convinced me to have the nurse call; she said it would be the simplest, quickest way to get you here to celebrate with us."

Celebrate? "Mason, I can't *see.*"

"That's because Saint Jude's is a rehab hospital."

It was like he was speaking a foreign language. "A rehab hospital?"

"Yeah," he said. "I didn't know that, either, when Ben was first admitted." He exhaled loudly. "Anyway, he got a lot of rest overnight. Between that and the good news, he's really starting to come around."

"Good news?" I murmured.

Mason's voice was dreamlike, almost hypnotic, as he said, "Ben's lab results came back today. The surgery removed virtually all the cancer. They're still running tests—I mean, he just came back from some sort of scan? So I guess we'll have to wait for those results, too, but right now things are looking good. Much better than the doctor had expected. He'll still need chemo, radiation, but his chances are good."

I couldn't let myself believe it. Not yet. I whispered, "But your mom was *crying*, Mason."

"She's a crier," he explained. "Happy tears, sad tears. You name it. Maggie," he said in my ear, and suddenly I was painfully, exquisitely aware that I was smashed up against him. "The doctor told us that Ben's chances of survival are seventy percent."

"And I can't see him," I murmured. I could come up with only one theory for these two things occurring in tandem. A theory so perfect that I could hardly even consider it.

Something warm was mushrooming in my heart. Something like hope.

"Thera," Ben slurred from across the room. "You just gonna stand there and slobber all over my brother or are you gonna come over and say hi?"

Mason and I sprang apart guiltily. I stepped forward, banging into Ben's bed rails. "Hey, Ben," I said, trying to sound as normal as possible but failing miserably. My brain kept repeating two words, over and over. *Seventy percent.*

But I knew otherwise. His chances were 100 percent because

I

could

not

see

him.

"Thera," Ben garbled. "You look like crap."

I laughed loudly, a combination of Ben's exclamation-point laugh and my own laugh. I liked the sound of it. "I imagine you do as well," I said, "but I can't see you."

Ben was quiet as he processed this information. "You can't?" he said finally.

I shook my head.

"Then I feel the need to inform you," he said, slurred yet serious, "that I'm the best-looking guy in the room."

45

Clarissa caught up with me a few minutes later, after Ben had drifted off to sleep. Mason gave us both a ride home, dropping Clarissa off first. He covered my hand with his as we pulled out of Clarissa's driveway, his skin sending me message after message—*I'm sorry for what you went through today* and *You're important to me* and *I care about you.*

"How are you doing?" he said softly, his thumb tracing tiny circles on my palm.

"Fine," I basically yelled. I cleared my throat. "I mean—Ben is okay, so I'm better than I've been in a long time." Understatement of the millennium. The sensation of his skin moving on mine was overwhelming, like nothing I'd ever felt before. Was he just being supportive and kind? Probably.

Didn't matter. My entire body was detonating.

"The thing is," Mason explained, "you won't be able to see anymore."

I started to refute this but then promptly stopped. He was right. Unless I deliberately hung around emergency rooms and hospices—a thought as disgusting as it was tempting—my eyesight was basically a memory.

Fact was, I was blind.

Mason's thumb hitched. "I didn't mean to upset you," he whispered.

I hadn't noticed the tears creeping up on me, but they were there now, falling slowing down my cheeks. "It's okay," I said, swiping them away. I tipped my head against the window and sighed.

One of the things I liked about Mason was that he knew when to leave me alone with my thoughts. He turned the radio on low and we spent the rest of the ride in silence. There was just me, propped against cool glass with a massive, heart-wrenching realization beginning to press down on me, Mason's hand on mine, and the music. As Mason came to a stop at my house, he said, "Um. There's a police car in your driveway."

Nerves fluttered in my stomach. "I didn't tell my parents I was leaving the house today," I said, my voice wavering. "They must've called in the cavalry."

I was in so much trouble.

"It's my fault that you ran off to Saint Jude's," Mason said in an exhale. "Want me to go in with you? Help you explain?"

I squeezed his hand once and then pulled away from him. "You're sweet to offer, but no. This thing with my parents goes way beyond today—and none of it is your fault." I yanked open the door and stepped out with one shaky foot. "Just keep me updated on Ben, okay? I have a feeling I won't be leaving this house for a long time."

I could hear Mason's car backing out of the driveway as I crept up the porch steps to the front door. Pausing for a moment, I drew in a deep breath, and then I turned the knob and stepped inside. I closed the door quietly with two flat palms and stood perfectly still, waiting for the screaming.

It didn't come.

What came instead was a sharp inhalation of breath, my father's collapsed "Thank God," and my mother's ragged "She's here." And suddenly Mom was closing in on me, all jagged bones and hair, embracing me fiercely and muttering, though seemingly not to me. She was either sobbing or laughing "She's okay" over and over. Eventually she stepped back, but her hand clamped down hard on my forearm, as though I were a balloon that might drift away.

I wanted her to yell at me. I was ready for her to yell at me. But the only words passed came from a rumbly-voiced police officer. He asked me only cursory questions—Where had I been? Had I been taken against my will? Was I all right?—and then he left the house in a trail of strident footsteps.

Then it was just the three of us.

And my mother's grip on my arm.

It was terrifying to me, that grip.

I heard Dad walking in my direction, stopping right in front of me. "Maggie," he breathed, "we were so worried about you. We thought . . ." He cleared his throat. Started again. "We kept trying to call you and you didn't pick up. We were so afraid that after everything . . ." He cleared his throat once more. "We were terri-fied that you'd run away. That you'd done something dangerous and gotten hurt."

My father's distraught voice, the way my mother was clutch-ing my arm—it all surged over me, and suddenly I felt my throat jam up. "I thought Ben was about to die, Dad," I explained. "So Clarissa and I took the bus to Saint Jude's."

"You took the *bus*?" Dad sputtered.

"Dad," I said. My voice was quiet. Small. We'd never spoken like this, Dad and I. We'd always been masters at avoiding confronta-tion. "I'm perfectly able to walk two blocks from my own house and catch a bus to Saint Jude's. If you don't believe in me, in my ability to get around, to live"—I tried to pull free from my mother's grasp, but couldn't—"how do you expect me to believe in myself? You have to let me figure things out on my own."

I heard him swallow. "I don't know how to do that," he said. He didn't sound much like my father. His voice was old and quiet and crumpled. "I don't know how to stand by and watch you get hurt."

"But Dad, your worrying about my getting hurt—*that's* what's hurting me." I felt my eyes well up. I knew that I'd already cried too much today, knew it was pointless to start up again. But I also realized that my next several sentences wouldn't come out without tears. "I'm still Maggie. I still want to spend time with you. I still want to search for music together on Saturday mornings."

He unloaded a heavy sigh. "After you . . ." He stopped and then started over. "Time and time again, I invited you to come along, and you always said no. I figured it was too painful for you, so I stopped bringing it up. I'm sorry, Mags. I guess I should have kept asking." He put a heavy hand on my back, let it slide around to my shoulder to give me a one-armed hug. He smelled like spicy aftershave and laundry detergent and sweat. I wiped the tears off my cheeks, struck by how small and young I felt in his embrace— like I was Ben's age, maybe even younger. He gave me one last squeeze before pulling away.

My mother's grip tightened on my arm, and I turned toward her. "Mom." It was just the one word, but sounded so much like a plea. Truth was, she was scaring me.

Seconds slid by.

"Maggie," she began finally, bordering on hysterical. She gulped in a breath before continuing on, her words choppy, rushed. "You were right, about how I left when you . . . when you were . . ." She stopped and sucked in a breath. I didn't move, just waited her out. "You were always the strong one. The strongest person I knew. So much stronger than I could ever be. It was terrifying to see you in that hospital, so sick and weak."

I nodded, though I didn't know why. Maybe I just wanted to encourage her to keep talking so I didn't have to speak. I was afraid to open my mouth. I could feel a sob surging up from my chest that was so massive, it was going to shatter me in half.

"I felt so goddamn guilty," Mom went on, her voice louder now, adamant. "I knew that if I'd taken you to the doctor that morning—if I hadn't gone to work—you probably wouldn't have been lying in that bed, fighting for your life. And the truth is, I just didn't know how to deal with all of that, so I stayed with my sister for a few days, trying to pull myself together." She paused, and I heard her take a deep breath. "It was an awful thing to do, sweetie. You needed me, and what did I do? I left you."

"You could have just told me all of that, Mom," I said, my words quiet, shaky. "I would have forgiven you."

"I know," she whispered. "I didn't know you were lucid enough to even realize I was gone. That sounds like an excuse—and I guess it is." She exhaled tiredly and was quiet for several heart-beats. Finally she said, "I've been waiting for you to stand up and dust yourself off, stronger than ever. You're Maggie, after all. Tough as hell." I heard her swallow. Take in a breath. "And you *have* started to move on; you've discovered new ways to do things. You've made new friends. I'm proud of you, Maggie."

"Are *you* moving on, though?" I choked.

"Of course I am. What do you—" She broke off, heaved out a breath, and started again. "Oh honey, is this about soccer? You think I'm disappointed that you can't play like you used to? Of course it's been hard to see you lose all that, hard to see you lose your . . . hard to see you . . ."

I just stood there, motionless, waiting for her to say it. But she didn't, and so I said it for her. "Blind, Mom. I'm blind."

And as I said it, I knew that it was true.

That it would always be true.

I couldn't cling to the scraps of my past while the present carried on without me. I'd had my sight. It had been fleeting and beautiful and overwhelming, and I'd loved every moment of it.

And now it was gone.

It struck me hard, that truth, and I crumpled from the weight of it.

Thank God she was still holding my arm, because she caught me as I fell and we went to the floor together. "I know you are,"

Mom said, rocking me back and forth, "and that's okay. You have to know that it's okay. That we are all okay."

I felt like she was giving me permission to let go of all the pain and guilt and fear—all the resentment and hurt I'd been carrying. Chest heaving, I collapsed into her and sobbed, suddenly aware that I'd been holding myself upright for seven-plus months, and I was too exhausted now to do it on my own. After my tears subsided, I untangled myself and sat up, wiping off my cheeks with the back of my hand. I drew in a deep breath, held it for just a moment. And then I exhaled, letting it all slip away.

46

B en started chemo after he got released from Saint Jude's. He spent most of his time lying in bed or hanging over a trash can, either sleeping or throwing up.

It was a Sunday, a couple weeks into his treatments, when I strode into Ben's room and ceremoniously deposited a heavy package on his bed. "Got you a present," I said.

Ben was quiet for a moment while he processed the information. Then, and with a yawn that failed to disguise the pleasure in his voice, he said, "For real?"

I sat down on the corner of his bed and tapped the top of the gift with my index finger. "Yeah. For real. Open it."

I heard the bed squeak as he sat upright, heard him wildly ripping away the wrapping paper. And then I heard a gulp. For a moment, I thought maybe he was puking. Which made me panic a little, because I wasn't sure whether to find him a trash can or to cover my mouth and get the hell out before I sympathy-puked. But then he said in a choked whisper, "The *Q*s."

My heart collapsed and inflated at the exact same time.

Yesterday I'd gotten up repulsively early, showered, and spent an hour combing through the local online classifieds. Then I'd burst into my parents' room and woken up my father, hollering, "There are fifteen garage sales today, Dad! Fifteen!"

Because sometimes, you need to be the one to take the first step.

To-go coffee cups in our hands, we'd wandered around garage sale after garage sale for the better part of the morning, chatting and meandering and goofing off. It hadn't been exactly like it used to be—*we* weren't exactly like we used to be—but it had been a start. And right now, that was all we needed. I'd found the *Q* encyclopedia at our fourteenth stop. It was part of a set, tucked underneath a table. I might've never even discovered it if my cane hadn't gotten snagged on a wire hanger.

Ben cleared his throat. "Thera," he said finally, all casually, like he'd known me for centuries and I'd spent most of that time surprising him with meaningful gifts, "want me to read you some of the entries?"

A laugh exploded up from somewhere deep inside me, a bubble bursting all over the room. I hadn't realized until that very moment how badly I wanted to hear the *Q*s. "Yeah, I do."

. . . .

I almost mowed Mason over when I walked out of Ben's room. Evidently, and due to a filing issue in my closet, we were wearing the exact same thing—jeans and plain black T-shirts—because he paused in the hallway for a moment and then said in a low voice, "You look a hell of a lot better in that outfit than I do." His words slid down my spine and made a hard landing at the backs of my knees. And I couldn't quite recover. Even an hour later, as we lay on the living room floor and babbled about music, my legs felt spongy and inept.

"How does anyone get to the age of seventeen without hearing a single Operation Scarce song?" I said. "It's un-American."

"I told you," Mason said. "I was sheltered."

I rolled my eyes. "Please. I have one of their songs on my phone if you want to listen to it."

"What I want to listen to," he said, and I heard him turn on his side to face me, "is the song you played that day on the piano."

"Oh no. No no no no," I said, laughing. "That's just something that's been circling in my head lately, is all."

"Just humor me, Maggie. Please?" he said, hitting me hard with that buttery voice.

I blinked. "Um. Okay."

I rolled upright, taking longer than necessary to make my way to the piano bench. Probably I'd played this song a thousand times over the past several weeks. I knew it backward and forward and backward again. But even so, Mason was a real, honest-to-God, brilliant musician, and I was just a girl who plucked notes out of the air and glued them together however she saw fit. I sat down clumsily on the bench, my hands in my lap. Mason walked up behind me, stopping close enough for me to feel the heat coming off his body.

I didn't move.

Reaching over my shoulder, he gently took my hands, one at a time, and placed them on the keys.

It was strangely intimate, that act.

Closing my eyes, I took a deep breath, tried to forget about everything but the music, and began to play. The music seemed loud for some reason, like it was rushing at me in a pair of headphones, like I was standing in the front row at a concert next to a massive speaker. So much so that I almost didn't hear Mason as he started singing the lyrics I'd read that day in his room, the lyrics for "November."

I stopped playing. "You're singing to my music," I said brilliantly.

He sat down on the bench beside me. His voice so close to me that I could feel the smile in it, he said, "I am. Keep playing."

"Right. Yes, of course. Keep playing. How silly of me." His non-reply told me he was waiting for me. I cleared my throat and forced my hands to move. He was singing again as I hit the third key, starting smack in the middle of the second verse. I stopped again. "This is weird."

Mason, sounding slightly embarrassed, said, "Sorry. I probably should have told you that I haven't been able to get your music out of my head since I heard it. It just feels right for this song, you know? Can you—can you keep playing?"

My music. Stuck in *his* head.

I took a breath, placed my hands in position, and we staggered through the rest of the song—me, trying to match his tempo, and him, trying to find mine. When we finished, Mason let out a little self-deprecating sigh. "This song has been sounding off to me, but I haven't been able to pin down why."

"It's the rhythm," I said.

I felt him twitch in surprise. "You think?"

"Yeah. I mean, try reworking it in three-four instead of six-eight. Your lyrics—they're so passionate. But the rhythm? Not so much."

"So you think if we match each other in a three-four, it would be . . . passionate?" he said softly.

I swallowed. Were we still talking about music? "Um. Yeah."

"I can do that," Mason said.

Silence floated around us for a moment.

"Right," I said, sort of loudly. I put my hands into position. Hacked out a little cough. "So in three-four, then?"

My original plan had been to hold back a little and let Mason find me with his lyrics, but as soon as I hit the first note I realized that I wanted to put my entire world into this song. Mason stepped in at the beginning of the second measure, draping his voice achingly over my every note. And the song spun out of us so slowly, so perfectly, so sinuously, that I wasn't sure if we were making the music or if it was making us. In it were our combined struggles, celebrations, losses. In it was everything we'd gone through, and every truth we'd come to know.

In it was us.

And when the last note faded away, when we turned to face each other, Mason's shocked breath mingled with mine. Suddenly the air between us was flimsy, uncertain, yet impossibly solid.

"Wow," I whispered, "that was . . ."

"Passionate," he murmured.

I wasn't sure how we got there—whether I leaned in or he

stretched toward me—but suddenly there was no space between us and we were kissing. His lips tasted like ocean salt and absolute submission, and I was worried that Mrs. Milton would walk in and see us, and all I could smell and feel and taste was him him him. And it was as though there were some sort of crazed lunatic inside me that was set free, because I was dying to run my hands through his hair and over his chest and under his shirt and around his shoulders, and then—oh, God—his lips parted and I just melted into nothingness. After my mind blew up and came back together again and then blew up and came back together again, we peeled apart.

"Wow," he breathed.

"Wow," I said. Or at least I thought I did. I was pretty sure my mouth made that particular motion. My mind was preoccupied, on playback, reconstructing and deconstructing the kiss, which then made me pick apart my kissing skills, which then made me extremely nervous, which then made me suddenly blurt out, "Are you still going out with Hannah Jorgensen? The model? From New York City?" Somewhere in the back of my mind, I was screaming at myself to shut up, but the words just kept on coming, tumbling out of my mouth before I could catch them. And what's worse, I could feel myself getting upset, tearing up at the thought of him with another girl. I blinked several times. "Because I heard that you were going out with her, and honestly, I'm not the sort of person who just . . . makes out with a guy who has a girlfriend."

Finally, I clamped my lips together to keep the *stupid* from coming out of my mouth.

A little bit of lighthearted air shot out of his nose. "A rumor. I don't even know Hannah Jorgensen."

"Yeah?"

"Yeah," he said, and he chuckled softly, just once.

"What?" I said.

"You're soft inside, Maggie Sanders," he accused, swiping the pad of his finger on the corner of my eye to whisk away the wetness.

"I am *not.*"

He laughed. "You are. You try to come off all badass and sarcastic, but inside?" He leaned toward me and kissed me again. I felt him smiling against my lips as he said, "You're a marshmallow."

A tap on the front door made us jump away guiltily. "Knock, knock," a woman said, and then the door squeaked open and the sharp click of high heels sounded in the entryway. "Teddy and Samantha wanted to stop by to drop off some balloons for Ben. Is it a bad time?"

Mason cleared his throat, sounding adorably flustered. "No, no. Come on in. Hey, Teddy. Samantha. Ben's in his room. Follow me."

I heard them barrel inside, heard a small set of footsteps stop beside me. "You," Samantha grumbled.

"You."

"I guess you aren't going away, are you?" she said stubbornly, but I could detect a hint of tolerance hiding in her tone.

"Not a chance," I said.

. . . .

When I got home that night, I called Hilda and asked whether she could squeeze me in the next day for a lesson in public transportation. Then, climbing the stairs and shutting the door to my room, I slid a college DVD out of its envelope and popped it into my computer, curling up under Gran's quilt to listen.

47

Like so many other twelfth-grade girls this crisp fall afternoon, I found myself standing on a soccer field, grass jabbing at my ankles and wind in my hair, a crowd of spectators watching. I never pictured myself here without a jersey, never thought I'd be positioned so closely to a goal without a ball between my feet.

Never thought I'd be doing something like this.

I swallowed. Wiped my palms on my jeans. The crowd here was massive—much larger than the crowd had been at Alexander Park. But then, the Loose Cannons couldn't just saunter onto UConn's campus without seizing a lot of attention.

I could almost feel Ben's smile as I shifted my weight, fingers hovering over the keyboard as I waited for David to kick off the concert. Ben had been claiming lately that the moments just before an impressive act were more amazing than whatever followed. I was beginning to believe him.

Despite the chemotherapy cocktail that continued to slither through his veins, Ben was doing well. Yes, he was still hurling. And yes, he'd lost all of his hair, even his eyebrows. And yes, I'd been wallowing in an unprecedented number of bald-eyebrow jokes. And yes, I still couldn't see him, a fact for which I was perpetually grateful.

I smelled Mason before I heard him—that musky scent that I'd been tumbling into ever since the first day I met him. "Clarissa just got here," he whispered in my ear. "She wanted me to give you this. For good luck." I knew exactly what it was when he placed it in my hand. I peeled the wrapper back, took an unhurried bite, and then, chewing slowly, intently, I handed it back to him. "You aren't going to eat the whole thing?" he asked.

"It's the first bite that's the best. The rest is unnecessary," I told him, and he rumbled a low laugh, whispered good luck, and kissed me on the forehead.

Mason and I had been dating for approximately a month, fourteen days, twelve hours, and thirty-two minutes. Give or take. I'd like to say that I'd gotten used to his larger-than-life persona, but even I couldn't tell that lie. Last night, he'd asked me whether I felt as though I'd changed over the last several months. I'd shaken my head no. I hadn't changed. Not really. I was still an extraordinary smartass. I still considered cookies one of the basic food groups. I still ignored strangers when they spoke to me. I still believed that flip-flops were my biggest fashion statement. I still got annoyed when my English teacher talked about his nutsack. What was different about me wasn't me: it was what I noticed. What I paid attention to. After all, circumstances don't change us. They reveal us.

If you'd told me several weeks ago that Carlos would storm away from the group, once and for all, leaving the Loose Cannons few options except the girl who knew their keyboards by heart—the girl who had been practicing their songs on her legs for months on end—I would've told you that you were insane.

But it was happening.

Right now.

David crashed the cymbals. My fingers spread across the keys and I hit the first notes of "Transcendence." I was nervous as hell and my hands shook on the wind-cooled keys, but the music found me anyway.

Like it had been living inside me my entire life, it found me.

Mason's voice rang out clear in the stadium, stunning the crowd instantly. Not just because it was gorgeously compelling—*holy crap*, it was gorgeously compelling—but also because it crooned out of every speaker in the stadium. Yesterday, Mom and I had come to the campus and cleared the concert with the dean, Mr. Seamen. I'd liked him, and not just because he had a hilarious last name—the sort of name I couldn't say without smirking. Fact was, he'd loved the idea of Coach Sanders's daughter standing on UConn's soccer field. He'd even let the band use the stadium's PA system.

All of which made it even more surreal.

As we segued into the next song, I heard my mother hoot my name. I smiled. Something had given way between us over the past several weeks, leaving a wide-open space that I wasn't sure how to fill. We still weren't perfect, but we were more *us* than we'd been in months.

As rehearsed, the band paused dramatically before "November."

And then the song unfolded just as it had in the living room that day with Mason—the keyboard leading into the song. I let the music unravel itself through my fingers, twisty and complicated and intense. Seconds later Mason joined me, slipping a hand in and unlocking an aching melody, and the song poured out of us: secretive, striking, longing, dark, beautiful.

Ours.

And as I stood on the field that day, a sharp breeze in my face and the grass cushioning my feet, I wondered how I'd given up on my Thing so easily all those years ago. I hadn't just given up on playing music. I'd given up on everything that it was to me—emotion, expression, synergy, life, love.

When the song ended, the last note of "November" hung suspended in the air over the stadium. Without the weight of it pressing down on me, so massive and so eternal, I was sure I would've soared up, away from this world. As the music faded there was only silence, working its way around me like a corkscrew. I stood there for a moment, just shifting on my feet.

And then it got loud.

The crowd erupted around us, screaming and stomping and hooting. I was shocked, startled, unsure of what to do.

But then it happened.

I heard Mom's enthusiastic voice in my ear, felt her arms wrap around me, felt her face, wet with tears, pressing into mine. It was the victory hug that I'd long been waiting for. It wasn't at all like I'd pictured it all these years. Not even close. It was better.

Acknowledgments

F air warning: these acknowledgments will be inadequate. Thanking everyone who has helped bring this book to the shelves would be nearly impossible, so please consider the following paragraphs just the frosting on the one-bite cupcake.

First and foremost, endless thanks to my family. To my parents, Janet and Merle, and my sister, Cari, I cannot thank you enough for your infinite support and encouragement. Your unremitting love is one of the biggest reasons you hold this book in your hands, and I will never, ever be able to repay that sort of debt. To my oldest son, Talon, I'm eternally grateful for your kindness and tolerance, for keeping me grounded through this entire process; and to my youngest son, Blaise, thank you for your bottomless enthusiasm, for taking it upon yourself to be my second publicist, my biggest promoter, my greatest advocate. I'm a better person because of you two boys. You are, and always will be, my greatest accomplishment. And lastly, to Paul, my husband and best friend. Thank you for your patience. Thank you for riding out both my celebrations and my tears. Thank you for letting each and every one of my days begin and end with you. Thank you, thank you, thank you. I am so very lucky to have you in my life.

I also owe tremendous gratitude to the Hyperion team. To my remarkable editor, Laura Schreiber, I cannot thank you enough for your wisdom, sense of humor, and love of my characters. You've pushed me far beyond what I thought I could do, something for which I will be eternally grateful. Your brilliance can be found hiding behind every sentence, every paragraph, every word. And to Emily Meehan, Kate Hurley, Whitney Manger, and the rest of the Hyperion team—some of whom I know by name, and some I will never know—I'm forever indebted to you for your support, devotion, and earnestness. I've been so fortunate to work with such a passionate group of people.

My undying appreciation goes to Kathleen Rushall, for being the most enthusiastic and dedicated agent on the planet. Thank you for your belief and patience in me, for your lightning-fast answers to my e-mails, for making every part of this journey a celebration, and for gently and persistently guiding me along. I trust you clear to the Milky Way. And also, speaking of agents, huge thanks as well to my foreign agent, Taryn Fagerness, for your diligence and commitment to my work. Because of you, my story has been shot out of a cannon to reach farther than I ever dreamed possible.

A massive shout-out to the amazing people the publishing world has brought into my life. To my critique partners: Lindsay Currie, Karen Rock, and Courtney Barrett, endless gratitude for your moral support, laser eyes, and never-ending exuberance; and to Lola Sharp, there aren't enough thanks for your hilariously inappropriate texts and e-mails, your ingenious insight, and your optimism. You've been my life raft time and time again, and I owe you an Everest's worth of cheese. Lastly, huge thank-yous to the insanely talented Team KRush, the agents and writers associated with MLLA, the Fearless Fifteeners, the Diversity League, and the Fall Fifteeners. You all have inspired and amazed me time and time again. I'm eternally indebted to you for the advice and encouragement you've given me. You are all gods and goddesses.

Buckets of thanks to my extended family and friends, all of whom have championed and cheered me on throughout this entire process. There are too many of you to name here, but please know that you mean the world to me. The friendships in this story were derived from you. I'm so very blessed to have had that sort of love in my life.

I'm infinitely grateful to the librarians, bloggers, booksellers, and teachers who have advocated this book. You've spread your enthusiasm with heart, excitement, and charm. Your kind words and support have amazed and humbled me beyond measure.

And lastly, I'm most appreciative to you, dear reader, for opening your heart to my story. I'm so very honored to have been invited into your life, if only for a little while.